TWISTER

TWISTER

Barbara
Block

KENSINGTON BOOKS

KENSINGTON BOOKS are published by

Kensington Publishing Corp.
850 Third Avenue
New York, NY 10022

LIBRARY OF CONGRESS CARD CATALOG NUMBER: 95-076006
ISBN 0-8217-4989-7

First Printing: July, 1995

Printed in the United States of America

DISCLAIMER

Although the city of Syracuse is certainly real as are some of the place names I've mentioned, this is a work of fiction. Its geography is imaginary. Indeed, all the characters portrayed in this book are fictional and any resemblance to real people or incidents is purely coincidental.

ACKNOWLEDGMENT

I would like to thank Paul Grover and Mark Fleischman for their automotive expertise.

To Bruce who told me to keep writing.
I couldn't have done it without you.

Chapter
1

Maria was crying. She'd been crying for the last five minutes. Her name, her address, her age—eight, and the fact she'd lost her dog were the only bits of information I'd managed to get out of her so far. But at least her sobs had subsided to a quiet weeping.

"We'll find him," I repeated as I patted her on the shoulder. God, it was hot out on the street. Ninety at least.

"Her," Maria corrected as she rubbed her eyes with grubby hands. Dirt streaks ran down her cheeks. "Her name is Gomez."

"And what does Gomez look like?"

"She's this big." She held out chubby hands to indicate a dog that weighed twenty pounds at the most. "And she's got brown fur that sticks up."

"Anything else?" I could hear my knees creak as I shifted my weight. I'm too old for squatting.

"She has two white paws and a big white star on her chest

and she sleeps on my bed every night." She smiled for an instant, then she remembered that Gomez was gone again and her face began to crumple.

"Don't worry," I said quickly to forestall another bout of weeping. "Did she have a collar and tags?"

Maria curled a lock of long black hair around a finger and looked down at the sidewalk.

"It's okay," I reassured her. "It doesn't matter. She probably just went for a walk."

Maria shook her head dolefully. "She was in the backyard. My mommy put up a fence for her and everything."

"She could have dug underneath it."

"I don't think so."

"What did your mommy say?"

"She's at work."

"Is there anyone else at home?"

"No." Maria's lip began to tremble again.

"Did you call your mom and tell her?"

Maria studied the grass growing out of the crack in the concrete. "No," she whispered.

I straightened up. Pins and needles ran up and down my leg. I pointed to Noah's Ark. "I'll tell you what. You go inside that store and tell the man behind the counter to call your mother and we'll see what she says, okay? And then we'll go from there."

"What if he won't call?"

I smiled. "He will. Just tell him his boss, Robin Light, told him to. If he has any questions he can come out and talk to me."

Maria's eyes widened. "This pet store is yours?"

I nodded.

"Wow. You're really lucky."

"Sometimes." I pushed her gently toward the door. "Now go on in there and make that call."

The girl nodded and ran off. Nothing like trying to set up a window display and seeing some little girl standing in the middle of the street crying to ruin your concentration I thought as I went back to trying to decide whether to put the bags of colored gravel next to the hexagonal or rectangular aquariums. Of course in the old store I hadn't gotten to do window displays because there hadn't been any display windows.

The shop had been located in a Victorian house five blocks away. The new Noah's Ark was in a plain-Jane commercial space, but I loved it. It didn't have the character the old place had, but it was cheaper to heat and easier to keep clean. I was just thinking about how the fire hadn't been all bad when I saw Lynn Stanley driving down the street. Or rather I saw her white Jag. It stuck out like a movie star at K Mart.

Come to think of it, she usually did, too. But not today. Strands of blond hair were escaping from her French braid, she wasn't wearing jewelry, and she had a smudge of dirt on the collar of her white suit.

I waved and she stopped.

"Finally come to ask me out to lunch?" I inquired as I ambled over to the parked car. "You've been promising for long enough."

Lynn and I were unlikely friends. Had been for seven years. A testament to the old saw, 'opposites attract.' She was the rich beauty queen and I was the slovenly working lady. But we enjoyed each other's company.

"No." Lynn fiddled with her sunglasses. "Actually I have to see somebody on Otisco Street."

My eyebrows shot up. "That's a little out of your way, isn't it?"

Lynn licked her lips nervously. "Robin, have you ever done something truly stupid?"

I laughed. "Let me count the ways."

"Because I have. God, have I ever. You see this guy . . . I gave this guy something . . ." She paused to take a deep breath. "Something of Gordon's." I groaned. Gordon was Lynn's husband. He had a bad temper and collected guns. Not a good combo. "I have to get it back before he finds out." I noticed her hands were shaking.

"You want me to come along for moral support?" I asked. She looked like she could use some.

"Would you?" She gave me a weak smile.

"Be right back." And I dashed in the store to tell Tim to hold down the fort.

He was standing in front of the counter, wiggling his eyebrows and his ears, while Abbott, our tokay gecko, was walking around the top of his shaved head. Maria was giggling and petting Pickles, the store cat. Tim blushed when he saw me.

"Her mother's on the way," he said in as gruff a voice as he could manage.

"Fine." I ruffled Maria's hair, told Tim I'd be back soon and left.

"So who is this man?" I asked when I got in Lynn's car.

Lynn didn't answer.

"Somebody interesting?"

Lynn put her foot on the gas and took off by way of a reply. I didn't press the issue. I figured I'd see him in a few minutes anyway.

Lynn drove down the streets as if she was running the course at Watkins Glen. The air-conditioning hadn't even had a chance to kick in by the time we reached Otisco. Lynn honked the horn and nosed the car through a group of kids playing baseball. Once we parked they converged on us like ants on a sugar cube.

"I hope you don't mind, but I think it would be better if I went in there alone," she said as she turned off the motor.

Actually I did mind, I wanted to see what was going on, but I couldn't say that. It would have been too crass.

"Are you sure?"

"Positive. I'll come back down if I need any help." She slipped her keys in her purse, one of those small jobbies you can just carry a lipstick and a credit card in, and got out of the car.

The kids parted like the red sea to let her through. The white linen suit Lynn was wearing didn't exactly hide her assets. She was a babe with a capital **B**. Unfortunately their awe didn't extend to me. Possibly it had something to do with my baggy jeans and T-shirt. Or the fact that I looked like a beanpole. Or the way my red hair was pulled back in a ponytail to get it off my face and neck in the heat. Or maybe it was the beads of sweat on my upper lip. Or the way my features disappeared without makeup. Or my freckles. Or all of the above.

"Hey, lady." A hand plucked at my belt as I got out. I looked down. A little kid, wearing a plaid shirt and striped shorts, was staring up at me. He pointed at the car. "I seen one of these in the movies."

"I bet you have." I moved onto the pavement. The kids, ten of them, moved with me.

Another tug at my belt. "It cost a lot?"

"A lot." I wiped the sweat off my face with the back of my hand. I'd have given anything for a cool shower.

"How much is a lot?"

"More than you'll ever see in your life," a kid wearing a Raiders baseball hat cracked.

The other kids laughed and poked one another in the ribs.

A little girl of about five or six worked her way to the front of the crowd. "How about giving us a ride?" she asked.

"This yours?" a voice behind me asked.

I half turned. It was Manuel. "Of course it's not mine," I replied.

" 'Cause if it was I'd ask you what you been stealing."

"Cute."

Manuel might be a neighborhood punk, but at least he was my neighborhood punk. We'd spent time together in the hospital. He'd been getting over a blow to the head and I'd been recovering from burns I'd received when someone had tied me up, left me in the old Noah's Ark, and set the building on fire. And since the same person had done both things, we'd developed a bond.

"I like the hairstyle," I told him.

Manuel preened. Since I'd seen him last he'd gone from a skinny teenager with bad skin in baggy pants and a fade to a skinny teenager with bad skin, sideburns, a pompadour, black jeans, a white T-shirt, and a garrison belt. The fifties revisited. He ran his hand over the Jag's hood.

"Boy, if I had something like this . . ." Manuel's voice faded away as his fancies took flight.

I glanced at my watch. Four minutes had passed since Lynn had gone in the house.

"Listen, Manuel." I interrupted his daydreams. "Who lives in there?"

"Nobody special."

"What do you mean nobody special?"

"Just some guy."

Manuel was echoing Lynn's words. "Some guy." What guy? God. Was she having another affair? But I couldn't imagine her sleeping with anyone who lived in a house where the porch was jacked up on cinder blocks and the windows were either boarded up or covered over with plastic. Lynn tended to go for the satin sheets, champagne, and red roses type. Whoever lived here looked as if they'd have trouble buying her a beer.

I lit a cigarette and thought of another explanation. Maybe this guy had been working for her and taken something of Gordon's and she'd come to get it back. No. She'd explicitly said she'd given him something. I sighed. When she came out I'd ask. I checked my watch again. Lynn had been in the house for six minutes now. I decided to give her another nine before I went in and got her. I didn't want to interrupt anything, but she *had* said she'd be right out. Plus I had to get back to the store. I had order forms to fill out, cages to clean, and most importantly, a shipment of lizards to pick up at the airport. It was days like this that made me wish I was still a reporter. I took a puff of my cigarette and rechecked my watch.

A whole minute had passed. The next time I glanced down at my wrist two more minutes had gone by. The hell with it. I threw my cigarette on the pavement and ground it out with my heel. I just couldn't stand waiting any longer. I handed Manuel ten dollars, told him to guard the car and went inside the house.

The door slammed behind me with a dull thud. I took a breath. The air felt viscous, as if I was breathing in pudding. Beads of sweat stung my eyes. I blinked them away and took a good look around. I was standing in a large, square entrance hall. Five feet in front of me was a staircase that led to the second floor. The first ten steps were visible, but after that they angled off and were lost to view. A small room lay off to my right, a larger one to my left. The room straight ahead connected up with the kitchen. Everything was paneled in dark wood.

Lynn was nowhere in sight. Neither was the guy she'd come to see. I yelled for her, but didn't get an answer. Jesus, where the hell was she? What the hell was she doing? I could feel myself getting more irritated and jumpier by the second. But then again, I reminded myself as I walked into the room on the right, Lynn never did have a sense of time. She never hurried. Anywhere. Ever. For anyone. She just wafted through life like a butterfly on the wind, stopping whenever and wherever she wanted, assuming that whatever she needed would always be waiting. The benefit of being a babe.

I should only be so lucky I thought as I fingered the venetian blinds covering the bay windows. The motion sent what must have been a year's worth of dust into the air. I sneezed and turned away. Except for several cartons stacked by the far wall, there was nothing here. Nor did it look like there had been for some time.

I wandered across the hall. Although the room was larger, it was equally dim. Two wooden chairs stood over by the fireplace. Next to them was a collection of weights and a steel bar. A sweat-stained weight belt was draped over it. A pair of fingerless gloves lay on the floor along with a water bottle. I took a closer look. The plates were twenty-fives and fifties. The gloves were ripped with use. The water bottle had Atilla's Gym printed around the middle. Lynn's friend, whoever he was, was a serious lifter. Atilla's was where the big boys went.

Next I went into what had once obviously been the dining room. The room contained more furniture than the other two. A beige couch lay against one wall. A fancy television and a stereo sat not too far away on wooden crates. A small Oriental, a good Kurdistan by the looks of it, lay between them. The three items appeared as out of place as tea roses in a bed of weeds. But I didn't think too much about the disparity because by then I was getting nervous. I mean Lynn had to have heard me by now. But then again maybe she hadn't. Old houses like this had thick walls that blocked out sounds.

I walked into the kitchen. The room was long and narrow. Dishes were soaking in the sink. Two dented-up pots sat on an old white stove that looked like it had been in use since the thirties. A scarred wooden table was pushed against the far wall. Half of it was piled with cartons full of papers. The rest of the space was taken up with weight-lifting magazines, cans of protein powders, amino acids, and bottles of vitamins. The medicinal smell of brewer's yeast hung in the air.

A small window gave a view of the backyard. Next to that was a door leading to the outside. Another door sat catty-corner to it. I went over and opened the second one. The room had obviously been intended as a pantry, but somewhere along the line someone had converted it to a half bath. In the back there was a set of steps that led upstairs. I stepped back out, closed the door, and opened the other one, thinking that perhaps, for some reason, Lynn had gone out of the house the back way.

But when I took a look it was obvious she hadn't. Six-inch spaces gaped where pieces of wood had rotted away. I put my foot on one of the remaining slats and bore down. The board groaned and wobbled and I quickly took my foot off. As I closed the door a flash of lightning shot across the sky. It looked like the storm the weatherman had been predicting for the last couple of days might be arriving after all. I was standing there watching the sky darken and trying to decide what I was going to do next when I heard a creak.

Then I heard it again.

I called out.

Dead silence.

I held my breath. I heard my heart beating as I stood there straining to hear. Something. Anything. But there was nothing. It's probably the house I told myself as I wiped my forehead with the back of my hand. The boards are settling or the beams are cracking in the heat. Everyone tells me that's when I should have gotten out of there and called the police. And in retrospect they're right. But second sight is always one hundred percent correct and it was a thought I never seriously entertained. For one thing I was too busy trying to convince myself that nothing was wrong. And anyway, I didn't think they'd come—not for something like this.

It had been a tough July in Syracuse. First it had rained for days on end, then it had grown hot and humid. It had been in the nineties or above for the past two weeks. Mold grew, the garbage stank, dogs snapped, and people fought. Down the block from the store we'd had one knifing and three shootings in the past week. The sound of the police sirens had become a constant litany as they sped by to answer one call after another. I was beginning to feel as if I were in L.A. So unless it was an emergency—as in shots fired and someone lying bleeding on the ground—I figured it might be hours before a blue and white rolled up. And I wasn't prepared to wait till then.

The back steps were narrow and curvy and I went up them slowly. I emerged on the second-floor hallway. Rooms, at least eight of them, radiated off to either side. The hallway was broken in the middle by the master staircase that led down to the entryway below. It was even hotter up here than it had been downstairs. The only sounds I heard were the kids playing outside and the crackle of the plastic over the windows. I yelled out for Lynn again. Again I didn't get a reply. By now I was getting seriously concerned. I only hoped something *was* wrong, because if she'd heard me all this time and hadn't answered I was going to kill her.

I entered the first room with my heart pounding. But it was empty. No one was there. The space was small, made smaller by two boarded-up windows. Directly across was another doorway. When I walked through it I found myself in another, even smaller room which, judging from the rods going from one wall to another, must have been used as a closet. I was just turning to go when I felt a tap on my shoulder. I screamed and whirled around.

"Sorry," Manuel said sheepishly.

"Jesus. What the hell is the matter with you?" My heart was still pounding.

"I was just checking on you. You were taking too long. Wouldn't want you getting lost." He grinned and gave me a playful punch.

I gave him a much harder punch back.

"Hey, watch the tattoo," he protested rubbing his forearm. "It's fresh."

I was still angry enough not to apologize.

He stroked one of his sideburns. "So what's the story? Where's your friend?"

"I don't know. I can't find her or the guy she came to talk to."

He cupped his hands and put them around his mouth. "Oh, Freddy," he yodeled. "Put on your fingernails. We're waiting."

This was not what I needed right now. I pointed to the door. "Just go out the way you came in," I ordered.

Manuel twisted the heel of his shoe into the floor. "Okay. That was pretty dumb. I'm sorry. Let me stay."

"No."

"Come on," he whined. "Be a pal."

I sighed. "Oh, all right. But no more funny stuff."

I mean what the hell. I could use the company, he was here already and the truth was: he had probably done and seen more in his sixteen years than I had in my forty.

We went through the next three rooms together.

It didn't take us long.

The first room was empty.

So was the second.

Then we got to the third.

Chapter
2

Lynn was kneeling on the far side of the bare room. Her head was lowered, her arms were stretched out on the floor, the palms of her hands were down. She looked as if she was offering obeisance to some unknown God. It wasn't until I took a couple of steps in that I saw the man lying under her.

He was splayed out across the oak slats. The upper half of his body was outlined by a petal-shaped pool of blood. A few tendrils of the stuff had begun winding their way down the cracks in the floor.

"Shit, that's the guy who lives here," Manuel whispered in my ear as I crossed the floor.

"You sure?"

"Yeah."

I squatted down next to Lynn. She didn't move, did nothing to indicate she was aware of my presence.

"She okay?" Manuel asked.

"I don't know."

I put my hands on her shoulders, raised her up slightly, then twisted her around. Her jacket was smeared with red. My stomach knotted. I thought she'd been shot. But when I asked her where she was hurt she told me she hadn't been in a voice so low it was practically inaudible.

But the guy underneath her sure had been. The left part of his chest was pulped. I thought of strawberry jam and felt the bile rising in my throat. I fought it, swallowing hard. A few seconds later when the nausea had subsided, I reached down and touched the man's shoulder. Though the odds against it were high, there was an outside chance he might still be alive. His skin was warm under my fingers. I fumbled around for the pulse in his neck for what seemed like forever. But no matter where or how hard I pressed I couldn't detect any movement.

The man was dead.

I turned back to Lynn and asked her if he had been like this when she came in. She didn't answer. I don't think she even heard what I was saying. She seemed to be looking right through me. Her eyes were glassy. Tears rolled down her cheeks and onto the lapels of her suit.

"You want I should get the cops?" Manuel asked. He was standing right beside me, looking dazed. He'd definitely gotten more than he'd bargained for.

I nodded.

He lingered for another moment before he took off. I could hear his feet thumping down the stairs as he ran and the sound of the downstairs door slamming against the wall as Manuel threw it open. Then, except for a torn piece of plastic sheeting from one of the windows flapping in the wind, it was quiet again. Outside the first drops of what promised to be a torrential downpour began to fall. I turned back to Lynn.

"You want to tell me what happened?" I asked again, pleaded really, but all I got was an almost imperceptible shake of her head.

As I sat with Lynn cradled in my arms waiting for the police to come I kept stealing glances at the guy lying on the floor. No matter how much I didn't want to look my eyes kept being drawn back to him. He was in his mid to late twenties. His hair was light brown with blondish streaks that could have come from a bottle or the sun. He had a strong jaw, a chiseled nose, odd, amber-colored eyes. And he was movie star handsome. Even in his present state that much was apparent.

And then I realized something else.

He looked familiar.

Only for the life of me I couldn't remember where I'd seen his face.

The question gnawed at me. I was still thinking about it when the police arrived ten minutes later. Lynn's eyes flickered when the cop came in the room, but she didn't say anything. Her complexion was getting ashier by the second. Her skin felt clammy. She was going into shock. The cop took one look and called for a stretcher. I caught a last glimpse of her being lifted into the ambulance, the raindrops running down her face, as the police hustled Manuel and I into a squad car and took us down to the Public Safety Building to make our statements. Neither of us said anything to the other on the ride down there. I think we were both still too stunned.

They separated us immediately. The room they put me in was small and stuffy. It smelled of Taco Bell, cigarettes, pine-scented air freshener, and body odor. I paced while I waited for Detective Connelly to appear, remembering the last time

I'd been down here. Then I'd been a suspect in a murder case. Now I was a witness. That should be better, but somehow they both felt the same. But if Connelly remembered last year's case, and he must have because it had made the newspapers, he didn't say anything when he walked in.

He had a short man's swagger, a sallow complexion, a receding hairline, and an unfriendly expression. He asked me what had happened and I told him. Again. And again. And again. By the time I signed my statement my voice was hoarse and the words had begun to lose their meaning. The process had taken two hours, but it felt like I'd been locked in that room for six. All I wanted to do was get out of the Public Safety Building and into the fresh air.

As I walked out of the lobby door I spotted Manuel. He was slumped against a marble pillar watching the rain sheeting onto the pavement while he waited for me. The kid looked exhausted and I'm sure that I did, too. I took my cigarettes out of my T-shirt pocket, lit two, and gave one to him. He nodded his thanks. I asked him if he'd been waiting long.

He took a puff of the Camel. "About fifteen minutes."

"So what did you say to the cops?"

"I told them what I saw." He paused to pick a strand of tobacco off his tongue. "And you?"

"The same."

"Boy." He shook his head and took another drag. "So what do you think happened in there?"

"I wish I knew."

"You think your friend killed that guy?"

"No." I watched the rain pelting down. It was almost tropical in its intensity. A clap of thunder reverberated. Then a zigzag of lightning lit up the sky. Suddenly the air smelled of ozone. "Definitely not," I repeated in response to Manuel's dubious expression. Whatever had happened I couldn't imagine Lynn killing someone. She was the kind of woman who cowered instead of striking back.

"Then who did?"

"I don't know."

"The detective I was talking to, he told me the guy had just been killed."

Connelly had said the same thing to me.

"No one else was there."

"No one that we saw," I amended remembering the thud I'd heard when I'd been downstairs. "Maybe the killer went out over the roof after I came in."

"I don't know, Robin." Manuel scratched at his chin. "I didn't see anyone when I was waiting outside."

"He could have jumped out one of the rear windows."

Manuel clicked his tongue. "The backyard's a long way down."

"Not if you've just killed someone and you want to get away."

"Maybe," Manuel said, but I could tell he was agreeing to be polite. Then he changed the subject. "So what kind of gun do think the guy used?"

"I don't know and I don't care."

"I bet it was a .357 magnum. Boy, there sure was a lot of blood, wasn't there? And all that red quivery stuff . . ." My stomach began to churn. "You think that was his heart we saw?"

That did it. I walked away. It was either that or throw up on the pavement. As I went back inside the Public Safety Building to call Tim and see if he could come down and get us, I decided that one thing was for sure. Manuel was a hell of a lot less squeamish than I was. I'd seen four dead people over the course of the year and the sight still made me want to retch. I was debating whether this was a function of age and sex or of personality when I spotted George Sampson striding across the lobby.

He was wearing khaki pants and a light green polo shirt that set off his black skin and highlighted his biceps and pecs. At 6´4˝, with weight to match, he made the lobby look smaller. I know if I were a criminal and he were after me I'd just lie down and cry.

"Coming or going?" I inquired of my friend.

"Going. I pulled early shift today. So what are you doing here?" His mouth set in a hard line as I explained. "What is it with you anyway?" he asked when I was done. "Can't you stay away from trouble?"

"I'm trying."

"Yeah, right," he said as he put his hand on my shoulder and propelled me toward the door. "Come on. I'll give you two a lift home."

George had been my husband's best friend. He'd stuck by me when Murphy died. He'd stuck by me when I'd been involved in a murder investigation. He'd stuck by me when I'd been in the hospital. But he hadn't liked it. Sometimes I had the feeling that if he could he'd wrap me in cotton wool and ship me off to Tibet.

Manuel, George, and I dashed to George's car. Even though it was parked just across the street we were soaked by the time we got in. The ride to Manuel's house was quiet. I spent it smoking and looking out the window, while Manuel and George confined themselves to bitching about the weather. Fifteen minutes later we dropped Manuel off at his door. Then George made a U-turn and headed toward Noah's Ark.

"So you really don't know what happened?" he asked picking up our previous conversation.

"No, I don't," I snapped. "That's what I said to Connelly and that's what I'm saying to you."

"Take it easy. I'm just asking." George tapped the steering wheel with his fingers.

I watched the windshield wipers arc back and forth. This rain had to end soon. It couldn't go on at this rate. After all this was Syracuse in July not India in the monsoon season.

"I wonder who the guy was?" I said a minute later.

George glanced at me. "Which guy?"

"The dead one in the house, of course."

"Of course. Well, I guess we'll find out soon enough."

"Because he looked familiar."

George stopped tapping. "How do you mean?"

"I don't know . . . There was just something about him . . . I think I've seen him somewhere."

"You don't remember where?"

"No."

George pulled up to the curb in front of the store. "You'll tell Connelly if you remember, right?"

"Right," I replied.

But I don't think George believed me because he just sighed, leaned across me and opened my door. I ran into the shop. The place was empty. No customers. This kind of rain was lousy for business.

Tim came out from behind the counter to greet me. "That was a long favor," he observed as he unwrapped a small Burmese python from around his arm.

Tim had worked with Murphy in the old Noah's Ark and had, thankfully elected to stayed on with me when I moved to the new store. He was reliable, knew his reptiles, and was

an all-around nice guy even if he did look like Ghengis
Khan, especially since he'd shaved his head, added three
more earrings, and pierced his cheek. Somehow I'd liked
him better with a ponytail and one earring, but he hadn't
asked my opinion so I hadn't given it.

I grabbed a paper towel and began blotting the water
from my hair. "Things didn't exactly go as planned," I told
him as Pickles wound herself around my legs and then sauntered back to her spot underneath the counter. Since I'd
found her she'd gone from skinny to round. All she did was
eat and sleep. As I watched her walk away I decided I wanted
a beer. Possibly several.

"You'll be happy to know I got one of my friends to run
out to Hancock and pick up the snakes," Tim said as I tossed
the paper towel in the garbage can.

"I take it that's one of them?" I pointed to the four-foot
python Tim had hanging around his neck.

He nodded. "Nice, isn't she?" he asked hanging the snake
around my neck as I passed by him on my way to the storeroom.

"Very." I stroked her, then handed her back.

"Her scales are glossy. No parasites that I can see. The
corn snakes are in good shape, too. Go on. Take a look,"
Tim urged.

"In a minute." Tim followed me into the back. I stopped
in front of the refrigerator, opened the door, took out two
bottles of Corona, knocked the cap off the first, downed it,
then sat down on a hundred-pound bag of cedar shavings
and started on the second. Through it all the python
watched me from her perch on Tim's shoulders. Her eyes,
flat and unblinking, took everything in.

Tim nudged a bale of hay over with his foot and sat down
next to me. I told him what had happened.

"Boy, you sure do have a knack," he said when I was done.

"So it would seem." What could I say? The man was right. For the past year every time I took a step I seemed to land in the muck. I took another gulp of beer.

"By the way, we never found that kid's dog."

"Maria's?"

"Somebody took her right out of the yard."

"That's too bad."

"I said we'd keep an eye out."

"Good." Outside of that there wasn't much we could do.

I finished the Corona and was just thinking of getting another one when the buzzer attached to the front door went off. Tim and I got up and went into the main room just in time to see Julio "Peewee" Menedez drip his way across the floor. He was a skinny, short, little nothing of a kid who tried his damndest to look as tough as possible. He had a buzz cut and a goatee. His arms were covered with tattoos. He was wearing a tight white T-shirt, black jeans, and cowboy boots. But his eyes, large and soulful and scared, betrayed him.

"Hey, Robin, I got something to show you."

"Not now, Julio. Another time." I just wasn't in the mood to deal with anything else.

Undeterred, he placed the small cardboard box he was carrying on the counter. "You're gonna love it," he confidently assured me as he opened the flaps, reached in and came back out with the biggest spider I'd ever seen.

"Meet Martha," Julio said sounding like a proud mother introducing her offspring. "She's a bird-eating Brazilian. Usually they're six inches across, but Martha's at least seven, maybe even eight. Pretty, isn't she?"

Pretty wasn't a word I'd ever use to describe a tarantula

and this one was particularly unattractive with its black hairy legs and reddish brown pulpy body.

"She can jump at least five feet. She eats good, too. I'm feeding her baby chicks. And she's real friendly." He stroked her back. "You wanna pet her?"

"Not really."

"Yeah, she's really great," Julio continued as Martha crawled up his arm, stopping at his shoulder. I tried not to flinch as she waved two of her legs in my direction. "But I got this problem with her I'm hoping you can help me with." He paused for a breath, then went on. "See, it's like this. I gotta move back with my mom until I'm eighteen. My probation officer says I got to live in a supervised situation. And my ma she don't want Martha in the house. Says she'd give her a heart attack."

"Understandable. So you want to sell her to us?" I asked, trying to clarify the situation.

"Not exactly."

"Then what?"

"I was talking to Manuel . . ."

"Manuel?" Already I knew I wasn't going to like what was coming next.

"And he said that maybe I could keep her here till I get out of the house again. You know, like you do with a dog when you go away."

"You mean you want to board her here?" I asked incredulously.

"Yeah."

"I'm sorry but I don't think it would work."

The smile Julio had been sporting died. I felt like a murderer. "I'll pay you."

"That's not the issue."

"I'll come here every day and take care of her."

"Come on, Robin," Tim coaxed. "Be a nice lady. It's not like it's a big deal."

I knew it wasn't. But I don't like spiders, especially hairy, fat ones.

"Please," Julio begged. "She's my friend. We're like Charlotte and Wilbur in *Charlotte's Web*. Close. Like this." And he crossed two of his fingers to illustrate.

"You read the book?" It had been one of my favorites.

"No, man." Julio looked at me as if I was crazy. "I watched the movie. Maybe twenty times. So how about it?"

I was about to say no, when I had an idea. E.B. White deserved as wide an audience as possible. Who knew, maybe Julio would like *Charlotte's Web* enough to go on to *Stuart Little*. I smiled. "I tell you what. You read the book . . ."

"I can do that," Julio said excitedly.

"In the next two weeks." Otherwise he'd finish it around Christmas if I was lucky.

"Okay," he agreed a little doubtfully.

"And take care of her and keep her in the back and we have a deal."

Julio grinned at me. "You're all right."

"I know." And I went over and turned on the radio. I wanted a little music, but I got the news instead. The reporter was talking about the construction on Route 690. What else was new? It was an annual Syracuse summer rite. I was about to turn the dial when he mentioned a possible homicide on Otisco Street.

"Oh wow," Julio said before I could say anything.

Tim and I both stared at him.

"You know I think I might have seen the guy that did it."

"Come again?" Tim said.

"No, really. See, I was coming out of A.J.'s house when this guy comes tear assing out of his driveway." Tim and I exchanged looks. A.J.'s house was right in back of the one I'd found the body in. "And I mean this guy was really traveling."

I reached for the phone and dialed the police.

Chapter
3

Connelly walked in the store thirty minutes later and headed straight for Julio. "Okay," he said whipping out a notepad and pen. "Give me your name and address and tell me what you have to say." This was obviously a man who didn't believe in preliminaries.

Julio took a deep breath and started. "See, like I told Robin, I was at A.J.'s house . . ."

Connelly looked up from his pad. "Were you there to maybe cop a nickel bag?"

"Hey, why don't you just listen to what he has to say?" I interrupted. If he started leaning on Julio, the kid would fold. He was nervous enough talking to the cops as it was. It had taken a lot of persuasion to convince him to stay.

Connelly folded his arms across his chest. "And why don't you just butt out," he snapped at me.

We glared at each other for a few seconds. I had to bite my lip to keep myself from telling him to go screw himself.

Finally he turned back to Julio. "Okay, so you were just hanging out?" he asked.

"That's right," Julio mumbled.

Connelly raised a sardonic eyebrow. "Cause A.J.'s your friend?"

"Yeah." Julio gave the detective a wary look.

"And you saw this guy running past you."

Julio pointed to me. "That's what she told you on the phone, isn't it?" he said to Connelly. "What's the matter? You got a memory problem or something?"

Connelly stuck his jaw out. "Maybe we should do this downtown."

Julio turned a shade paler but he clung to his attitude anyway. "Hey, I'm doing you a favor. I don't got to stand here and take this shit."

"Please." I put a hand on his shoulder. "For Martha's sake. After all," I reminded him, "she *is* staying here."

For a moment Julio's expression vacillated between anger and resignation. Finally he gave in. "What you want to know?" he asked facing Connelly again.

Connelly glanced at his watch. "Good. Maybe we can wrap this thing up. Now was this guy Hispanic? Caucasian?"

"Caucasian," Julio replied biting on his thumbnail.

Connelly began writing. "How tall would you say he was?"

"I don't know."

Connelly looked up. "Taller than me? Shorter?"

"Taller." Julio started on his other thumbnail.

"How much taller?" Connelly put his hand up over his head and raised it. "Here? Here?"

"Like that," Julio said when Connelly's hand hit the 5´11˝ mark.

"Okay." Connelly nodded. "Was his hair light or dark?"

"Dark."

"Eye color?"

"I don't know. He was moving too fast."

"Dress?"

Julio smirked. "He wasn't wearing one."

"Cute." Connelly put his pen down. "No smart ass. I mean what kind of clothes did he have on?"

"Pants," Julio answered. "Some sort of shirt."

"What color were the pants?" Connelly asked.

"Light brown. I think."

"And the shirt?"

"White."

"Anything else?"

"I couldn't see. Like I said, he was running too fast."

Connelly stopped writing and slapped his pad against his hand. "You don't happen to know this guy's name by any chance?"

"I already told you I don't."

"That's right. I forgot. And you saw him running out the driveway?"

"Yeah."

"About what time?"

"I don't know. I don't got a watch. See?" And Julio held out his arm to show Connelly.

Connelly's mouth twitched. "Or were you too stoned to care?"

"I wasn't smoking," Julio yelled.

Connelly scratched his cheek. "Excuse me. I forgot. Anything else you want to tell me?"

Julio shook his head.

"Then I guess that about wraps it up," Connelly said and slipped his notebook back in his pocket.

"Maybe you should take him downtown and have him go through mug shots," I suggested. "He might . . ."

Connelly's mouth tightened. "So now you're doing my job?"

"No. I just . . ."

"Listen, you stick to your animals and let me stick to my investigations. We'll all get along better that way. I know you think you're real hot after what you pulled off last winter, but in my book all you did was make a mess." I opened my mouth to say something but before I could he was talking to Julio. "And you'd better stay away from A.J.'s. I catch you down there and I'm gonna run you in, understand?" Julio looked at the floor. "Understand?" Connelly repeated in a louder voice.

"Yeah, I understand," Julio said sullenly. Connelly turned to go. "Fat fucking faggot," Julio whispered under his breath.

Connelly wheeled around. "What did you say?"

"Nothing. I didn't say nuthin," Julio stammered.

"Good. Because I don't like garbage mouths." Then Connelly left.

I followed him out five minutes later. That scene had taken my last bit of strength out of me. Suddenly my knees were aching and the scars on my legs were itching so badly I wanted to tear my skin off. All I wanted to do was go home, get out of my clothes, fix myself a large Scotch, lie down on the sofa, and watch the rain fall. Which is what I did after I called the hospital to see how Lynn was doing and was told she was resting comfortably. Whatever that means.

Surprisingly I managed to get a good night's sleep. Usually when something goes wrong I toss and turn. I see walls dissolving into flames and timbers crashing to the ground. Or my dead husband leans over and whispers in my ear telling me all the things I'm doing wrong. But this time there were no bad dreams. No dreams at all. Or at least none that I could remember. When the alarm went off at 7:30, I was still asleep and it took me a minute to rise to the surface.

As I pulled myself out of bed, I reminded myself the first few steps of the day were always the worst and that the stiffness in my legs would disappear as I got moving. I turned on the shower. Then, while I waited for the hot water to kick in, I studied my right leg. Again. It was a morbid fascination I couldn't seem to control. A quarter of the skin on my calf was as shiny and taut and hairless as a marble's surface. There was another skin graft on my upper thigh and a couple of smaller patches on my other leg. I still hadn't accepted the scarring and I had to keep reminding myself that I'd been extremely lucky to get out of the fire with as little damage as I had.

I suppressed a shudder, grabbed the shampoo and stepped into the stall. No matter what the therapist had said, as far as I was concerned some memories were better left unremembered. And then I thought about Lynn and wondered how she was doing and whether or not she'd agree with that sentiment. As I ducked under the spray, I decided I'd sneak into the hospital and say hello before I went to the store. Usually the staff was pretty good about that kind of thing.

I closed my eyes and stood under the shower. While the water cascaded down me, I recalled how the nurses had let George come and visit me whenever he'd gotten off his shift. He'd just sat next to my bed and held my hand. I don't think I would have gotten through it without him. But then, I reminded myself, I hadn't had anyone else. And Lynn did. A minute later I got out, dried off, slipped on an old cotton T-shirt and a pair of underpants, and went down to the kitchen.

I was sitting at the table, legs wrapped around the chair rungs, reading the *National Enquirer* and dunking a chocolate bar into a cup of coffee and sucking off the liquid when the phone rang. I tipped my chair back and reached for the receiver. It was Tim.

"What's up?" I asked.

"Pardon me, but weren't you supposed to deliver two bags of birdseed to Mrs. Z. yesterday?"

I groaned. They were still in the trunk of the cab. With everything that had happened I'd forgotten all about them.

"Because she just called me wanting to know where they were."

I scratched the bridge of my nose. "Okay. Listen. Call her back and tell her I'll be right there." My visit to the hospital was obviously going to have to wait till later in the morning.

"Customers," Tim cracked. "You can't live with 'em and you can't kill 'em." Then he hung up.

I lit a cigarette, pushed myself away from the table, and went upstairs to get dressed. I put on a black tank top, a baggy pair of khakis, and some sandals. Then I combed my hair and pulled it back into a ponytail and started looking for my keys. Ten minutes later I was out the door. The wet grass lapped at my toes as I walked over the front lawn to get to my driveway. One week and the grass needed mowing again. Incredible. Everything had gone into a growth frenzy.

As I neared my checkered cab, I spotted my cat, James, skulking underneath the laurel hedge. The moment he saw me, he turned around and ran. The sound of peeping hung in the air. The creep had caught another bird, a baby by the sound of it. I just hoped it wasn't a finch. But I had a horrible feeling it was. Last year, I'd watched helplessly as he'd decimated the nest they'd made in the blue spruce in front of my house. You'd think they'd learn. But then, I reflected as I got in my cab and pulled out of the driveway, people don't, so why should birds?

It was a fresh, crisp morning. Washed clean by the storm, the houses, the cars, even the mica in the sidewalk glistened in the morning sun. The air was filled with the scent of honeysuckle and lily of the valley. Down the block three giggling children on Big Wheels chased one another up and down a driveway enjoying the respite from the hot humid weather. I hummed as I drove toward Agatha Zabreski's house.

Mrs. Z., as I called her, lived on Ontario, which was perpendicular to Otisco. Her house, a small colonial, was freshly painted, her little patch of grass always mowed, the flowers always tended, in contrast to most of the other houses on her street which leaned toward the rickety, the run-down, and the garbage strewn. She was sitting on her porch in a rocker waiting for me when I pulled up. She was seventy-five. A stereotypical little old lady with white hair, blue eyes, and a whispery voice. She had outlived a husband and a sister and, despite her constant protestations of ill health, I wouldn't be surprised if she outlived me as well. She was like the engine in an old Ford. No frills. Just the basics. But it would go on forever.

"Sorry I'm so late," I said as I got the birdseed out of the cab trunk and lugged it up the stairs.

"That's all right, dear." Agatha plucked at the cuff of her long-sleeve blouse. Even in the summer she was always cold. "I wouldn't have called, but you know how my babies get about their food."

Mrs. Z.'s babies consisted of a ten-year-old Moluccan, a Hyacinth Macaw, an African Grey, and two lovebirds, all of whom she shamelessly spoiled.

I gestured to the bags with my chin. "You want me to put them in the usual place?"

"Please, dear, if you would."

I pushed the screen door open with my shoulder and went inside. My arrival was greeted by a deafening cacophony of shrieks and squawks. But in spite of the birds, notoriously messy pets, the house was spotless. The floors were waxed to a high gloss, the cabbage-rose wallpaper was seamless, the mahogany furniture had been polished until it shone. In the living room the sofa and armchairs were slipcovered in chintz, their arms and backs protected by crocheted doilies. Family photos dotted the mantel. The smell of lemon oil lingered in the air, bringing back memories of my grandmother. She had kept a spotless house, too. Unlike me.

I skirted an ornately carved end table and walked through to the tiny study where Agatha kept her birds. The racket was deafening. Eardrums vibrating, I deposited the sacks of food on top of a chest of drawers that housed Mrs. Z.'s supplies, opened one of them up and filled all the food dishes. A merciful silence fell as the birds began to feed.

"Thank you, dear," Mrs. Z. said when I came back out on the porch. "You're very sweet. There's just one more thing, if you could." And she pointed down toward the sidewalk in front of her house. "My eyes aren't as good as they used to be, but I think I saw a puppy crawling under my steps while you were inside. I was wondering if you would mind terribly checking? It would make me feel better. I'd do it myself, but I'm feeling a little poorly this morning."

I sighed. That was one of the things about Mrs. Z. She always had another little thing or two for me to do whenever I came. But what the hell. I only hoped somebody would do this for me in my old age. So I told her it was no problem and went down to take a look. I had to get down on my hands and knees. The space underneath the steps smelled of dried leaves and mouse droppings and cat piss. It was dark and it took a minute for my eyes to adjust to the gloom, but when they did I saw the animal Mrs. Z. had been talking about. The puppy was cowering on the far side of the steps. It looked very young and very scared.

"Come on," I coaxed.

It didn't move. I made friendly noises. It stayed where it was. Finally I lost patience and hoping it wouldn't bite me reached in, grabbed the poor thing by the nape of its neck, and dragged it out. In the light I could see it was a cocker spaniel, three months old at the most. The puppy was a mess. It was so skinny its spine was sticking out. Its red fur was matted and clotted with dirt. And it had the biggest ears, feet, and eyes I'd ever seen.

I scrambled up off my knees. "You were right, Mrs. Z.," I said, showing her the dog.

She frowned and leaned forward. "I wonder if that's the one that's been yelping over in Joe Davis's backyard for the last three days? Maybe that's why it's been so quiet all of a sudden."

"Joe Davis?"

"He lives around the corner." And she compressed her lips into a thin line of disapproval.

"Well if he comes around asking for the dog you can tell him she's at the store."

Mrs. Z. sniffed. "I'll do no such thing. As far as I'm concerned that man couldn't take care of a flea, much less anything larger." Then she leaned back and fanned herself with the back of her hand. "My, it's heating right up again, don't you think?"

We chatted for a few more minutes, mostly about her birds, and then I left. As I pulled out into the street I caught a last glimpse of her sitting in her chair. There was little, I'd be willing to bet, that went on that she missed. It took me longer than usual to drive to the store, because I had to drive with my right hand and hold the puppy with my left otherwise she would have been down on the floor around the brakes. By the time I arrived at Noah's Ark I'd decided to keep her. Whoever had had her didn't deserve her. And anyway I'd fallen in love. I think it was the ears that did it. I had just gotten out of the car and was heading up to the store when a patrol car pulled up behind me. George Sampson hopped out.

He didn't look happy. I knew this because he was scowling and when a 6´4˝ three-hundred-pound man scowls you tend to notice. I told him he looked like he needed to take a day off.

"You know, spend some time at the beach, dig in your garden," I added even though I knew he didn't have a garden and hated the sun. But it was such fun teasing him—he was an easy mark—that I could never resist.

He grunted by way of reply. His uniform strained at the seams as he marched toward me. His skin was slick with sweat.

"So what you been doing down here anyway? I thought you were working the East Side."

He swatted at a fly. "I'm covering for Zimmer. He's out for the week getting his balls tied up." His voice was hard and flat.

"My condolences."

He brushed my comment aside, hooked his thumbs into his belt, and planted his feet on the sidewalk. "You know how you told me you didn't know the guy your friend found. He looked familiar, but you didn't know him."

"I remember."

"Well I ran into Connelly this morning and he told me

they were going through this guy's clothes and guess whose name they found in one of his pockets?"

"Madonna's?" I asked hopefully.

"Yours."

"Oh dear." I shifted the puppy to my other arm. "Maybe he wanted to buy some cat food. Or a chew toy."

"Robin, he didn't have any pets. And the note didn't say Noah's Ark. It said Robin Light. And it had your home number on it, not the store's."

"Well, who knows? Maybe he wanted a private consultation? Maybe he was interested in setting up a two-hundred-gallon fish tank."

George looked me square in the eye. "For your sake, I hope you're telling the truth."

"Why shouldn't I be?"

"I don't know." George pointed a finger at me. "I never know with you. But I do know this. Connelly's gonna be calling to ask you about this and if he finds out you've been lying to him he's gonna haul you down and charge you with 'obstructing' and anything else he can think of. So don't piss him off. He's already plenty pissed off with you from yesterday. He told me and these are his exact words, 'that you're an arrogant know-it-all bitch.' "

"I'm flattered."

George smiled in spite of himself. "And do me a favor. Don't let him know I told you. I don't want to get called down."

"You know I won't say anything."

"I know," George said. "Just making sure."

"Connelly didn't happen to tell you this guy's name, by any chance?"

George shook his head. "Sorry." Then he gestured at the

pup who was now wiggling in my arms. "So what have you got there?"

"My new dog."

"Where'd you get him?"

"Her. She was hiding under Mrs. Z.'s porch. Tell me, who's Joe Davis?"

George gave me a funny glance. "Why do you want to know?"

"I was just curious. Mrs. Z. mentioned him."

"In connection with what?"

"Nothing. He's a neighbor of hers."

"Just stay away from him."

"Well I wasn't planning on inviting him over for dinner."

"Because he's a mean mother."

"How mean?"

George stroked his chin. "They say he sucked a man's eyeball clean out of his head once."

"Is that physically possible?"

"I don't know and I don't want to find out."

I was about to agree with him when the squad car radio started making noises. George looked at it in disgust.

"You'd better go," I said when he made no move to leave. "You don't want to get written up."

"Yeah. Yeah. I know." He started for the car. "Listen, I'll give you a call later. See how things are going."

"Do that."

He nodded, got in the squad car and drove away. The puppy let out a squeak and licked my chin. But as I turned and went back inside the store I wasn't thinking about the dog, I was thinking about what George had come by to tell me.

My name being linked with the body, even in a tangential way didn't please me. At all.

That meant another chat with Connelly.

A prospect in which I was not anxious to indulge.

I decided I'd better get down to the hospital and find out from Lynn who this guy was and what the hell was going on.

Because as far as I was concerned the only thing worse than sitting in the Public Safety Building answering stupid questions, was sitting in the Public Safety Building answering stupid questions I didn't have the answers to.

I had just walked in the store and was still thinking about what I was going to ask Lynn when Tim came bounding out of the storeroom to tell me that Connelly had called and that he wanted to speak to me ASAP.

The man was fast. I had to give him that, I thought as I filled Tim in on what George had told me.

"Not good," he said when I was done. "Not good at all."

No kidding. But I wasn't in the mood for one of those long on speculation and short on fact discussions, so I held up the puppy and asked Tim what he thought about her instead.

"Pickles will be *so* pleased."

"She'll adjust," I said impatiently, disregarding his sarcasm. "Besides that."

"She's filthy. Where did you find her? At the garbage dump?"

"She was hiding under Mrs. Z.'s porch."

"Too bad she's not Gomez."

"Yeah. Isn't it?"

"I'll tell you one thing. She definitely needs a bath."

"I totally agree," I said plopping the puppy in Tim's arms. "Have fun. And don't forget to clean the wax out of her ears."

"Me?" he squeaked.

"And use some conditioner on her coat. It'll make it easier to get the knots out," I continued. "Then give her some food, not too much, since we don't want to upset her stomach," I continued blithely. It's always so much easier to give orders than to carry them out.

Tim began tapping his left foot on the floor in annoyance. "And where are you going to be while I'm doing all this, not to mention mopping the floor and waiting on customers?" he demanded.

"Talking to Lynn."

Tim scowled. He didn't like my answer. Even though he hadn't said anything, I knew he thought I should stay away from the whole, sorry mess. "And what about Connelly?" he demanded.

"What about him?"

"Aren't you going to call him back?"

"Maybe later." I didn't want to talk to Connelly. At the moment I didn't have anything to say to him and I didn't want to hear what he had to say to me.

Tim pressed his lips together in disapproval. "And what do I say if he calls again?"

I shrugged. "Lie. Tell him I haven't been in and you don't know where I am." I ruffled the puppy's ears. Then I left before Tim could reply. Whatever he had to say could keep until I got back.

Chapter
4

I looked at my watch as I drove down Genesee Street. Even though it was only eleven, I was beginning to sweat. The cars around me shimmered in the sun, but I noticed that toward the west the sky had begun to gray over. Yesterday's rain had given us a small reprieve, but it obviously wasn't going to last. By this afternoon we would be smothering under another blanket of hot, humid air.

I was thinking about how Syracuse weather only seemed to come in two modes—freezing or boiling—as I pulled up in front of St. Ann's. There were no parking spaces in front of the hospital, but then there never were. For a moment I thought about parking in a No Parking area, but I remembered my fourteen unpaid parking tickets and headed for the garage. I could have saved myself the three bucks though because the nurse on the eighth floor told me that Lynn had checked herself out at nine o'clock that morning. I got back in the car and headed toward Dewitt.

The drive over to Woodchuck Hill Road took about twenty minutes. Most of the houses along the lane were expensive and secluded and Lynn's was no exception. The access road to it was narrow, the sign bearing the number was small and unobtrusive. If you didn't know what you were looking for, the chances were you'd miss it.

The house stood in the middle of a heavily wooded lot. It was cedar shingled and aggressively modern with sharp corners, two cathedral ceilings, and lots of windows and skylights. The landscaping had the same minimalist feel. No blowsy perennial English borders here. Just arbovitea and massed white impatiens. I parked my cab in back of the white Jag, got out, and rang the doorbell. A chime sounded above the drone of the insects. But no one answered.

After a moment I walked around to the back. My sandals made a faint crunching noise on the small black stones that lined the path I was following. Otherwise everything was still. Even the birds seemed to be dozing in the heat. When I came around the house I saw a large expanse of golf course-perfect grass going down to the woods. The new tiled oval-shaped swimming pool was set three-quarters of the way up toward the house. Dark green tables and lounge chairs were scattered around the water's edge.

Lynn was lying in one. She was wearing a black bikini and a vacant expression. When she saw me she raised her hand in a greeting, then let it drop back down again. As I got closer I could see her face was drawn, her eyes puffy from crying. I drew up a chair, sat down next to her, and asked how things were going.

She shrugged her shoulders and went back to studying the trees.

"Are you okay?"

"What do you think?" she replied glaring at me.

"I think you've probably been better."

"If you know, then why did you ask?"

Great. Just what I wanted. Lynn in a pissy mood.

"The pool came out well," I said, backtracking to a more neutral subject. "I like the tiles." They were aqua and white.

"They're Italian."

I nudged her. "Hey, remember the summer you worked on the *Herald* and we used to sneak off and meet your brother out at Green Lakes and spend the day swimming?"

Lynn's eyes came alive at the memory. She managed a half smile. "Sometimes we'd just ride around."

"Get an ice cream cone."

"Play miniature golf."

"We had fun, didn't we?" I asked.

"Yes, we did."

"That was the summer before you got married," I reminded her.

"And you got married the year after," she recalled.

I gave a regretful laugh. "Boy, was that a mistake."

Lynn bit her lip and turned her head away.

"Why'd you marry Gordon anyway?" I inquired. I'd always been curious, but Lynn wasn't one of those people you asked personal questions of.

"I was pregnant," she whispered, still not looking at me.

"You never told me." How many other things I wondered didn't I know about the woman sitting in front of me?

She gave a small shrug. "It was a long time ago."

"What happened to the baby?"

Lynn's fingers whitened as she gripped the edge of her chair. "I had a miscarriage when I was four months along." She gave a bitter laugh and turned and faced me. "Gordon was supposed to take me away, we were supposed to go to California. He was going to get a job in an insurance agency, he had one already lined up, and I was going to stay home and play happy housewife. But after the miscarriage," Lynn stumbled over the word, "my father offered him a job with the company and he took it." She looked down at her nails. "I guess Gordon couldn't resist the money. He'd never had any growing up." Lynn's voice grew fierce. "He should have said no. I told him to, but he said he was just going to take the job for a little while. Things would have been different if we'd gone away," she cried. "I know they would have been. He should have listened to me. He should have." As she hit the side of her chair for emphasis, her face crumpled.

Embarrassed, I tried to distract her by changing the subject. "Hey, remember when you were seeing Michael?" I asked.

Lynn gave a half sob, half laugh. "And you said I could use your house and Murphy walked in on Michael and me. You should have seen the expression on your husband's face."

"I bet. Whatever happened to Michael anyway?"

Lynn shrugged. Whatever she'd been feeling was gone. She had herself under control again. "He got transferred to Atlanta."

"You ever hear from him?"

"He called a couple of times, but I never called back. He never did much for me anyhow."

"You're lucky Gordon never found out."

"Sometimes I almost wish he had." And Lynn reached over to the table next to her, lifted up a tall frosted glass and took a long sip out of it. "Gin and tonic," she explained after she'd put it down. "And don't say it's too early."

"I wasn't going to."

"Good. You want one?"

"Sure. Why not?"

I watched Lynn hoist herself out of her chair and walk

into the house. Her gait was a little wobbly. I wondered how many she'd had. As I waited for her to come back I thought about what it would be like to be Lynn. To have her money, her looks, her lovers. I could handle it, I decided.

Very easily.

Except for Gordon.

I didn't think I could deal with him. Correction. I could deal with him if I had to, I just didn't want to have to.

I'd heard the rumors and I'd seen his dark moods, the way he'd slam into the house when he was mad, the way Lynn shrank from him then. Once in a while I'd see black-and-blue marks on Lynn's arms, but if I asked about them she'd always laugh and say she'd bumped into something. And maybe she had. It was possible. The fact was I really didn't know what happened between Lynn and Gordon. The truth was neither she nor I talked about our marriages. We both had lousy ones and we both went out to forget about them. I sighed thinking about all the years I'd wasted with Murphy.

When Lynn returned a few minutes later I'd taken my sandals off and was dangling my toes in the water. She handed me my drink, got hers, and sat down next to me. We drank in silence. For every sip I took she had four. I'd been hoping she'd start the conversation, but it was clear that that wasn't going to be the case. If I wanted to dance, I'd have to call the music.

"We have to talk," I finally said after another minute had elapsed.

"About what?"

"About what happened yesterday." What the hell did she think I'd come to talk about? The latest charity ball?

Lynn licked her lips nervously. "Of course. What do you want to know?"

I twisted my body so I was facing her. "Why don't you start by telling me why you didn't come out of the house when you found that guy?" I asked, figuring I'd work my way up to the more important stuff.

"I just . . . I couldn't. . . ." She ducked her head as she searched for the right words. "I saw him like that and I knew. I knew just by looking. But I had to make sure. And then I don't know. Something happened. I got down on my knees and I couldn't get up. I felt so heavy. I couldn't move. It was like I was paralyzed. I heard you calling, but you sounded so far away. And there was so much blood. It was on my hands. Over my suit. I couldn't get it off."

"It's okay." I patted her shoulder.

"I kept seeing it last night." She shuddered and took a swallow from her glass.

A dragonfly flitted by and we both watched it for a few seconds.

"Who was he?" I asked when it had disappeared.

"Who?" Lynn said. Her eyes took on a blank look.

"The guy whose body you found."

"Oh, him." Lynn licked her lips again.

"Does he have a name?"

"Of course." She gave a shrill little laugh. "Everyone has a name."

"Then how about stopping the bullshit and telling me what it is." I mean enough was enough. It wasn't as if I was asking for the combination to her safe-deposit box.

Lynn started to get up.

"Where are you going?"

"To freshen my drink," she stammered.

"That can wait."

A shiver went through her body. "Can't we do this another time?" she pleaded.

"No, we can't." I put my face close to hers. "One of Connelly's men . . ."

"Connelly?"

"The detective assigned to this case found my name and phone number in a pocket in one of this guy's shirts and now he wants to talk to me."

She made a fluttering motion with her hands. "I don't feel very well. I need to go upstairs and lie down."

"You're not going anywhere until you tell me what I want to know," I said, resisting the urge to slap her silly. "You can't drag me into something and then leave me hanging out to dry."

Lynn moistened her lips again. "I didn't drag you in. You offered to come."

"Is that a fact?" I could feel myself growing hot with anger. "I came because it looked like you needed some support."

She looked away.

"Tell me, I'm curious, did you give the police and Gordon the same runaround you're giving me?"

"No." Lynn swallowed. "I told them Brandon . . ."

"That's his name?"

"Yes."

". . . Had stolen something and I was trying to get it back." Lynn covered her face with her hands and started sobbing.

"Here." I handed Lynn her gin and tonic. "Take some more of this."

She grasped the glass with two trembling hands and took a big swallow. "He was so sweet. And he reminded me of . . ." Her mouth began trembling again. "Of someone. Not the way he looked, you understand. But there was something about him. A quality. God, I never should have given him Gordon's shirt. But his had gotten wet in the rain. And I never thought Gordon would miss it. He's got so many. But he kept asking and asking." Lynn buried her head in her hands. "This is all my fault. Why does everything I do turn out wrong?" she moaned.

"Lynn, that's not true."

"No. Don't say that. You can't possibly imagine." And she raised her head. "I know what I did was bad, but I can't help it . . . I can't." And she started sobbing again.

My stomach was knotting as I put my hand over hers. My God, I thought. Had Manuel been right? Had she killed that man? No. I pushed the thought away. She was talking about something else. She had to be.

Suddenly I was sorry I'd come.

I didn't want to hear any more.

I wanted to leave.

But I couldn't walk away from Lynn when she was in this state so I stroked her arm and told her to hush. After a minute or two her crying subsided. I was just about to help her up when I saw her husband, Gordon Marshall, and her brother, Ken Stanley, striding toward us over the grass.

Once again I was surprised at how much Ken looked like Lynn. He had the same slender build. The same hazel eyes. The slightly upturned nose. The cleft in the chin. Except for the ten-year difference in ages and the fact that he had brown hair and hers was blond, he could have been her twin. Gordon, Lynn's husband, reached us first. With his dark hair, electric blue eyes, regular features, even teeth, and lean, well-exercised body he could have been a model. But the perpetual look of disdain that he wore made him, to my lights, a cold and unattractive man.

"What are you doing here?" he snapped at me.

"Talking to Lynn."

"You should have called first. It's obvious she's in no condition to see anyone now." Then he turned toward his wife. "Are you okay?"

Lynn looked up and nodded.

"You don't look it." He shot me a venomous glance.

Lynn's brother held out his hand. "Come," he murmured to his sister. "I'll take you upstairs."

She rose slowly.

"There's no reason why you have to be bothered by all of this nonsense," Gordon said to her as he clucked her under the chin. "The death of a boy that works on the line out at the plant has nothing to do with you."

Now that was interesting. This guy worked in the family business.

"But . . ." Lynn protested.

"No, Gordon's right," Ken said, giving Lynn's arm a sympathetic pat. "What you need now is rest."

"My wife," Gordon explained to me as he put his arm around her shoulder and gave her a proprietary hug, "feels things very deeply. But," Gordon continued, "her brother and I have been telling her that she must learn to gain some perspective, isn't that right, darling?"

Lynn nodded weakly.

"She's really had an awful shock." Did Lynn flinch as Gordon stroked her hair or was I just imagining it? "But she'll be fine in a few weeks, won't you, sweets?"

"Yes," Lynn whispered.

Gordon and her brother began leading her off. I'd walked a couple of feet when Lynn yelled for me to wait. She shrugged off Gordon's arm, ran back to me, and gave me a hug.

"I'll call you later," she whispered in my ear. "There's something I have to tell you."

Something was very wrong here, I thought as I watched

Lynn being led away. The whole thing stank. Her being down on Otisco Street. Her reluctance to give me the guy's name. Her convenient fits of crying. Her brother's and her husband's descents. Their whisking her away. And now this. None of it added up. What the hell did she want to tell me anyway? I wanted to run up and tear her away from the two men, but that would only have made things worse. I'd just have to call her later on. I was meandering back up the garden path, kicking the black stones in a fit of frustration when I ran smack into Connelly.

"You," he said, shaking a fat finger at me, "are in serious trouble."

Chapter
5

I decided to play dumb.

"And why's that?" I asked him. Connelly looked worse than yesterday if that was possible. His suit was even more wrinkled, his hair or what there was of it was even more disheveled, and his eyes were redder. He'd definitely been putting in some hours.

"Remember what you told me yesterday about not knowing the identity of the guy whose body you found?"

"I remember."

"Well, then how come your name and phone number was in one of his shirt pockets?"

"Oh my God! Was it really?" I cried, taking the naive route. He peered at my face while I talked, searching it for telltale signs of lying. But I managed to keep my eye blinks under control. Which was good. George didn't need any additional aggravation and he'd sure as hell get it if Connelly found out he'd been feeding me information.

"So you're saying you don't know this Brandon Douglas?" Connelly repeated when I was done.

"That's right."

"You're sure?"

"Yes."

"Absolutely?"

"That's what I just said, didn't I?" I replied with as much conviction as I could muster. After all, I told myself, thinking someone looks familiar and knowing that you know them are really two different propositions.

"Because," Connelly informed me, "if you know and you don't tell me that's obstructing an investigation."

"Really? Are you threatening me?"

Connelly gave a little tight-lipped smile. "What I'm doing is reminding you of what can happen if I find out you haven't been telling me the truth." A pause. Then, "Which I don't think you are."

Maybe it was the heat, maybe it was my nerves, maybe I was reacting to my visit with Lynn, but suddenly my patience went. "Listen," I snapped. "I just told you I don't fucking know for the last time. Now get off my back."

"Hey! Watch the language."

"Oh, excuse me," I sneered. "I forgot you don't use words like 'fuck' down at the PSB."

Connelly's cheeks reddened. "I should run your ass in right now."

"For what? Using the 'F' word?" Connelly's cheeks turned scarlet. His face was beginning to look like a bing cherry. "If I were you," I continued, even though I knew I should stop, "I'd spend more time looking for the guy Julio told you about and less time harassing Lynn and me. Then you might actually solve the case."

Connelly opened his mouth to answer, but no words came out.

It was time to leave.

In fact, it was past time.

I thought about waving as I pulled out of the driveway, but the shred of common sense I had left made me repress the impulse. Then as I drove toward the store I thought about how good what I had just done had felt and about how stupid it had been. I should have just answered Connelly's questions and shut up. But for some reason ever since my husband had died, I seemed to have lost a lot of my ability to let things slide, to not comment, to not see, to be put upon. I don't know, maybe it was because I'd done too much of that stuff when he was alive. Or maybe not. The reasons didn't really matter. All I knew was that I was changing in some fundamental way. But I didn't know how. Or whether the change was going to be good or bad.

I was still mulling over that question when I stepped into Noah's Ark. Three people were standing by the counter: Tim, Manuel, and some guy who I didn't know. The guy who I didn't know looked angry. The other two looked nervous.

"Here's the owner," Tim said to the stranger.

The man turned and glared in my direction. He was 5´10˝, with a hard, stringy body, and greased-back black hair. His gray T-shirt was smudged with dirt and so were his jeans. As I walked toward him I realized what it was about him that disturbed me. His face was slightly lopsided. It looked like it had been taken apart and sewed back together by someone who hadn't quite mastered his craft.

"Yes?" I said brightly, giving him my best customer-pleasing smile.

He scowled. "I understand you have something that belongs to me."

"I don't think so." I couldn't imagine having anything this man owned I decided as Pickles jumped on the counter. She meowed and I gave her an absentminded pat.

"That's not what some of my neighbors say. They say they saw you driving away this morning in that yellow cab of yours with something of mine in it."

"I'm afraid I don't understand, Mr. . . . ?"

"Davis."

"Joe Davis?" I hazarded, hoping I was wrong.

"That's me."

OhmyGod. Not for the first time, I damned the checkered cab I drove. It was just too conspicuous.

"I want my dog," Davis repeated.

"I'm sure you do," I heard myself say in a surprisingly firm voice. "But I don't have it. Your neighbors made a mistake."

Davis thrust his chin out. "You'd better not be lying to me."

"Now why would I do that?" I protested as Pickles turned and jumped off the counter. She landed with a loud thud and trotted, tail held high and belly swinging, into the backroom.

Davis's face hardened. "I'll be back if I find you got her," he warned. "You can bet on it. And boy," he continued, "I sure wouldn't want to be you if I do." Then he pointed to an aquarium at the end of the counter. "What's that?"

I followed his finger. "That's Martha." Great. Tim had put the spider out front after I'd told him to keep her in the back.

"She bite?"

"Only when she's upset."

Davis reached in his pants and whipped out a roll of bills. "How much?

I took a deep breath and let it out before replying. "She's not for sale."

Davis's eyes narrowed into slits. "I said how much?"

"I'm keeping her for someone," I hurriedly went on. "A policeman. He's very attached to her, isn't he, Manuel?"

Manuel swallowed hard and nodded. He looked more frightened now than he had yesterday when we'd found Brandon Douglas's body.

"That's two strikes for you. One more and . . ." Davis shrugged. "Well, I think I'll just leave that to your imagination."

"Don't bother," I retorted. "I have a bad one. Now get out of here before I call the cops." And I pointed to the door.

He leered. "You and me. We're going to have fun." Then he turned around and sauntered out of the shop. As soon as the door slammed I collapsed against the counter.

"Jesus," Manuel whispered. "You have Joe Davis's dog?"

"Puppy," I corrected mechanically.

"You know what that guy did?"

"Yeah, yeah. I know. George already told me. He sucked some guy's eyeball right out of his head."

"And swallowed it," Manuel added.

Tim turned white.

"I don't think that's physically possible," I answered as I reached under the counter with shaking hands for my pack of Camels and took out a cigarette. "He's just got some good PR."

"Maybe you should give the dog back," Manuel suggested. "You know, say you found it wandering around somewhere."

"No." I found my matches in my pants pocket and lit up. "I'm not doing that."

"Robin, be sensible," Tim pleaded.

"It's not a matter of sensible." I watched the smoke I'd exhaled drift toward the ceiling. "You saw the condition that animal was in. Forget it. I'd rather kill her and give

Davis back her corpse than return her. It would be kinder."

"But, Jesus, Robin," Manuel moaned. "Joe Davis."

"He'll forget about her," I predicted with more confidence than I felt.

"But what if he comes back here and sees her?" Tim asked.

"He won't. He's never been in the store before, so I don't see why he should start coming here now. And even if he does, big deal. After the pup has had a few good meals and gained a little weight, he won't recognize her. I mean really, one red cocker spaniel puppy looks like another."

"Well, I hope you're right," Tim said.

"Me, too." I looked around. "By the way, where is she?"

"Sleeping in the back. Fortunately for us."

"You know what?" Manuel said to me.

"What?"

"I got a present for you." And he took something out of his pocket and pressed it into my palm. "It's a stiletto," he explained. "Just in case."

"Just in case what?" I teased.

"Whatever. Go on. Press the button."

I did as I was told. The blade jumped out. "Nasty."

"Eight inches. Go on, take it."

I decided he was right. Having it couldn't hurt. Especially with Joe Davis running around. I thanked Manuel, retracted the blade, and was putting the knife in my pocket when the door opened and Maria came in. Her face was clean, but her eyes were sad.

"Did you find Gomez yet?" I asked.

She shook her head and played with the pleats in her skirt.

"Did you call the ASPCA?"

"We went out there."

"No Gomez, hunh?"

She put one pink sandal behind the other. "We walked all over, too."

"Don't worry, she'll show up."

"My mommy says she thinks she was stolen. She said Mrs. Roble's dog is missing and so is Mrs. Myer's." Her lower lip started to tremble.

"Would you like to see our new puppy?" I asked, trying to distract her. "I think she could use a hug."

Maria nodded.

"Good." I turned to Manuel. "Please take her out back and show her where the dog is."

"Me?" His voice quivered with indignation. "I ain't no baby-sitter."

"Well, you are now," I retorted.

I expected another comment, but he just bit his lip and stalked off.

"That was silly," Tim said when they were gone.

"What?"

"Telling Maria to go in and play with the puppy."

"Why?"

"Well, she lost her dog and this one's so cute . . ."

"You're right." I hadn't thought of it that way, but by trying to help I might have just made things worse.

"I mean what if Gomez doesn't turn up?"

"I guess we'll deal with it then." And I went into my office to look through the mail.

I shooed Pickles off my chair and sat down behind my desk but I couldn't concentrate. I kept thinking about Lynn. Finally I tried to call her but I got the answering machine instead. I left a message, hung up, and studied the new price list from Herps Of The World. If she didn't call back, I'd try again tomorrow when things had calmed down. And with that decided I went back to my price list. I was in the middle of figuring out whether or not we really needed a wide-striped ball python when the phone rang again. I picked it up. Lynn's father's secretary was on the line. It seemed Mr. Stanley wanted to see me. Today.

I agreed to go. Actually I was happy to go. Maybe he had a few of the answers I needed. After a little haggling we set up a mutually agreeable time and I hung up. The rest of the day went by quickly. I phoned in orders for crickets and mealworms, talked to the air-conditioner repair man about coming to check the leak in our cooling system, did a little bookkeeping, and rearranged the displays in the salt water aquariums. At seven I left Tim in charge of closing up the store and walked out the door. It was hot and hazy. The smell of barbecuing meat hung in the air, making me realize how hungry I was. But I didn't have time to eat. I sighed and got in my cab.

The drive over to the Stanley Pharmaceutical plant took me a little over a half hour. The traffic was light and as I drove I took the opportunity to review the little I knew about the business. Stanley Pharmaceuticals was a family owned operation that manufactured generic drugs—mostly cold remedies—for places like Fay's and RX. But recently it had been doing a little dabbling in the biotech business and according to an article I'd read in the *Herald Journal,* the company was, 'poised to take off,' although where it was poised to take off to the article didn't say.

As I pulled into the parking lot, I was surprised to see it was full. Somehow at 7:30 at night I hadn't expected that, but then I realized the place probably ran double, or even triple shifts. I got out and looked around. Then I spotted the doors marked RECEPTION and headed toward them. They were locked and I had to buzz to be let in. The woman who opened the door looked meaningfully at her watch, then escorted me through the silent office. I realized as we walked down the darkened corridors that even though I'd known Lynn for a little over seven years, I'd never met her father. But I'd seen his picture. It appeared in the *Herald* on a regular basis. The man was a player in the local political game, a supporter of the 'right' charities.

Mr. Stanley rose from his desk as his secretary ushered me in. He had a moon face with a big nose, small ears, hard eyes, and a little pinched mouth. His suit was well tailored, his nails manicured, his hair, or what there was of it, expensively cut.

"Come in, come in," he said, motioning me forward.

I took in the furnishings as I made my way over to the chair he had indicated. The furniture was genuine Chippendale, good Orientals blanketed the floor, and the walls were covered with shelves full of blue and white Chinese pottery. It was a beautiful room, one I would have expected to find on Park Avenue instead of in the middle of a manufacturing plant.

"Thanks for coming." Mr. Stanley sat back down while I lowered myself into a hunter green leather chair off to the side of his desk. The desk itself was enormous. And bare. A crystal pen and pencil set, a green felt blotter, and a silver framed photograph of Lynn gazing up adoringly at her elder brother were the only items on it. He coughed into his hand. "I just wanted to thank you personally for what you did for Lynn and to apologize for any inconvenience you've experienced."

"But I didn't do anything," I protested.

"You stayed with her. You comforted her. That's enough." Lynn's father leaned forward. "She's a very sensitive individual." It struck me I'd been hearing that a lot lately. "She always has been. This is a dreadful thing for her to have to go through." I managed to refrain from saying how much worse it must have been for the guy who got killed. "Naturally her mother and I want to do everything we can to get this . . . mess cleared up."

"Naturally."

Lynn's father puffed his cheeks in and out. "We've already spoken to a lawyer, of course."

"Of course."

"One who specializes in criminal law." And he mentioned the name of the best one in Syracuse. "He seems to feel we have nothing to worry about."

"That's good," I murmured.

"And, of course, the fact that Connelly had my son-in-law's gun collection checked and found that none of them had been fired certainly helps our case."

I wanted to slap my forehead. How could I have forgotten about those?

"But our lawyer did indicate that things might be resolved in a more expeditious manner if the police found the young man you mentioned seeing."

"Actually I didn't see him."

"You didn't?" Mr. Stanley raised an eyebrow. "Ken told me you had." Since I hadn't told Ken or Lynn I could only assume Connelly had.

"He's mistaken. A kid called Julio did."

"Aha." Mr. Stanley made a steeple with his fingers and rested his chin on it. "And this Julio . . ."

"Menedez."

"You feel his information is trustworthy?"

"I do, but the police don't." And I told Mr. Stanley about my conversation with Connelly. "Maybe you should talk to his superior," I suggested.

"Thank you. I definitely will." Mr. Stanley nodded his head vigorously. "Yes, I definitely will. You can be sure of that."

Poor Connelly. I managed not to smile at the thought of the dressing-down he was going to receive. "I understand the man who was killed worked here."

"So the police informed me." Mr. Stanley scratched at his cheek. "Evidently he worked on the line. But I can't honestly say I could put a face to the name. These days the people out there tend to come and go." Then he reached in his desk, took out an envelope, got up, and walked over to me. "Here. This is for you," he said, handing the envelope to me. "As a token of my family's appreciation."

"But . . ."

"No buts." He shook my hand. "And if there's anything I can ever do for you," he said as I rose, "please let me know. I do have some influence around this town." Then he buzzed for his secretary, who escorted me out.

I tore open the envelope as soon as I got out into the parking lot.

There was a four-thousand-dollar check inside and the word, 'thanks.'

I was nonplussed.

But then I saw something that surprised me even more.

Joe Davis was striding across the far corner of the parking lot with a group of men. They were all laughing and talking and slapping one another on the back. Most were carrying Thermoses and brown paper bags or lunch boxes. Just as he got to a set of big double doors at the far end of the building he turned. Our eyes locked.

A smile flitted across his face.

Then he puckered his lips and made a sucking motion.

Suddenly my mouth felt like the Sahara.

Chapter
6

I was still watching Joe Davis—I couldn't seem to take my eyes off of him—as he gave a slight bow, turned, and disappeared inside the factory with the rest of the men.

For a few seconds all I was conscious of was the racing of my heart. As I started walking toward my cab I told myself that I was being ridiculous.

I told myself I was just letting Davis's PR get to me.

But I had to admit it was doing a good job.

As I went to get a cigarette out of my pocket I realized I still had Stanley's check clutched in my hand.

Which got me thinking about other things.

Like exactly why had Lynn's father given me this money?

Where I come from most people say thank you with a bouquet of flowers or a box of candy.

This felt like a payoff. But why? For what? It's not like I'd done anything for the man. Or had I, in some way? Only I didn't know it.

But then again Stanley was rich.

Maybe four thousand dollars to him was like a hundred dollars to me.

Maybe he was really grateful.

And this was his way of expressing it.

A little crude, but effective.

And then my mind wandered back to Joe Davis again.

I couldn't seem to help myself.

He obviously worked at the factory.

Which meant he probably knew Brandon.

In fact, I'd bet on it.

No. There were just too many coincidences, I decided as I swatted at a mosquito flying around my head.

And I don't like coincidences. They make me uneasy.

Especially when their numbers start getting up into the double digits.

And of course there were the other questions, the ones running around in the back of my head that I still hadn't gotten the answers to.

Like why had Lynn come running back to me as Gordon led her away?

What was it she had wanted to tell me?

God, she had looked so sad, so lost.

And who was this Brandon Douglas anyway?

What was his relationship to Lynn? Why was she so upset? Why had she wanted to see him so badly?

And then I came to the sixty-four-thousand-dollar question: why did he have my name and phone number in his pocket?

Speaking of sixty-four-thousand-dollar questions, I sighed and looked at the check in my hand again. And what the hell was I going to do with this? Deposit it? Return it? I didn't know. And I was too hot, hungry, and tired to make a decision.

I folded it up and stuffed it in my T-shirt pocket. I'd do a Scarlett O'Hara and think about it tomorrow. I got in the cab and drove off. I'd been planning to stop at Howie's, a trendy little restaurant in Armory Square, and get myself a bite to eat, but once I got there I realized I really wasn't up for something like black pasta with baby corn, nasturtiums, and goat cheese so I made a U-turn and headed off to my old standby, McDonald's—I tend to alternate between them and Kentucky Fried Chicken—where I got my usual: a double cheeseburger, a large french fries, two apple pies, and a Coke, after which I headed back toward Noah's Ark and picked up the puppy.

She peed in greeting the moment I came through the door. Then she came running toward me in an odd, stiff-legged, sideways gait, her body folded like an accordion. I knelt down and picked her up. She licked my chin, then gnawed on my finger while I got the paper towels from underneath the counter. Wouldn't you know it? I thought as I threw some down on the spreading puddle and mopped it up. I have a piddler. Then I locked up and headed on home. It was nine-thirty by the time I pulled up to my house.

I live on the East Side in a neighborhood just far enough away from Syracuse University to avoid the students, but close enough for faculty. The houses run from modest wood-sided colonials to ornate stuccos. Mine is somewhere in between. It's a medium-sized three bedroom, two-bath brick colonial. Nothing special. But I like it because it's light and cheerful and easy to take care of.

As I walked up the driveway I heard a hoot of laughter coming from the Myersons' screened-in porch. Somewhere down the block two cats screeched at each other. I stood on my bottom step and breathed in the perfumed night air. It was slightly cooler now, but the day's heat still lingered on, a promise of what tomorrow had to offer. I heard a drone in the sky and looked up. A plane flew by, its green and red lights twinkling against the ebony sky. For a moment I wished I was on it. After it was gone I fitted the key in my door lock, turned it, and went inside.

I'd thought I'd get the puppy settled down, eat my dinner, glance at the paper and watch a little TV, but I'd thought wrong. Because it turned out I had an uninvited guest: Manuel. I was not pleased.

He was sitting at the kitchen table with his feet propped up on one of its corners and his chair tilted back.

"Hey, it's about time," he said when he saw me.

I could feel my jaw muscles tightening as I strode toward him. "First of all get your feet down and second of all what the hell are you doing here?"

"Relax." He lowered his feet and sat up.

By now my hands were on my hips and my foot was tapping out a rapid rhythm out on the floor. "If you don't mind, I'd like an explanation."

Manuel stretched. "What does it look like? I came to see you, of course."

"Of course. Tell me, does the concept waiting to be invited in mean anything to you?"

He shrugged. "I got bored outside. Nothing to do. And anyway, there were too many flying things."

"Too bad."

"Hey," he protested, "don't get pissed at me. It's not my fault you have a lousy lock on your back window."

"Right. I forgot. Nothing is ever your fault." I set the puppy down on the floor. She began sniffing around my feet.

"You should thank me for coming here." Then Manuel stood up. "Seem familiar?" he asked, waving a small grayish-colored card around.

"I don't know. Should it?"

"Take another look," he instructed, practically shoving the thing under my nose.

"Jesus. Is that one of my business cards from when I was working at the *Herald Journal?*"

"Could be," Manuel sang and danced away.

"Where'd you get it?"

He did a little jig. "Five beans and Master Manuel will reveal all."

"Manuel," I warned, taking a step toward him. "Don't play games."

"All right. All right. Chill out." He waltzed over and handed me the card. "You know, you got no sense of humor."

"None. Now where'd you get it?"

"On Otisco Street."

"Where on Otisco Street?" I asked even though I had a pretty good idea what the answer was going to be.

"Where do you think? In the house you and I were in, of course."

"Of course."

He pointed to my soda. "Can I have a sip of that?"

I took the top off of the cup and pushed it over.

"How'd you get in? The place is still sealed off."

"Through the back." He took a gulp of Coke, then continued. "See I thought I lost my cigarette lighter there so me and Rabbit went in to look for it."

I rolled my eyes. "Give me a break."

"What? You don't believe me?" Manuel asked, trying to play the injured innocent and failing.

"Not even this much." I put my thumb and finger together an eighth of an inch. He pretended to sulk. I ignored him and continued. "What were you guys looking to rip off?"

"I don't do things like that anymore," he protested. "Ask my probation officer."

I managed not to laugh.

"Okay, okay," Manuel conceded after a few more seconds of silence on my part, "so big deal. Yeah me and Rabbit went in there looking to boost the CD player and TV. See he and Raven . . ."

"Raven?"

"The girl Rabbit's seeing. They ain't been gettin along too well lately. He thought that if he gave her the stuff it might sweeten her up, if you get my drift. I mean the guy was dead anyway, right? It wasn't like he was going to need it." Manuel stopped and took another gulp of soda.

"Go on," I prompted.

"And then, I don't know, we got to looking around . . ."

"To see if there was anything else worth taking?"

"Well yeah. Kinda. But there was nothing else there. Just clothes, weight-lifting stuff, that kind of shit. Nothing good. So we decide to leave. Well we're walking out when I spot these cartons stacked over by the kitchen wall and I figured why not? You never know, right? So I start going through them. The first and second ones are filled with more junk. The third one is, too—but guess what? Your card is in the bottom of the box along with all this other paper. So I took it. I figured you'd be interested."

"I am. What else was in there?"

"Like I said, junk. Crap."

"What kind of junk?"

"Ah, let's see." He tapped his cheek with his fingers. "A

high school yearbook. Some sort of scrapbook. A couple of old T-shirts. A couple of stuffed animals." He pointed to the McDonald's bag. "Listen, if you're not going to eat that hamburger . . ."

"Go ahead." I pushed the sack toward him and lit one of my cigarettes. "Take it all." Suddenly I wasn't hungry anymore. "Anything else?"

"A notebook. Like the kind my teachers were always after me to get." Manuel opened the bag, unwrapped the hamburger, and stuffed it in his mouth.

Looking at him eat, I wondered if his mother had made dinner that night.

"Sure," he answered when I asked. "She makes dinner every night. I just don't like what she cooks. Too many beans, man."

While Manuel polished off my food, I paced around the kitchen trying to make sense out of what Manuel had just told me. The puppy followed along, playing tag with my sandal.

What the hell was my card doing in that box, especially a card I hadn't used in a good four or five years?

I didn't have an inkling of an idea, but since this was the second time in two days my name had surfaced in connection with Brandon Douglas my alarm bell told me I'd better start looking for an answer. And fast. It was a miracle Connelly hadn't found the card already. I guess his evidence tecs hadn't done as good a job as they should have. But they could come back. And if they did who knew what else they were going to find in those cartons. No. I had to beat Connelly back in. And anyway I was curious. I wanted to get a handle on who this Brandon Douglas had been. He seemed to know who I was. I wanted to do the same for him.

I turned and walked over to the kitchen table. "Manuel," I said. "What did you do with the stuff?"

"What stuff?"

"The stuff you found in the carton you were telling me about."

"I left it on the kitchen table, why?"

"I want to see it."

He half turned. His mouth was full of french fries. "I'll take you in, but it'll cost you."

"Why should I pay you to do that?" I asked indignantly.

"The yellow tape is up."

"So?" I raised my eyebrows. "That didn't stop you, it's not going to stop me."

"Come on, Robin, be a pal," Manuel whined. "I need some money."

I gave an exasperated sigh. "You always need money. Why don't you get a job? You'd probably spend less energy working than you do hustling."

Manuel grabbed another handful of french fries and shoved them into his mouth. "Nobody wants to hire me," he informed me after he'd swallowed.

"Could it be because your appearance doesn't exactly inspire trust?" I asked sarcastically.

Manuel hung his head. "Don't be like that." For a moment I felt guilty until I realized he was just trying to put me on. Then he pointed a finger at me. "And anyway, you owe me. After all I *did* do you a favor. Plus I know where everything is. Think it over."

I did. Much as I hated to admit, I came to the conclusion that Manuel was right. Things would be simpler with him along. I stubbed out my cigarette and flicked it in the sink. "Okay. How much do you want?" I demanded.

Manuel got a sly expression on his face as he calculated his worth to me. "Thirty bucks," he finally said.

I snorted. "Thirty bucks? You've got to be kidding."

"Okay." Manuel rubbed his hand across his chin. "I'll do it for twenty."

"You'll do it for ten," I countered.

"Fifteen," Manuel shot back.

I nodded. Fifteen was a fair price. "You're on."

Manuel smiled. "Cash up front."

I laughed. "You think I'm that dumb. Half now, half later."

"Done," Manuel said.

We shook hands. Then Manuel started eating one of the apple pies and I reached over and grabbed the other.

It took me about fifteen minutes to settle the puppy down and another five to pull Manuel out the door. It was almost ten-thirty when we reached Otisco. The moment I saw how busy the street was, I realized I'd made a tactical error. Everyone was still out. Clusters of men and women leaned against cars or sat on porch steps, their voices rising and falling in the dark. A pack of screaming kids dodged in and out of the shadows spraying each other with water guns.

Toward the end of the block another group of kids were squealing with excitement as they set off M-80s and Black Cats. The fireworks popped and crackled and sparked in the street. I was debating whether to go or to stay when a squad car rounded the corner. The kids took one look and scattered. The cop pulled over to the side, got out, and ran after them. The decision had been made for me. I put my foot on the gas and sped off.

Manuel and I caught a late movie at the Carousel Mall. He wanted to see *Night Stalker,* a movie about a vampire that kills everyone in a town. I wanted to see the latest Harrison

Ford movie. Since I was paying, I won. But it was a Pyrrhic victory. Manuel didn't stop talking all the way through it. I was ready to slap duct tape on his mouth by the time we got out of there. Naturally though once we got in the car he had nothing to say. We drove back to Otisco in silence. The street was now empty, the only noise the electric hum of the street lamps. I parked the cab in the shadows and we got out. The house looked bigger than it had in the daylight.

The thing loomed. The scaffolding, the windows, the gabling all made it look like the house in a horror movie. Suddenly I was glad I had Manuel's knife in my pants pocket.

"Changed your mind?" Manuel whispered in my ear.

"No," I replied even though at that moment I would have liked to. "Let's go."

We walked up the driveway single file keeping as close to the side of the house as we could manage. Then we hit the backyard. It was even darker, the light blocked out by the surrounding trees. I'd taken about five steps when I stumbled over something hard in the grass, a cement block as it turned out, and stubbed my toe. I cursed under my breath.

"You okay?" Manuel asked as he hoisted himself up onto what was left of the porch.

"Fine," I answered through gritted teeth. A few seconds later, I followed him up.

We inched our way along one of the support beams, stopping every four or five steps to test for rotten wood. Then Manuel got to the door, opened it and we slipped inside. The first thing that struck me was the blackness. It was so dense it was almost palpable. Then there was the heat. And the silence. It was almost as if the house was waiting. I swallowed hard.

"The table's right next to you." Manuel's disembodied voice floated through the air.

"I remember."

"All the stuff's on it." Then I heard a click and saw a small spurt of flame. Manuel's face flickered in the yellow light cast by his cigarette lighter. "It wasn't this dark in here before," he complained as he held the lighter over the table so I could see.

"That's because you were here earlier," I pointed out.

"Hurry up," he urged. "I'm burning my fingers."

"I'm doing the best I can," I retorted.

Then I heard the noise.

Chapter
7

It sounded as if someone was tapping on the walls with the tips of their fingernails.

And it was coming from somewhere close by. Somewhere in the living room. Or near the kitchen door.

My skin prickled. The hair on my arms stood up.

Even though I knew it was probably a mouse trapped in the walls.

Or a rat.

Or a chipmunk.

It didn't matter.

Because I couldn't keep myself from remembering the noise I'd heard in the house on the afternoon that Brandon Douglas had died and wondering if maybe the killer had come back.

So I did what anyone else would do. Caught somewhere between fear and reason, I grabbed everything I could on the table, threw it all into the carton, and ran.

"Shit," Manuel gasped out when we got back to the car. "I wonder who that was?"

"Probably nobody."

"It sounded like someone to me."

"Come on," I said, opening the cab door and sliding in. "Let's get out of here."

I'd been planning on dropping off Manuel at his house, but when we got there he couldn't find his key and since he didn't want to wake up his mother and get yelled at I ended up taking him back home with me. Great. Just what I wanted. More Manuel. This, I decided as I turned the car around, must be my punishment for contributing to the delinquency of a minor.

It was a little before two o'clock by the time we rolled up to my place. I should have been exhausted, instead I was excited. I could hardly wait to sit down and go through everything in the carton. Manuel, on the other hand, was so tired he was having trouble keeping his eyes opened. He'd been nodding off in the cab on the drive over and when I opened my front door he marched straight into the living room and plopped down on the sofa. A moment later he was asleep, a slight snore issuing from his lips. Which suited me just fine. It would be easier to concentrate without Manuel's running commentary.

By that time the puppy was yipping in the kitchen, so I put the carton down on the end table next to the club chair and went and got her. She nestled in my arms as I poured myself a Scotch. Then I carried her back into the living room, sat down, and took my first good look at what I'd taken.

I pulled out two small stuffed purple teddy bears, the kind you get at the State Fair, a couple of tortoiseshell barrettes, some rubber bands, and lots of sheets of paper with doo-dlings on them. Then came two T-shirts, one pink, the other purple. The pink one had a picture of a dog, the purple one had a sleeping kitten. I looked at the labels. The only thing I found out was that you should wash them inside out. I threw them on the coffee table and went back to my digging. And that's when I hit pay dirt.

The loose-leaf album was covered in brown leather. The word REMEMBRANCES was embossed in gold. I opened it up. It was filled with black pages. I flipped through them. Each page was covered with a thin transparent plastic jacket. Inside each plastic sheath was a newspaper article. Each article dealt with the Janet Tyler murder. I closed my eyes and thought back.

It had been a simple, common story. Too common. An eighteen-year-old college student named Janet Tyler walks into a bar, has a couple of beers, and walks out never to be seen again. Two years later a birder stumbles over her body at the Montezuma Wildlife Reserve. All that's left are bones, a white plastic comb, and a pink bandana tied around a skeletal wrist. He throws up and calls the cops.

It takes them almost a month to ID the body. They finally do it from dental records. The family is notified. The investigation begins. Statements are taken. People are questioned. Lots of people. Periodic reports are issued to the newspapers declaring that an arrest is imminent. Only nothing happens. The leads dwindle. The reports are issued less frequently. The story moves off the front page to the second page of the metro section.

Then suddenly something new occurs. Big headlines. The killer has turned himself into the cops. Says he couldn't stand the strain. The photos show him as a skinny man who wears thick glasses and blinks a lot. Turns out he's the girl's cousin and he's had a thing for her for years. One day he finally works up the courage to put the moves on her, but she laughs at him, so he gets pissed and kills her. The cops buy the story. So does the judge. The guy, one Matt Lipsyle enters a guilty plea and is sentenced to twenty-five to life and is sent off to Attica. And that should have been the end of the story. Only it wasn't.

Not at all.

I quickly turned the pages. If I was right the column I'd done should be somewhere in the middle. I slowed down. Yes. Here it was. I took the paper out of its plastic jacket. It was yellow with age, crumpled around the edges, and smudged with greasy fingerprints. I didn't read it immediately. I pretty much remembered what I'd written. Instead, I closed my eyes and thought back to the day I'd driven down to Weedsport. It had been unseasonably warm for early October. The trees had looked burnished. Everything had been bathed in a golden light. I'd been happy to get the assignment. Actually, I would have been happy to do a story about a church Bingo tournament if it had gotten me out of the building for the afternoon.

My editor, who was on one of his periodic human-interest kicks, wanted me to do a follow-up piece on the Janet Tyler murder.

"Go down," he'd said. "Write about how everyone has put the murder behind them and is getting on with their lives, etc., etc., etc."

The only problem was: they weren't.

The reason was simple.

Nobody I spoke to thought Lipsyle had done it.

No one.

It wasn't in him to do something like that, they'd said.

He'd been too sick, they'd said.

And everyone had a different theory about why he'd confessed.

And there'd been no shortage of suggestions about who'd committed the murder, either.

They'd ranged all the way from a judge's son to a distant cousin to a drifter who came through the area every once in a while looking for work.

Everyone had been willing to talk.

Except Janet's mother.

She'd told me she had nothing left to say. Everything was all used up.

I'd spoken to her in her house on Angel Street as she scrubbed storm windows that already sparkled.

A gawky teenage boy, around sixteen or seventeen, had hovered in a corner by the door. Listening. Not saying anything.

"Janet's brother," the mother had explained as she went after another nonexistent smudge. "He hasn't been right since the day she disappeared. Spends most of his time in her room or moping around the house." She rubbed her reddened knuckles against her chin. "I've tried to get him out, but he just won't go. He don't listen to no one no more. He don't talk much, either."

I'd turned and asked him if he wanted to tell me anything.

But he hadn't answered. He'd just glared at me with amber-colored eyes. The same color as Brandon Douglas's I suddenly realized. My God. I took another sip of Scotch. Then another picture popped into my head, a picture of Brandon Douglas whirling around and running back inside the house.

His mother had shaken her head as she watched him go. "Just like his father—my second husband. He died four years ago. Now Janet's gone. That boy's all I got left and I'm afraid I'm going to lose him, too, and Jesus that ain't right."

"No it's not," I'd stammered.

Then I'd hurried away wanting to get as far away from her pain as possible. The boy's expression had stayed with me on the drive back to Syracuse. It had stayed with me as I'd written my story and filed it. When my editor read it he'd wanted me to go down and interview Lipsyle.

"Get a hot quote," he yelled at me as I went back to my phone to make the arrangements.

But there were no arrangements to make. Lipsyle hadn't wanted to talk to me. The warden I spoke to told me Lipsyle was HIV postive, was recovering from a bout of pneumonia, and never granted interviews to anyone. I wrote Lipsyle a couple of letters trying to get him to change his mind, but when he didn't answer my editor told me to forget about it. Which I did.

Until now.

The puppy rubbed her head against my hand as I absent-mindedly scratched behind her ears. One thing was for sure: Janet Tyler's little brother certainly hadn't gotten very far in this life. He was what? Twenty-two? Twenty-three at the most. But he'd looked older lying on the floor. His body had filled out, his features had grown into his face. The only thing that had been the same had been the eyes. Cat-colored eyes.

I took a sip of Scotch and thought that it was times like these that really made me want to believe in the possibility of an afterlife, to hope that we all get a second chance, if not a third and a fourth, and to wish that in some cosmic way everyone connects up with the people they loved again. I drained my glass and lit a cigarette. Then I nudged Manuel with my foot because I had to talk to somebody about what I'd just found out.

He moved slightly. I nudged him again.

"Whaz's up?" he mumbled in a voice hoarse with sleep.

"Wake up."

He opened his eyes, shut them, turned over, and buried his head under a throw pillow.

This time I leaned over and poked him in the ribs. "I know who Brandon Douglas is."

"That's nice," he murmured into the material.

"He's Janet Tyler's younger half-brother."

But Manuel didn't answer. I lifted the pillow. His eyes were shut, his mouth was slightly open. He was sound asleep again.

I turned back to the puppy who was now sitting in the club chair. "At least you care," I told her.

She wagged her tail in agreement. Just looking at her put me in a better frame of mind. When she cocked her head and gave me what could only be called a come-hither glance, I suddenly knew what I was going to call her: Miss Zsa Zsa after Zsa Zsa Gabor. Zsa Zsa for short. Then she yawned, her pink tongue curling in her mouth, and jumped onto the floor.

I scooped her up just as she was starting to pee, ran outside, and deposited her in the grass. She squatted, then when she was done began attacking a large dandelion. As I watched her, my mind went back to what I'd just been reading, what I'd been remembering.

And I wondered why Brandon Douglas had kept my card, the card I'd given to his mother so many years ago.

Had he wanted to talk to me about his sister's death? Because that's what the article I'd written had been about: everyone's suspicions.

Did he have some new ideas about who killed her?

Could those ideas have gotten him murdered?

I took a puff of my cigarette while I thought.

At first that concept seemed improbable.

After all the murder had happened almost ten years ago. My column was five years old.

A fair amount of time had elapsed.

But still. There were the articles. There was my card. He had saved it.

But if Brandon had wanted to speak to me, then why hadn't he called? He had my home number. The cops had found it in one of his shirt pockets.

Or maybe he had and couldn't get me. My answering machine had been out of commission for three or four weeks before I'd gotten around to buying a new one. Or maybe he'd just gotten disgusted and quit trying. Or maybe he was trying to gather evidence to back up his claims.

Which meant that the person he was interested in probably lived here, in Syracuse.

I flicked the cigarette onto the grass. The butt glowed among the tight little white balls of clover. Then I ground it out with my heel and I picked up the puppy and went inside. I'd just shut the front door when the phone started ringing. Who the hell could be calling this time of night? I wondered as I dashed into the kitchen to get it. God, I hoped it wasn't something awful, like Tim calling to tell me the store was on fire.

"Yes," I said into the receiver. "Talk to me."

"You see, Robin," Lynn said, "I'm calling like I said I would." Her speech was slurred to the point of near unintelligibility.

"Jesus, how much have you had?"

"About half a bottle. I just can't sleep," she cried.

"Neither can I," I said through gritted teeth.

I'd had enough. Why couldn't she just pass out quietly on the bathroom floor and leave me alone?

"It's all my fault. Everything."

"Lynn, go to bed."

"I don't know what to do."

"Go to bed," I repeated. "You're drunk. I'll talk to you tomorrow."

"I'm sorry, so sorry." She began to sob. Then the line went dead.

She'd hung up.

Good.

But then I started to worry.

What if she did something like fall and hit her head or take a couple of Valium?

I redialed.

Gordon answered.

"Listen . . ." I began.

"I know, I know," he replied, his voice sounding as sweet and sticky as liquid cough syrup. "It's all right. We've called a doctor. Everything is under control." And he hung up.

I called back.

The answering machine clicked on.

I tried again and got the same response.

So I ended up standing there at three in the morning, with my stomach churning, the receiver clutched in my hand, trying to decide what the hell to do.

Chapter
8

In the end I did nothing.

A fact which still makes me squirm whenever I think about it.

But it was late. I was exhausted. And I guess if we're doing truth-telling here, it was just easier and more convenient for me to tell myself that Lynn was hysterical and that her husband, even if I did think he was a world-class putz, would take care of her than it was to tell myself something was really wrong.

Because that would have meant I would have had to have hauled my ass over there and seen what the hell was going on.

A thing I wanted very much not to do.

Like I said: I was tired, it was late, and Lynn was drunk.

By the time I got there she'd probably be passed out anyway.

Instead, I told myself I'd check in on her first thing in the morning and put the receiver back on the hook. Then I closed the front door, locked up the house, and trundled off to bed. But I had trouble falling asleep. The sheets felt gritty, the air conditioner in my window seemed to be blowing out hot air instead of cold, and the puppy kept chewing my hair. After I finally did manage to doze off Lynn and her brother kept floating through my dreams. Her father was there, too. A baby kept crying in the distance. Only it sounded like a dog barking and even though I knew I had to find it, I couldn't.

I woke up groggy when the alarm went off at eight, feeling as if I could have used another three hours' worth of sleep. I managed to drag myself out of bed anyway and stumble outside with Zsa Zsa. After she peed I shook Manuel awake and called Lynn. I kept on getting a busy signal though. Finally I stopped trying and took a shower instead.

I washed and dried my hair and went rummaging through my closet and drawers looking for some clean clothes. Everything I had was either in the dirty laundry pile or too warm to put on. Time to do the wash, I told myself as I found a last pair of jeans hiding in the back of my closet. They were a little loose, I'd lost about ten pounds in the last eight months, but what the hell. Since I had no more T-shirts, I put on an undershirt and one of Murphy's vests—I still hadn't been able to part with all of his clothes—and studied myself in the mirror. Not bad, if I had to say so myself. I had nice arms, nice shoulders, good breasts, and the pants hid the scars on my legs.

I brushed my hair, did it up in a French twist and in a burst of enthusiasm put on some blusher, eyeliner and shadow. Absurdly I felt better. I should definitely do this more often I decided as I dialed Lynn's number again. The line was still busy. I hung up and went downstairs. I'd try from the store.

Manuel was peering in the refrigerator when I walked into the kitchen.

"Don't you have anything besides chocolate bars and soda in here?" he groused.

"I've got some coffee in the freezer."

"That's a big help." He shut the refrigerator door. "How about cereal?"

"Sorry. Never eat the stuff."

"Bread?"

"Nope."

"You must have something else?"

"Cat food. I understand the tuna isn't bad."

He groaned.

I laughed and nodded toward the door. "Tell you what. We'll pick up something at McDonald's before I go to work."

It was cooler outside the house than in. A convocation of crows blanketed the oak tree across the street. Their cawing filled the air. On either side of me, my neighbors were pulling out of their driveways and going off to work. I waved to them and called for my cat, who was crouched under the tree, tail twitching, eyes fixated on the branches above. But he gave me a look of disgust and ran off. Probably Zsa Zsa racing around in front of me had something to do with that. Well he'd come home sooner or later. He always did. As I headed toward the cab Zsa Zsa kept weaving in and out of my feet and I had to be careful to keep from stumbling over her.

We made McDees in five minutes. Manuel ordered enough food for three people, while I got an Egg McMuffin and two coffees. We ate while I drove to the store, which wasn't the best idea. I was still trying to get the egg off my jeans as I pulled up to Noah's Ark. I don't know why I'm such a slob.

As soon as I parked Manuel took off down the block and Zsa Zsa and I went inside. Suddenly Pickles was there meowing. Zsa Zsa squirmed out of my arms and ran toward her. Pickles arched her back and hissed. That stopped Zsa Zsa for all of two seconds. Then she decided the cat couldn't possibly mean what she was saying and bounded toward her. Pickles gave me a black look and leaped up on the counter. She stalked over to the far corner and jumped onto the shelving while Zsa Zsa raced after her below.

"Sorry," I told the cat as she sat there rigidly, her tail twitching in outrage. "She's young yet. You just have to give her time to learn some manners." Pickles just stared at me balefully.

"One of these days you're really going to get it," I told the dog as I picked her up and flicked on the lights.

Then I turned the air conditioner up a couple of notches because it felt stuffy in the store. The machine wheezed and gasped. I crossed my fingers. After another thirty seconds I heard a clunk as it turned over.

I let out the breath I didn't know I'd been holding and put the dog back down on the floor. She ran off to find her chew toy and I took a sip of coffee and unlocked the cash register. Hopefully by next summer I'd have enough money to get a new machine, a good one. Till then the air conditioner would just have to limp along—like the rest of us. I stretched, clicked on the radio and began reconciling the drawer. It was one of my least favorite tasks. I always lose track and have to start counting again. I was doing the tens for the second time when I heard the announcer on 94.5 FM saying, ". . . confessed to the homicide on Otisco Street. And now on to the weather."

Damn. I spun the dial to the other stations hoping to hear another report, but it was too late. The news was over. All I got was weather and traffic.

"I guess you heard." Tim was standing in the doorway. The iguana he'd taken home for the night was draped over his shoulder. He fingered the gold ball in his cheek.

"Only the end. Who confessed?"

"Lynn."

My stomach knotted. "You're kidding," I told him even though I could tell from the expression on his face that he wasn't.

He shook his head. "The announcer on the radio said manslaughter."

I picked up the phone and dialed Lynn's house. No one answered. I tried Stanley Pharmaceuticals. The receptionist told me that Mr. Stanley was out for the day.

I put down the receiver and began pacing back and forth. I couldn't stand still. Christ, what a mess. Obviously Lynn had finally gone over the edge. In a big way.

Tim put the iguana on the counter. "Calm down."

I stopped. "I just don't believe it." I took another turn around the store. "Damn, I should have gone over there last night." And I told him about the phone call.

"What difference would that have made?"

"Maybe I could have talked her out of doing this. She's so doped up on pills and alcohol I don't think she knows what the hell she's saying let alone what she's doing."

And Gordon had said everything was under control. Some control. Then I wondered what Mr. Stanley thought about this. I absolutely had to talk to Lynn. I reached for the phone again, but stayed my hand when I realized it would be pointless.

Right now she'd be down at the Public Safety Building being processed. She'd be out by late afternoon though. They wouldn't hold her. On that I'd be willing to bet. Her father would make sure of it. After all, she was an upstanding citizen, on the A list, with roots in the community and all the rest of that crap. I was also willing to bet that the judge wouldn't set bail too high, either. And even if he did, it didn't matter. Her family could certainly afford to pay it. I was wondering how much money Papa Stanley was going to have to fork over when George walked into the store.

"So what do you think about Lynn?" Tim asked George.

George looked puzzled. "Why should I think anything about her?"

"You mean you haven't heard?"

"Hey, I've been writing reports all morning about people getting their dogs stolen. Jesus, it's like a fucking epidemic."

"Tell me about it," I said. And I filled him in on Maria and Gomez and what Maria's mother had told her.

"So no one has been trying to sell you guys any puppies?"

"They wouldn't," I told him. "We don't carry dogs. Where do you think they're being taken?"

George sighed. "I don't know, but I tell you I'm going to do some research and find out. Now what's this about your friend Lynn?"

"They arrested her."

"For what?"

"She evidently confessed to killing the guy on Otisco Street. It was on the news."

"Now why doesn't that surprise me?" George scratched under his collar. "I thought her story stank from the first time you told it to me."

"Well, I still believe it."

He raised an eyebrow. "I know she's your friend and all, but come on."

"Lynn's afraid of guns," I explained. "She made her husband put his gun collection in the garage."

George's eyebrows shot up. "Her husband has a gun collection?"

"None of them have been fired."

"How do you know?"

"Lynn's father told me. It was the first thing Connelly had his men check."

"That doesn't mean anything. Her husband could have had a few unlicensed ones floating around. Most of those types do."

"Well, I don't think they found any. And even if they had it wouldn't matter. Lynn hates guns. She'd never pick one up, much less shoot it."

"That's what I heard about the seventy-year-old grandmother I arrested last week for shooting her husband. But somehow she managed to take her old man's .45 and blow off the side of his head."

"Lynn was in shock when I found her."

"Trust me, so was this grandmother."

"She asked me to come down with her. If she was going to kill someone, why would she do that?"

"She probably didn't plan on killing the guy. Most times people don't. You fight. Things just get out of hand. Or maybe she did and she was just setting you up so she could use you when she copped to manslaughter. . . ."

"Okay," I interrupted. "I get the point. But the fact is she wasn't carrying a gun."

"And how do you know that?"

"I didn't see it."

George rolled his eyes. "Did you search her?"

"No, but she was carrying one of those small bags, the kind that's just big enough for a lipstick, a compact, and a couple of dollars."

"Oh. Just like yours."

"Very funny." When I carried a bag, which wasn't often, I carried a backpack big enough to stuff my house in.

"Have you considered that maybe the gun was his?" George asked. He sighed in relief as he unbuttoned his collar.

I put my hands on my hips. "So what happened to it?" I demanded. "It should have been lying on the floor."

George shrugged. "Who knows. Maybe your friend tossed it somewhere. Maybe she hid it in the house. From what you told me she had time to do it before you came in."

"Not that much," I argued. "And if that's the case, why haven't the police found it?"

"How do you know they haven't?" George countered as he gently scratched the place on his neck where his collar had dug in.

"Obviously because they would have arrested her if they had instead of waiting for her to confess," I retorted.

George stopped scratching and shook his head. "Not necessarily. Ballistics tests, fingerprints, all that lab shit takes time. So even if they did find the weapon, Connelly might have decided not pick her up right away. I wouldn't have if I were him. I mean this lady isn't going anywhere."

I leaned forward. "Look, when I found Lynn she was paralyzed. She couldn't move. She couldn't even yell."

"Have you ever heard of acting?" he inquired, hooking his fingers in his belt and rocking back and forth on the balls of his feet. It was a habit of his that I found particularly irritating.

"She was going into shock," I insisted. "The paramedics took her away in an ambulance."

"Robin, Robin." George sighed. "Don't be so naive."

"Listen, I know what I saw and I'm telling you she wasn't faking," I repeated stubbornly even though I could see from George's expression he wasn't convinced.

Suddenly Tim chimed in. "Then how do you explain her phone call?" he demanded, pointing a finger at me. "Why did she tell you she was sorry? What was it she couldn't bring herself to say?"

I glared at him. He opened his mouth to say something else, thought better of it, and started rearranging the display of chew toys by the counter.

George's eyebrows went even higher. If he'd had more hair they would have been buried under it. "Do I get an explanation?" he asked.

Reluctantly, because I knew what he would say, I told him about Lynn's three o'clock phone call.

"Well, there you have it," he replied when I was done, a triumphant note in his voice, which got me really annoyed. "I rest my case."

"She was drunk," I protested. "She was doped up. She didn't know what the hell she was saying. She could have been referring to something else."

George gave me a long almost pitying look. "Robin, I hate to tell you this but a lot of times that's when people come out with what really happened. Look, I know she's your friend, but you've got to face the facts."

"I am," I continued. Looking back I realize I was talking as much to convince myself as to convince George but I didn't want to admit that then. "There are too many loose ends. Too many things that don't add up."

George snorted in disgust. "I'm right. You just don't want to accept it."

I bridled, especially since way deep down inside me I was afraid that what he was saying was true. For some reason the more unsure I am of something the more defensive I get, which was why before I knew it the words, "You wanna bet?" were flying out of my mouth.

George snickered because everytime I'd bet with him I'd lost. "Remember the 1990 Super Bowl pool?"

"This is different," I assured him.

His grin got wider. "And last year's World Series?"

"Every one is entitled to a few bad calls."

George closed in for the kill. "What about the little bet you made with me about whether or not Murphy would win the car rally down in New York City?"

"He lost by five seconds," I protested.

George crossed his arms over his chest. "He still lost."

But this *was* different. This time I knew I was right. "A hundred bucks says she's innocent," I challenged.

George shrugged. "Hey, if you got a hundred to spare, I'm not going to say no."

We shook hands, while Tim shook his head in disapproval.

"And how, oh great detective, are you going to go about proving your case?" George asked, rubbing his hands together in ill-concealed glee.

"Simple. I'm going to Weedsport."

Chapter
9

George chortled. "Weedsport? What the hell is in Weedsport besides the speedway?"

"Brandon Douglas's mother."

I was hoping that she would be able to tell me why her son had come down to Syracuse, I was hoping that she knew what had been on his mind. The way I looked at it was that this case was like a skein of yarn. There were two possible ends to pull on and since I couldn't do anything with Lynn's at the moment I might as well tug on Brandon Douglas's end and see what unraveled. But evidently George didn't share my conviction.

"Have fun," he said, his tone conveying what he thought of my idea.

"I intend to." Although even I had to admit that Weedsport wasn't known for that commodity.

"And by the way . . ."

"Yes?"

"You look very nice."

I felt a surge of pleasure. It had been a long time since anyone said anything like that. Certainly Murphy had never been big in the compliment department.

"You should get dressed up more often."

I smiled.

"You're both nuts," Tim said after George left.

"No. Just him."

"I hope you know what you're doing."

Of course I didn't, but I had absolutely no intention of telling Tim that.

I didn't get around to leaving for Weedsport till much later that afternoon. Right after George left we got a rush of customers in. Then one of the salt water aquariums developed a leak in one of its seals and I had to help Tim transfer the fish and break down the tank, after which I spent an hour on the phone trying to locate five pairs of mated veiled angels for one of my better customers. As I worked I half expected Connelly to come waltzing through the door with more questions, but he didn't. Which pleased me immensely. I needed some breathing room.

It was a little after four when Zsa Zsa and I left the store. I was heading toward the parking lot when Julio came up beside me.

"Hey, I got a baby chick for Martha in here." He shook the shoe box he was carrying for emphasis. "Want to watch her eat?"

"Another time, thanks." Like never, I thought. Keeping the spider in the back room was one thing. Watching it eat was something else. I was about to continue on when I remembered something. "Did Connelly ever get back to you?"

"Connelly?" Julio asked.

"You know. The cop you told about the guy you saw running through A.J.'s yard."

"Oh, him." Julio picked at a pimple on his cheek with his free hand. "No. Why?"

"Just curious." I guess Connelly hadn't thought it worth his while. I looked Julio in the eye. "Now you were telling the truth, weren't you?"

Julio bristled. "Fuck, yes."

"Good," I replied thinking that I might want to track this guy down at some point.

"Okay then." Julio relaxed. "No problem. You sure you don't want to see Martha eat? It's very educational."

"I'm sure it is. How's *Charlotte's Web* coming?" I asked changing the subject.

"I'm on page seven." He shifted his weight from one leg to another.

"Page seven? I can see you've been putting in a lot of time on this."

All of a sudden Julio started to stammer. "Listen, I've got to go. Can't keep Martha waiting."

I grabbed his shoulder as he went by me. "You haven't even opened the book, have you?"

He lifted a hand. "I've been busy. I'll start today."

"You'd better." I let him go. "Otherwise Martha's going to be out on the street."

"I promise." And he crossed his heart. Then he turned and practically ran into the store.

Maybe I was better off not having children I reflected as I opened the cab door and got in. I put Zsa Zsa next to me and she settled down, closed her eyes and went to sleep.

Maybe dogs were better. If Julio were mine I'd have strangled him by now. I should have just said no to his request to keep Martha at the store. But then that was my problem: I never said no. Or rather I said no when I should say yes and yes when I should say no.

I swerved to avoid a group of kids throwing water balloons at the corner and made a left onto Grant. Ten blocks later I took a right onto Oneonata. I had one more stop to make before I hit the thruway. A perch that I had ordered last week for Mrs. Z. had just come in and since I knew she was anxious to get it I figured I'd swing by her house on my way out and drop it off.

"You're a sweet child," she said when I handed her the package. "Fenton will be so pleased. Can I get you anything? A glass of lemonade perhaps? Some iced tea?"

"I'd love to, but I'm on my way to Weedsport."

"Weedsport?" Mrs. Z. exclaimed. "Why I have family there."

"Really?" I said politely.

As things turned out, I should have taken the time to talk to her. I should have sat on the porch and sipped lemonade and listened to what Mrs. Z. had to say. God knows I would have saved myself a lot of aggravation if I had. But I was in too much of a hurry, so I just said goodbye, got back in my car and continued on.

Weedsport is a small town located about half an hour's drive out of Syracuse. Its one main street contains a grocery, a video store, three places to eat, a dollar store, and a few other assorted shops. The houses range from one-story Cape Cods to large Victorians. The lawns are neat, the streets are tree-lined and everyone knows everyone. It's the kind of place, I recalled thinking the last time I was there, where they probably still have ice cream socials on Saturday afternoons.

Brandon Douglas's house looked exactly as I had remembered it. It was an old red Victorian with a white wraparound porch. The only thing different were the baskets of pink fuschias hanging from the hooks in the porch ceiling. Last time the flowers had been geraniums. As I let Zsa Zsa out of the car, I began having second thoughts.

I should have called first. This was the wrong time. Mrs. Tyler wouldn't want to talk to me. It was too soon after her son's death. But then, I decided, I'd made the trip, I was here, so I knocked. The worst thing that could happen was that she'd tell me to go home. A few minutes later the door opened and a plump woman dressed in flowered shorts and a lime green T-shirt came out. She was holding a dish towel and a metal bowl in one of her hands.

"Yes?" she said. "Can I help you?"

"I'm looking for Mrs. Tyler."

"Well, you won't find her here," the woman informed me tartly. "She died three years ago. Heart attack."

"I'm sorry to hear that." And I was, too.

"We all were." The woman threw the dish towel over her shoulder and gave me an appraising glance. "Now exactly what was it you wanted with her?"

"I just wanted to ask her some questions about her son."

The woman's jaw tightened. "What about him?"

"You know that he died, Mrs. . . . ?"

"Raus. Emma Raus. Yes, I know. It was in the paper. And I'll tell you something. His being killed like that didn't surprise me one bit. No, ma'am. Not at all."

"Why's that?"

" 'Cause he was always poking around where he shouldn't. He wasn't content to let things rest."

"You mean in relation to his sister?"

"I used to tell him that everything in this life happens for a reason. And you just have to accept it and trust in the Lord Jesus. But he couldn't do that. Not him. Always asking this and that. And look what happened to him. Where did all his questions get him? That's what I'd like to know. All I can say is thank God his mother died first and was spared the pain of seeing what happened to her son."

"Did he have any friends around here?" I ventured, figuring that whatever Brandon had been thinking the odds were great that he hadn't confided it to her.

"None his mother would have been proud of that's for sure."

Now why didn't her answer surprise me? I asked for their names anyway.

"They use to hang out at Zeke's. Ask down there. Driving around. Drinking. Getting themselves into trouble when they should have been working and studying, trying to make something of themselves. Oh, his mom tried," the woman went on. "But after his sister died, she just couldn't do nothing with him. Nothing. You ask me, I think it's what killed her." And then she turned and went back in the house slamming the door behind her, a punctuation mark for her disapproval.

I scooped up Zsa Zsa and walked back to the car. Hopefully I'd do better at Zeke's. I certainly couldn't do worse. It took me a couple of minutes at the most to drive over since the place was less than seven blocks away. The square building was covered with rectangular pieces of white tile, now stained yellow with age. On my way in I avoided the weeds growing through the cracked asphalt on the parking lot and the yellow jackets buzzing around the empty soda cans standing on the picnic tables.

A bored-looking teenage girl with mall-hair and a bad case of acne was leaning against the counter putting polish on nails that would have done a Chinese empress proud. Except for her and a harried-looking woman with red blotches across her cheeks and the bridge of her nose drinking coffee the place was deserted. This did not look promising. I ordered a Coke and two pieces of fried chicken and asked the girl if she knew Brandon Douglas.

"You one of those reporters?" she asked capping the bottle of polish.

"Yes," I lied, figuring that this was not someone who was going to ask to see my press pass.

"You doing a story?"

"Maybe."

"Would you put my name in it?"

"If you have something to say."

She brightened. "You know my sister used to go out with him," she proclaimed, basking in the reflected glory.

"Really?" My hopes rose then fell with the next sentence.

"But she's out in L.A. Which is where I'm goin' as soon as I'm old enough to get out of this crummy place." The girl waved her nails in the air to dry them. "I got to tell you though, I never liked Bran Muffin much."

"Bran Muffin?"

"Brandon," she said impatiently. "He was always weird, but then he got really strange, really *out there* if you know what I mean."

"I don't." I rested my forearms on the counter. "Why don't you tell me?"

"He was just strange." She raised her voice. "I mean the guy's been a nut job ever since his sister got whacked by that weirdo. Whoops." She clapped her hand over her mouth in a showy gesture as the woman sitting down, her face now a bright red, got up and practically ran out the door. "Sorry," she called after her. Then she turned back to me a smile playing around her lips. "I guess I shouldn't have said that, hunh?"

"You don't look too sorry to me. Who is she anyway?"

"That is Norma Lipsyle, the wife of the guy who killed Brandon's sister?"

"Really?"

The girl nodded. "She thinks she's so high and mighty just 'cause she's read all those books," the girl added, tossing her hair out of her eyes. "But she's on welfare so she can't be that smart. So she went to college. Big deal. That don't mean she knows everything. I mean she went and married a faggot, didn't she?"

"I heard he had children."

"Yeah. Four." She leaned forward. "But that don't prove nothing. My cousin says the guy has AIDS now and we all know how you get that. And she's got some weird disease, too. I wouldn't be surprised if she got it from him."

"I've heard people say he didn't do it."

"That's what my mom says," the girl replied as she took my chicken out of the microwave and threw it on a paper plate.

"And what do you say?" I asked as I paid for my food.

"I say he should have fried for what he done, but I hear he's dying now so I guess it don't make no difference."

Only to his wife, I thought as I watched her slam the door of her Saab station wagon shut and drive off.

"Listen," I asked the girl as she handed me a plastic knife and fork. "Are any of Brandon's friends around? Maybe I could talk to one of them."

"Nah." The girl got me a Coke. "They all left. I mean

what's to stay for? There's nothing here. No jobs. No nothing."

Great. Score zero for me. Then I had another idea. "Do you know where Norma Lipsyle lives?" As long as I was here I decided I might as well talk to the woman. Who knew? Maybe something interesting would emerge.

"Sure. Out on Selic Road." And the girl gestured in the direction I'd just come from. "My mom says she moved there after her husband got put in jail. Didn't want to live in town no more."

"I can't understand why," I observed as I took my food.

"Neither can I," the girl said.

The fried chicken was tough and greasy—although Zsa Zsa didn't seem to care. She ate as much as I gave her. Even the Coke tasted bad—not enough syrup—though I drank it anyway because I was thirsty. After I was done I got back in the car and even though it was late in the afternoon I stopped at a gas station and asked the attendant for directions to Selic Road. I don't know whether it was his directions or my mistakes but I spent the better part of the next two hours driving up and down unmarked country roads trying to find the damned place. Finally I said the hell with it, my patience and the gas in my car were both running low, and headed toward Syracuse. The sun was in my eyes most of the way back. Which didn't increase my good mood. I really had to remember to replace the sunglasses I'd lost three weeks ago.

When I hit Syracuse, I stopped at R.J.'s for a beer instead of going directly home. A blast of cold air hit me as I walked into the bar. I reveled in it while I looked around. The place was deserted. I guess everybody but me had better things to do on a hot summer night.

"New friend?" Connie, the bartender, asked as I sat Zsa Zsa on the stool next to me.

"Kind of," I replied as she slid a mug of Molson's across the counter. Zsa Zsa looked at the beer mug and barked.

"You think she wants some?" Connie asked.

"Let's see." I held out the mug. The puppy took a tentative lick. Then another. And another.

Connie laughed. "She likes it."

"I'm glad one of us found something they want," I said and told Connie about my day.

"So what are you going to do now?" she asked after I was done with my tale.

"I don't know. Go home. Get out of these clothes. Take a bath. Call Lynn."

I left half an hour later. By then I was feeling tired and Zsa Zsa was having trouble sitting on the stool. Maybe giving her half of my beer hadn't been such a good idea after all, I decided as I pulled up to my house. I parked the car in the garage, retrieved the mail, and went inside. I had put the puppy down and was studying my phone bill when I heard a crash.

I glanced at the living room.

A small circle of flames was flickering by the window.

Chapter
10

At first I was paralyzed.

I couldn't believe what I was seeing.

No. I didn't want to believe what I was seeing.

It had to be something else.

A bad joke.

Some strange optical illusion.

Then I smelled the gasoline and I knew it wasn't.

Somebody had thrown a firebomb through my window.

That had been the crash I'd heard.

Who said TV wasn't educational?

Only my feet still wouldn't move.

And my heart was fluttering in my chest like a caged bird.

I just stared, transfixed in horror, by the flames. Then Zsa Zsa barked and the spell was broken.

I ran to the hall closet for the fire extinguisher, raced back, turned on the nozzle and aimed.

Nothing happened.

I depressed the lever again. No result. I shook it. Hard. Nothing. The damn thing wasn't working. As I flung it down I heard a sob and realized it was mine.

By now the circle of flames was expanding. Little tongues of fire were eating the floor quarter inch, by quarter inch. I was running for the phone to call the fire department when I spotted my big old Mexican blanket, the one I'd bought down in Cancun five years ago, on the back of the club chair. I'd been meaning to take it back upstairs for months. Thank God I hadn't.

I grabbed it and threw it over the flames.

The smell of burning wool filled my nostrils. As I began stamping out the fire, unwelcome visions of Noah's Ark engulfed in flames ran through my mind. I saw the parakeet vanish in a ball of fire, heard the cry of the rabbits burning to death, saw the beam from the ceiling falling on my legs.

I took a deep breath and pushed the picture away.

Not again, I thought, as I stamped harder.

My rage grew.

"Not this time," I heard myself say aloud as I danced out the fire.

Noah's Ark had been enough.

I was not going to be burned out of my house as well.

Not if I could help it.

The heat made the scars on my legs tingle.

Sympathy pains.

I ignored them.

And kept going.

Finally after what seemed like an eternity, but was probably no more than five minutes, the fire was out. I stood there panting, watching a plume of black smoke twirl up to the ceiling and smelling the burnt wood. My eyes were stinging.

I touched my cheeks. They were slick with tears and sweat. My legs were trembling. I felt a rush of nausea.

I took a deep breath and then another and another after that. I told myself to get under control. I told myself the blaze had been small. I told myself I was reacting to the past and that I'd done okay.

I should be proud of myself. I'd been terrified, but I'd done what had to be done anyway. I thought wryly that the therapist I'd gone to see after Murphy's death would be pleased. She'd been after me to think positively—"treat every problem as an opportunity for new growth," she'd said. Which was why I'd left. The saccharin content in the office had been too high for my blood. I like my sugar in candy, not in some pompous, simplistic bromide delivered by an idiot who doesn't know what the hell she's talking about.

I nudged the blanket with my toe. It looked like it had been eaten by giant moths. So much for Cancun. Then I noticed the shards of glass lying on the floor. The remnants of the firebomb. I squatted down to get a better look. The fragments lay scattered between the back of the sofa and the window. It looked like it had been a beer bottle—an imported beer bottle. At least whoever had thrown it had had good taste. It was nice to know I was dealing with a high-class arsonist.

As I reached for a piece of glass it suddenly occurred to me that whoever had done this might still be lurking around outside. I sprang up and backed away from the window. But then I recalled that I'd heard the sound of squealing tires right before I'd heard the crash of broken glass. I hadn't paid the noise any mind, though, figuring it was just one of my neighbor's kids doing his usual number. Wrong.

What I'd heard was the guy who'd done this. He'd driven by, stopped just long enough to throw the bottle through my window and raced away. And then I wondered if the fact that I'd just walked in the door when it happened was coincidental or if he'd been following me. I hadn't spotted anyone behind me. But then I hadn't been looking, either.

I knew I should call the police. Only I didn't want to. Not yet. I still wasn't up to dealing with them. And anyway the guy who'd done it was probably on the other side of town by now. I know I would be if I were him. So I did the next best thing. I walked into the kitchen and called George.

"Be right back," the message on his machine said.

Great. When I finally did need him he wasn't there. I told him to call me as soon as possible and hung up. Then I went over to the sink, and turned on the tap. I cupped my hands and let the water fill them and sluice down my arms. The sound was comforting. I bent over and splashed cold water on my face and neck. Finally when I'd had enough I turned the tap off, dried my face with a paper towel, and grabbed the bottle of Scotch sitting on the counter and took a healthy gulp. And another. The familiar warmth spread through my body. I began to feel semihuman.

Zsa Zsa peeked out from under the kitchen table.

"So what do you think of all this?" I asked her.

She cocked her head, ran over to me and scratched on my legs with her front paws until I picked her up. Obviously, she wasn't too pleased with what had happened, either. I took another gulp of Scotch, then got a beer out of the fridge and popped the top. I was just finishing it when George banged on the door. It seems that I hadn't put the receiver back on the hook all the way and when George kept getting a busy signal he'd gotten concerned. He must have gone ninety all the way to get to my house as quickly as he had. I guess I'd sounded more freaked out than I'd thought.

"What's going on?" he asked when I answered the door. He was wearing paint-splattered shorts and a T-shirt and he had a streak of white paint running down the length of his cheek. I'd obviously interrupted him in one of his rare house-improvement moments.

"Somebody threw a Molotov cocktail through my living-room window."

"Shit, Robin. What did you do?"

"What do you mean what did I do?" I cried as he brushed past me and went into the living room. But he didn't answer.

"It came in there, right?" he asked instead, pointing to the broken window."

"Right. You know I'm the victim here."

He scanned the room. "Whatever you say." His eyes narrowed as they lit on the broken pieces of the bottle on the floor. "Did you touch any of these?"

"No."

"Good. Maybe we'll get lucky. Maybe Midgley will be able to lift some latents off of them."

"That would be nice," I said sarcastically. I was still angry, but George didn't seem to take any notice.

"I don't think there's much point in my looking around outside now." He peeled a dab of paint off the back of his hand. "Whoever did this is probably long gone and I don't want to mess up any footprints. You didn't happen to notice anyone outside as you were coming in, did you?"

"No."

"Maybe a strange car parked on the street?"

"The only thing I heard was the sound of squealing tires."

"I see." He prodded the burnt blanket with his toe. "We don't see this type of thing too often. Maybe we can work that angle," he muttered to himself. Then he turned and looked at me. "You must have really pissed someone off."

"So it would seem."

"Give me some names."

"Joe Davis comes to mind."

"That's right. You had that thing with him about the dog. Okay. Anyone else?"

I shook my head.

"Who'd you speak to when you went down to Weedsport?"

"Nobody who would do something like this."

He took out his pad. "Give me their names anyway. I want to have them checked out."

"I'm telling you they didn't have anything to do with this."

"You're sure, are you?" And he slapped his pad against his hand. Whap. Whap. Whap. "I mean some guy didn't suddenly wake up and say, 'Boy I'm bored today. Wait.' " George held up a finger. " 'I know. I have a great idea. I'm going to throw a Molotov cocktail through Robin Light's window.' "

Suddenly I burst into tears.

George looked mortified. I *was* mortified. I hate crying in front of people. I hate being that out of control. When I'd been married to Murphy I'd always gone for a drive or a walk whenever I'd had to.

"It's okay," George murmured as he hugged me. "It's just shock." Or too much Scotch I thought as he stroked my hair.

Finally I quieted down.

George got me a tissue and a glass of water. "I'm calling this in now," he said as he handed them to me.

The cops arrived five minutes later. By then I'd blown my nose and given my face a wash. There were three of them— one evidence tec and two patrolmen—standing at the door. George immediately took charge. Which was fine with me. He knew them and anyway I felt so spent that even talking was more of an effort than I had the energy for. The tec collected the glass fragments and looked for footprints outside, while one of the cops canvassed the neighbors and the other stayed to talk to me. But I couldn't tell him much and my neighbors hadn't heard or seen anything unusual. The three of them left an hour later with not much more than they'd come in with.

George insisted on staying and I was glad that he did. But even if I hadn't been I wouldn't have had the wherewithal to argue. I just told him where the clean sheets were and stumbled upstairs to bed. I fell asleep instantly. But my dreams were all bad—I was in front of Murphy's tombstone and he was angry at me because I hadn't brought flowers, I bought a fancy new car, but they hadn't given me the key so it wouldn't run, I opened a green door only to find nothing was there—and I was glad to wake up.

George was gone by the time I got downstairs. He'd left a note on the fridge telling me he'd gone to work and that he'd see me later. As I walked through the living room the odor from last night's fire hit me. Which really annoyed the hell out of me. The last thing I needed was to be reminded of the fire every time I walked in the door. After I took Zsa Zsa out, I came back in and opened all the windows, got a couple of fans out of the closet and turned them on. Then I put the wool blanket in a garbage bag and threw it out. The charred floor presented more of a problem. I didn't know what to do about that. Then I remembered Robert DiMario. His number was in my book with a star next to it. I called expecting to leave a message on his machine, but he answered instead. Even more surprising, he said he'd drop by on his way to another job he was doing and have a look at what needed to be done.

I hung up and took a container of coffee yogurt out of the fridge. While I ate I thought about Lynn and Otisco Street and Brandon Douglas's death, but whatever angle I came at it from I just couldn't see any connection between that event and last night's firebombing. But George had been right.

This hadn't been a random act. Zsa Zsa barked and I held out a spoonful of yogurt for her. No. I really had to talk to Lynn and try and find out what was going on. Obviously I'd stumbled on someone's toes. But whose? I was still pondering that question when Robert DiMario rang the doorbell.

DiMario was in his early fifties, though he looked about ten years older. He'd been a manager for New York Telephone and had taken early retirement when the company had offered him a deal he couldn't refuse. Then he'd started doing carpentry as a hobby. The hobby had turned into a successful business. He was nice, did good work, and came when he said he would. In short, he was a rarity.

"No problem," he said when I showed him the spot. "This will take me about half an hour. At the most. Tell you what, I'll run over here on my lunch hour and get you fixed up." He clicked his tongue against the roof of his mouth. "A hundred bucks should cover everything."

I would have given him two hundred just to get the smell out of my house.

I went to shut off the fan.

"And," he added as I walked him to the door, "I got some stuff in my other truck that'll get this smell out. I'll bring it along and leave it for you."

I could have kissed him. Instead, I gave him a spare key. After he left I put Zsa Zsa in the car and we headed out to Dewitt. The traffic was light. Everyone was coming into the city. I spent the twenty-minute drive rehearsing what I was going to say. By the time I got to Lynn's house I had my questions all worked out. Too bad I never got to deliver any of them. I parked the car, walked up the flagstone path and rang the bell. A set of chimes played something classic sounding somewhere in the house.

A few minutes later Lynn opened the door. Which surprised me. I'd been expecting Gordon. I'd even had my little speech all worked out. Only now it looked as if I wouldn't need it. The crimson silk robe she was wearing made her white skin look even paler. I could see that she'd lost more weight. Her cheekbones jutted out. Her eyes seemed to receded into their sockets. We were now beyond fashionably thin.

"Lynn," I began.

"I'm sorry," she whispered. "But I don't think talking now is a good idea."

"Good idea or not, we're going to."

She licked her lips nervously. "We can't. Gordon told me not to."

"Screw Gordon." Like when had she ever listened to him anyway?

Lynn's eyes glazed over. "I made a mistake," she said in a wooden voice. "And now I have to pay."

"What mistake? Fucking Brandon Douglas? Is that what we're talking about here?"

"A mistake," she repeated in a robotic voice. "I made a mistake. You have to go now. I can't talk anymore." And she closed the door in my face.

I stood there stunned. What was she taking? Thorazine? I'd seen zombies on the late show who looked more alive than Lynn did. Well zombified or not I still needed some answers and I certainly didn't like having the door slammed in my face. I rang the bell again. No answer. I put my finger on it and kept it there. A few seconds later the door flew open and Ken stepped out. Lynn had sent her brother as an emissary. He was wearing a pair of red swim trunks. His white polo shirt had damp patches around his chest. Little beads of water clung to his hair. As he moved toward me I could smell a faint odor of chlorine. Lynn must have gotten him out of the pool.

"So you're living here, now?" I said as he closed the door behind him.

"Only for the moment. My dad and Gordon asked me to stay and keep an eye on Lynn. She's not well you know."

"No kidding. What the hell are you giving her?"

He folded his arms across his chest. "Nothing the doctor hasn't prescribed I can assure you."

"Really?"

"Yes, really. She's close to having a nervous breakdown."

"That's too bad, but I still have to talk to her."

"I'm sorry but you can't do that."

"Watch me." And I started for the door.

Ken grabbed my arm. "Before you go bursting in there, there's something I think you should know, something that will help you understand what's going on."

"All right."

"Not here. Over by the garage. I don't want Lynn to overhear us."

"I'm waiting," I said after we walked over there.

Ken coughed. "This is hard to talk about."

In the spruce overhead a mourning dove twittered. To my left a robin was searching for worms in the grass.

"Try." By now my foot was tapping out a staccato rhythm.

He took a deep breath and let it out. "It's just that I still think of her as my baby sister."

"Well, she's not anymore."

"I know." And he smiled ruefully.

My patience was at an end. "Look," I told him. "If you don't start talking, I'm going to go back to that house and climb in through the window if I have to."

"No, you don't have to do that," he said quickly. "I'll tell you. When Lynn was younger she killed a man."

Chapter
11

I just stared at him. I felt as if someone had punched me in the stomach. Whatever I'd expected to hear this wasn't it. How could I have not known? But then why should I have?

"It was terrible." Ken's hands fluttered in front of his face as if trying to brush away the memory. "She was fifteen. She was taking pills, lots of pills. We never could find out who she was getting them from," he murmured. "Although God knows we tried.

"They were uppers. I think she started because she wanted to lose weight. It's hard to imagine Lynn chubby, isn't it? But she was. She was this round little kid. Everyone used to tease her about it. Including me." He compressed his lips into a thin line. "Boy how I wish I'd kept my big mouth shut. Then she started dropping acid. Doing a little coke. Drinking. Sleeping around. I remember the night she snuck out, took my father's Jag, and wrapped it around a tree. It was terrible. I tried to talk to her. My mother tried. My father tried.

The school psychologist tried. We got her into counseling. Nothing made any difference. Nothing. She'd become a stranger. It was as if someone had clicked a switch and a whole different person, someone no one knew, emerged.

"And then to cap it all off she dropped out of school and went to live with this older guy, a real sleazebucket. He was a night clerk in a convenience store somewhere out in Liverpool, lived in a trailer park out in B'ville. It was incredible that she should do that." Ken's voice quivered with outrage at the memory. "My mother nearly had a nervous breakdown and my father just about stopped talking. Then one night we get a call from PSB."

He swallowed. "I don't think we'll know what really happened out there in the trailer. The only thing I do know is that Lynn's face was swollen, both eyes were black and blue, her lip was bleeding, and the guy was dead. She'd shot him with his own gun. And she was hysterical. She was screaming and crying. Finally they sedated her. It took two people to hold her down so they could give her the shot." He shut his eyes, then opened them again.

"So what happened then?" I prompted.

"My father talked to the DA. Considering the circumstances, no charges were filed. Lynn went to a psychiatric hospital. That was part of the deal. she was institutionalized for about a year and a half someplace in Connecticut that specialized in adolescents. It was very posh. Very expensive. I used to go up and see her twice a month. When she came out she was a different person. Not the old Lynn, not the new one, but someone else." He sighed and ran his finger along the hood of Lynn's Jag.

"When she came back she just drove around in this dark green Morgan my father got her. They're the boxy sports cars with the strap on the hood. Round and around, day after day. She still has it, you know. It's stored in the garage. She won't sell it. She says it marks her becoming another person." Ken ran his hand through his hair. "My sister is too sentimental for her own good."

"I'm surprised it's in there with Gordon's gun collection. I mean considering the way she feels about it and all."

"God those." Ken groaned. "I can't figure that man out. Why anyone would want to spend the kind of money he does on something like that is beyond me."

"I'm surprised the cops didn't take them."

"Why?" Ken looked genuinely surprised. "They don't have anything to do with the shooting. None of them have been fired. None are missing. The police have already checked. All of Gordon's paperwork is in order." He looked at his watch. "God. I didn't realize the time. Excuse me. I'm going to be late." And he gave me a dazzling smile and walked back to the house.

I didn't say anything.

I couldn't.

I was still too stunned.

My mind was churning as I drove to the store. Try as I might I couldn't picture Lynn fat, I couldn't picture her out of control, I couldn't picture her living in a trailer park in B'ville with a convenience store clerk. I don't know. Maybe the old cliché is right. Maybe you really never do know somebody. I was still trying to picture Lynn twenty years ago as I pulled up in front of Noah's Ark. The day had gotten hotter. Whatever breeze there was had vanished. The leaves on the trees were absolutely still. To the west gray clouds were massing. It looked like we were in for another storm.

When I walked inside George was leaning against the counter talking to Tim. He had shaved and showered. His uniform was freshly ironed. He looked crisp. Alert. Ready to roll. I wondered how he did it because I, on the other hand, looked like hell.

"I just came by to tell you Midgley hasn't picked up any latents," he said as I put Zsa Zsa down. She immediately ran off searching for things on the floor that she could eat.

"Nothing?"

"Not even a partial."

I wasn't surprised. These days everyone knows enough to wear gloves.

"And I haven't been able to turn up any reports of similiar incidents in the city in the past two years, though the secretary said she'll do another computer search," George continued. "I also talked to Dalton, the fire department's arson inspector."

"And?"

"Basically he feels it was meant as a warning. The bottle was small, the quantity of gasoline was limited, it didn't really do much damage."

"No. It just scared the shit out of me."

"I think that was the point."

Zsa Zsa pranced up to George and sniffed his pants legs. But when he bent down to pet her, she ran behind my legs. I picked her up and scratched behind her ears.

George's walkie-talkie came to life. He ignored it. "They're going to run a patrol car by your house on a regular basis just to keep an eye on things."

"Thanks."

"And I'm going to pick up Davis for questioning."

"That's going to put him in a good mood."

"I know. So watch your step."

"I intend to."

"Speaking of which, where were you? I called earlier and no one picked up."

"Actually I was over at Lynn's."

"You're kidding." He looked at me in disbelief.

"I wanted to ask her some questions."

"You just don't learn, do you?"

"It's not that."

"Then what is it?"

"Let's just say I have more faith in my own ability to figure out what's going on than I do in the police department's."

"You don't think they're going to take this seriously?"

"Not as seriously as I will."

George opened his mouth to say something, changed his mind, closed his mouth, and left.

"Don't say a word," I warned Tim as the door closed. "I just don't want to hear it."

"Fine." And he went into the back to take care of the lizards.

"Or think about it," I added silently.

I was just going to check the heat rock in the anoles cage when Lola Martinez's little brother came in. He had ten dwarf Russian hamsters to sell. I bought them all. Then I put the carton on the floor. Not a good idea. Especially when Zsa Zsa decided to investigate. I found four, Tim found two, and the puppy located one under the fish tanks. Then while we were still searching for the other three little rodents, some guy came in and wanted to buy the ferret we had on display and I had to tell him he couldn't do that without a license and then he wanted me to hold it for him and I said I couldn't do that either, so he started yelling and I had to threaten him with the cops to get him to leave. All together it was not a great morning.

The afternoon didn't turn out much better. A woman wanted a refund for two dead salt water fish despite the fact that they'd been purchased almost a month ago and that we had a clearly stated 'buy at your own risk' policy when it came to fish, reptiles, and snakes. When I told her I couldn't give her her money back she called me a cheap bitch and stormed out, slamming the door behind her. Then one of my suppliers called to tell me that my best-selling dry cat food was on back order and wouldn't be available for another two to three weeks—if I was lucky.

While I was arguing with him I started cleaning off the top of my desk. Somewhere near the middle of the pile I came upon Mr. Stanley's $4,000 "thank you" present. With everything that had been going on, I'd forgotten all about it. I couldn't believe I'd been that careless, but then what with finding the body, having Lynn admit to a homicide I didn't think she committed, and having my house firebombed, I could see where Stanley's check might slip my mind. After I hung up I stood staring at it as I tried to figure out what to do. Finally I decided I had to give it back.

I didn't want to, I could definitely use the money but I felt funny taking it then and I felt funnier now. I thought about writing a note and explaining why I was returning the check, but after a couple of tries I decided to do it in person. At this point any excuse to get out of the store was a good one. And besides maybe Mr. Stanley could answer a few of my questions. I told Tim I'd be back in an hour or two and took off. As I was heading out Maria was coming in to visit Zsa Zsa. Apparently Gomez hadn't turned up yet.

I was halfway to Stanley Pharmaceuticals when the storm broke. The rain came down in opaque sheets, drumming on the cars, turning the world watery. Traffic slowed to ten miles an hour. I crept along, peering through my windshield, trying to make out the road's contours. Ten minutes later the storm settled into a regular, steady pulse and I picked up speed. It was still raining as I pulled into the factory parking lot. The place was full—I guess the factory was working at capacity—and I had to park on the lot's outer perimeter and run toward the building. An umbrella would have been helpful, but mine had broken. The shaft no longer extended, and I'd forgotten to buy a new one.

The receptionist, the same older woman who'd let me in the last time I was here, managed to convey by facial expression alone that I wasn't worth Mr. Stanley's time. I think the only reason she finally checked with him was because I threatened to sit there until she did.

"You have five minutes," she said to me at Stanley's door before she clomped off in her sensible one- and one-half-inch heels.

"You'll have to forgive Grace," Stanley told me as I walked across the room. "She was with my father. Sometimes she gets a little overprotective. Especially now. Especially with all the calls I've been getting about Lynn. The TV people are the worst."

"I'll bet."

"It hasn't been easy." He leaned back in his chair and balanced his pen between his two fingers. "On anyone. No sir. No siree." The circles under his eyes had grown and his face looked a little less round. "So." He sat up. "What brings you here? What can I do for you?"

I put the check on his desk. "I'm sorry, I should have done this earlier but I've thought about it and I can't take this money."

His eyebrows shot up. "Why ever not?"

"Because I haven't done anything to merit it."

"I see." He tapped his pen on the desk. "I see." Then he pushed back his chair, got up, and walked over to the shelves full of blue and white pottery. "You like these?" he asked gesturing to the collection.

"Very much."

"So does Lynn. They're eighteenth century you know. Some of the pieces even go back to the seventeenth century. I've had offers from curators of several reputable museums. But I've told them no. I've told them I hope to give them to my daughter one day. She's very important to me." He fell silent. I could hear the sounds of the factory in the background. "Listen." Stanley crossed over to the desk, picked up the check, pressed it into my hand, and curled my fingers over it. "I want you to take this back. I want you to consider this a payment."

"For what?"

"Something doesn't make sense here. I feel it in my bones. I want you to find out what's happening to my daughter. I want to know the truth. I have to know the truth." And he pounded on his desk.

"What about the police?"

"What about them? They accepted her confession. The case is closed as far as they're concerned."

"Then hire a private detective."

"No. You're her friend. You care. And you were with her before she went into that house. You found her. And you have experience," he added, referring to the case I'd solved last year.

"What you say is all true," I replied slowly. "But I was just at your daughter's house. She doesn't want to talk to me. She doesn't want to see me."

"I'm sure she will when she's calmed down a bit." I forebore from pointing out that if she were any calmer she'd be in a coffin. "You can talk to her friends in the meantime."

"Her friends?" I asked, wondering what they could possibly know about Lynn and Brandon Douglas and what had gone down on Otisco Street.

"Just a figure of speech. I meant people. Please do this for me." There was a quaver in his voice.

"I don't know."

I knew I should refuse.

George would be really pissed.

And since I didn't have a private detective's license this wasn't strictly legal.

And there *was* the firebombing.

The firebombing. I had to think about that.

Okay, I thought. Suppose George was right. Suppose it was tied up with the Brandon Douglas-Lynn Stanley thing. Then I should really back off. But if I backed off I wouldn't find out who had thrown that Molotov cocktail.

And I wanted to find out.

Real bad.

Not to mention learning why the hell my name was in Brandon Douglas's pocket. I still didn't have an answer to that question, either. And unless I did some poking around I wasn't going to find out.

So I said yes.

I just wouldn't tell George what I was doing.

And after all, four thousand dollars was four thousand dollars.

Chapter
12

The rain had stopped by the time I left the building. But the heat still hovered, an oppressive force. Plumes of steam were rising from the asphalt as the water on the ground evaporated in the hot, humid, air. Overhead a hazy, tired sun watched me thread my way through row after row of parked cars to my cab. I lit a cigarette and inhaled and thought about what I'd done. I'd come in planning to do one thing and left doing the exact opposite. Oh well. Who had said that consistency is the hobgoblin of little minds?

I sidestepped a puddle. Anyway it wasn't as if Mr. Stanley wasn't asking me to do something I wasn't already doing. It's just that this way I'd get paid for it. I reached my cab and opened the door. A blast of hot air greeted me. Wishing for air-conditioning, I gritted my teeth and got in. The steering wheel was hot under my fingers. Sweat was dripping down my forehead and into my eyes. I blinked it away and sped out of the lot and headed to the store.

Tim, Julio, and Manuel were huddled at one end of the counter when I walked in. Their eyes were focused on the quivering baby guinea pig at the other end. In between was the tarantula. She was standing still. Her front two legs were up. The hairs on them were erect. She was testing the air currents.

"Exactly what do you think you're doing?" I demanded, hurrying over to the counter. I guess the baby chick hadn't been enough of a show.

"Er . . . nothing," Tim said. Then he plastered a smile on his face. "We . . . I . . . didn't expect you back so soon."

Martha put her two legs down.

"Surprised?" I reached the counter and was picking up the guinea pig when the spider leaped into the air. "Jesus," I yelled jumping back.

Plop. The tarantula hit smack where my hand had been.

"Don't scream like that," Julio chided running up beside me. "You'll scare her. They're very sensitive."

"Sensitive is not exactly the word I would have chosen," I replied when my breathing returned to normal.

"There, there," he crooned to the spider. Then he put out his hand, palm up. Martha clambered on. "It wasn't her fault. You shouldn't have taken her lunch."

"I'm sure the guinea pig doesn't see it that way," I retorted as I put the quivering little mammal back in its cage.

"Martha has to eat, too, you know."

"Not when I'm watching she doesn't. Julio, you promised you'd keep her in a cage."

"Oh. I thought you meant I couldn't have her out when you were here," he stammered.

I turned on him. "That's bullshit and you know it. I feel like throwing both of you out."

"Don't," Tim said coming up behind me. "It was my fault. I was the one who suggested it."

I hesitated.

"Please," Julio begged. "One more chance. It won't happen again. I swear. And I read five more pages in *Charlotte's Web.*"

I folded my arms across my chest. "Okay. Tell me what happened."

"I just finished the chapter where Wilbur escapes."

"Can you be a little more specific."

"Sure." Julio favored me with a smug smile. "The goose tells Wilbur to push on a loose board so he can get out of his pen. Wilbur does but when he gets outside he feels kind of weird."

"How do you know Wilbur feels weird?"

"Because he says he feels queer and he ain't talking about the gay kind of queer, either."

"I guess you did read it, didn't you."

"Yeah. That's what I said. So how about it?"

I relented against my better judgment. "But this is it. No more mistakes."

Manuel let out a cackle, then quickly stifled it by covering his mouth with his hand when I glared at him.

"I mean it," I called after the three of them as they drifted out back. I do, I told myself as I went into the storeroom to check on Zsa Zsa. The puppy and the cat were sleeping next to each other. Miracles can happen, I thought as I stood there and watched them snoozing. Then I went back out and started thumbing through the newest issue of *Vivarium.* I was busy reading about how thanks to Hurricane Andrew there were now a number of large boas and pythons loose in the Florida area and how authorities were afraid they might establish breeding colonies when Julio and Manuel reappeared.

"We're heading out," Manuel informed me as they went toward the door.

They were midway when Julio snapped his fingers and turned toward me. "Damn," he said. "I knew I forgot to ask you something."

"Yes?" I closed the magazine.

"I told A.J. I'd ask you if you got any rattlers for sale."

"You know I don't carry stuff like that."

"But you can get it."

"But I'm not going to." I threw down the magazine to emphasize the point. "Hell will freeze over before I give someone like him something like that."

I loved this latest craze. Drug dealers were now using venomous snakes to booby trap their stash. I was surprised A.J. hadn't asked for a Gaboon viper. Or a black mamba.

"Jeez." Julio held up his hands and backed away. "Don't go spastic. I'm only asking."

"And I'm only telling. Now I have a question for you." The mention of A.J.'s name had jogged my memory. "Did the cops ever talk to A.J. about the guy you said you saw running through his yard?"

"You already asked me that."

"No, I asked you if they talked to you."

Julio glanced toward the door. He was anxious to leave. "Yeah. You're right."

"Well, did they talk to A.J.?"

Julio shrugged. "I don't think so."

"Then I will."

"Whatever," Julio said and left.

Maybe Connelly was too busy to go over there, but I sure as hell wasn't. Talking to A.J. probably wouldn't turn up anything useful, but at this point I needed to take advantage of every bit of information I could gather, no matter how tangential it was.

It turned out to be a slow evening. No customers. Just another kid coming in asking about his lost dog. George was right, I decided as I gave the kid the number of the ASPCA. This was turning out to be an epidemic. I sent Tim home at seven-thirty and closed the store a little before nine. Outside the heat had abated slightly. I stood for a moment studying the crimson-slashed sky. Then I put Zsa Zsa in the car and drove over to see A.J.

The seventy something-year-old house A.J. was living in had been built as a one-family Victorian. But time and the economy had changed that. Investors had moved in, bought the lumbering white elephant—because who could afford to live in something that large in this day and age—subdivided the inside, and rented the 'apartments' out to whomever they could. Now the paint was peeling, the gingerbreading was being eaten by carpenter ants, half the windows were covered with plastic, and beer cans littered the front yard.

A.J. was sprawled on his porch steps nursing a forty when I pulled up. His shirt was hanging opened and his skin was covered with a sheen of sweat which made the web of keloid welts running over his chest and arms even more apparent. I'd heard the scars were from knife fights. But I didn't know for sure. I didn't know A.J. well enough to ask him. I just knew him well enough to nod to when I saw him down at the convenience store. His face was impassive as I walked up the path toward him. No smile. No frown. No nothing.

"What you want?" he demanded when I was about five feet away.

"I want to talk to you."

"So talk," he said, his eyes scanning the people and the cars going by.

I folded my arms across my chest. "It's about the guy Julio says he saw the afternoon Brandon Douglas got killed."

"What guy? I know lots of guys."

"The one that came running through your backyard."

A.J. leaned over and spit onto the grass. "I don't remember."

"Did you see him, too?" I persisted.

"I just told you I don't remember," A.J. repeated taking another gulp of his forty.

"It wasn't that long ago."

"Around here a day is a long time."

"I suppose that depends on what you're on," I observed as I swatted at a mosquito on my wrist.

"What's that supposed to mean?" A.J. snarled.

"Nothing." I hurried on. I'd forgotten rule number one. People who do dope didn't talk about it with people who don't—unless they initiate the conversation. "This guy. Was he tall? Short . . . ?"

"Listen," A.J. said interrupting me. "Why don't you just take your skinny white ass and plunk it back inside that car of yours. I don't got to talk to you and I ain't."

"So what would it take to make you want to?"

At that he laughed. "How about you get me one of those diamondback rattlers like I seen on TV? A big one."

"Julio already asked me and I'll tell you what I told him. No. They make lousy pets. Any other requests?"

"Yeah. I got one." And he leered. "How about bringing your friend around . . ."

"Friend?" I asked wondering who in God's name he was referring to.

"The blond bitch with the fancy car. The one you was with the other day."

"You mean Lynn?"

"If that's her name. Then maybe we got something to discuss."

"How do you know her?" I asked even though I could guess at the answer.

"I used to see her down here two or three times a week—visiting." A.J. rolled the word around on his tongue, savoring it. So I had been right. Lynn was seeing Douglas. "She be a hard bitch to miss," he continued as he took another gulp of beer. Then crushed the can, and tossed it away. "Look, I'm a businessman, just like you." He stood up obviously regretting telling me the little he had. "And right now you're cutting into my prime selling time."

"Well, I certainly wouldn't want to do that."

"You're right, you don't," he replied as he brushed by me.

I watched him pimp roll his way down the block. When he turned the corner I left. As I threaded the cab through a group of kids playing tag in the street I thought about what A.J. had said. In my book seeing a guy two or three times a week means a serious affair. And even though the Plaza was more Lynn's style, I could see the appeal of coming down here. Nobody who mattered would see her. And it was exciting. A walk on the wild side.

And then I got to thinking about what Lynn had told me when she picked me up. She'd said, 'she had to get something back, something that belonged to Gordon.' Well, whatever it was it wasn't one of Gordon's shirts that was for sure. Had Lynn given Brandon Douglas something of her husband's and then changed her mind? Or had Brandon Douglas stolen something of Gordon's and she was going to get it back? Of course I could always ask Lynn. I could ask, but I didn't think I'd get an answer. I sighed. Nevertheless I had to try. But not tonight. Maybe tomorrow. And with that thought I turned onto Erie Boulevard and headed toward Dragon Gardens for some Chinese takeout.

Once I got home I locked the door and pulled down the shades. I didn't want to make myself a target for another attack. Even though I didn't think there'd be one, I didn't want to take any chances. Then the dog and I split two egg rolls and an order of Happy Family. We ate in the kitchen, because the living room still smelled of smoke. The new patch of floor had helped, but I still needed to wash the room down with the enzyme cleaner DiMario had left for me. That took me a good hour and a half. My back was aching but at least the smell was gone. I lay down on the sofa and watched TV for a while but nothing interested me.

I kept thinking about Brandon Douglas and Lynn. Finally I got up and got the carton I'd taken from Brandon Douglas's place out of the closet and put it on the kitchen table. It was time for a second, closer look at the stuff inside. Especially since I couldn't help feeling that in some way Douglas's death, his sister's murder, and Lynn's confession were all connected. I just didn't know how. Yet. I picked up Janet Tyler's composition book and opened the black and white cardboard cover and began reading.

The first page of the composition book was inscribed in a neat rounded script. Janet Tyler. Mrs. Palmer. Grade 11. Weedsport Central High. I flipped through it. There were several attempts at haiku, things like: *Rain dancing/ tears on my cheeks* or *Golden leaf/ floating down*. I turned more pages and read a short composition describing her cat. Then more poems. A description of her house. Her mother. Zeke's. A stab at an essay on Mark Twain. And so it went. A full year of high school compositions. A few good. Most mediocre. Judging by the condition of the pages they'd been read a lot. Probably by her brother. They must have made him feel closer to her. But all they did for me was make me feel sad.

I closed the notebook and took out the scrapbook that contained the Janet Tyler murder press clippings and began going through them again. This time with more attention. As I read I kept realizing how much about the case I'd forgotten over the years. The pleas to find her. Her description. The headlines when the skeleton was discovered out at Montezuma. More headlines when the bones were proved to belong to Janet Tyler. And then the conjectures, the hints, the statements. Lots of statements. But two of them interested me in particular.

One was Howie Kaplan's statement. Kaplan, a forensic anthropologist who'd been brought in to examine Janet Tyler's bones, had reported to the ME that he'd found gravel and sand as well as dirt in them. Meaning Janet Tyler had been buried twice: first in a gravel pit that turned out to be owned by a Syracuse-based construction firm by the name of Pearson and then at Montezuma.

The second statement that interested me was the one by Norma Lipsyle, the killer's wife. She claimed she'd seen Janet Tyler on the night she disappeared getting into a dark green MG TA. Then she'd retracted her statement right before her husband had confessed. Evidently nobody had followed through. I got up and poured myself a shot of Scotch and lit a cigarette. An MG TA was a pretty specific identification. It wasn't like she'd said, 'Janet Tyler got into a dark blue car.' No. she'd said an MG TA.

I wanted to speak to her and Kaplan.

I closed the scrapbook and stubbed out my cigarette.

Fortunately they were both around. Kaplan still taught at Syracuse University and of course I'd just seen Norma Lipsyle the other day. If I could find her damn house I'd be all set.

I took another sip of Scotch, put everything back in the box and went upstairs to bed. Suddenly I was so tired I could hardly walk.

Chapter

13

I had a lousy night. I kept on thinking I heard someone in the house, someone coming up the stairs. When I finally fell asleep I dreamt of purple and scarlet flames licking at the windows and doors of my room. I woke at three, heart racing, drenched in my own sweat, positive that someone was standing in the corner leering at me. I scrambled up and turned on my reading light with shaking hands. No one was there. Of course. I gulped down a Valium and sat for a while studying the shadow thrown on the floor by the dust ruffle on the bed while Zsa Zsa licked at my fingers and wagged her tail. Somehow just having another living thing nearby made me feel better.

Finally my heart rate returned to normal and I went into the bathroom and took a shower. Then because I had no clean clothes to put on I did my laundry. While I waited for the washing machine to finish, I made myself a pot of coffee, ate a couple of frozen Snicker bars, and then sat out on the back porch steps in my nightshirt and watched the puppy jump at the white moths dancing in the night air as I smoked one cigarette after another and wished that I hadn't given up grass and wondered who I could buy a nickel bag from now that Murphy was dead. A few minutes later James skulked out of the bushes. Zsa Zsa took one look and froze. So did James. Then she bounded toward him. James gave me a dirty look and scooted off into the underbrush.

"Sorry," I called after him.

He didn't reappear. Maybe if I put out a can of tuna he'd find it in his heart to forgive me. I got up, put my clothes in the dryer and went outside again. By now the sky had begun to lighten. Streaks of yellow showed on the horizon. I smoked another cigarette and thought about Lynn and Brandon Douglas and Lynn's husband, Gordon, and wondered if I wasn't missing the most obvious explanation for what had happened down on Otisco Street.

Wife has affair. Husband finds out. Husband goes ballistic and kills the guy. Wife confesses to the crime in a misplaced spasm of guilt. Why not? I stood up and ground my cigarette out. Why not indeed. By now the sky had turned into a pale gray canvas streaked with thick blue, yellow, and red lines. The finches were singing. A squirrel chattered in the fir tree overhead.

I went inside reluctantly and got my clothes up from the basement and dressed. Then I puttered around the house. But I couldn't keep my mind on anything. Finally I decided to drive over and talk to Lynn. I'd tried midmorning, afternoon, and early evening without success—maybe early morning would yield better results. Maybe Lynn hadn't taken whatever drugs she was on yet. Maybe if I woke her up I'd be able to get a straight sentence out of her. Boy, wouldn't that be a novelty. I was halfway there when I realized I had two problems: Gordon and Ken. They'd still be home. For a moment I thought about turning around, but then I decided if they didn't like what I was about to do, they could call Lynn's father and complain. The dew was still glistening on the grass when I got to her house.

I rang the bell. The chimes sounded inside. A minute or two later I heard footsteps approaching. Then the door opened and Lynn's brother stepped out. Well at least it wasn't Gordon. Thank God for small favors. Ken was wearing striped pajama bottoms and no shoes. And even though his hair was mussed and his eyes still caked with sleep, he moved with the lithe grace of a big cat.

"Jesus," he said when he saw me. "What the hell are you doing here at this hour of the morning?"

"I want to talk to Lynn."

"I thought we settled this the other day."

"I guess you thought wrong."

He folded his arms across his chest. "She's asleep."

I sidled past him into the house. "Then I guess I'm going to have to wake her up."

He grabbed my wrist. "Where are you going?"

"I told you," I said, twisting out of his grasp. "I need to speak to your sister."

Ken's eyes blazed. "If you don't get out of here I'm going to call the cops."

"Hey go ahead. But before you do I suggest you phone your father."

"Why?"

"Because he'll tell you I'm working for him," I called down to him as I bounded up the stairs two at a time. They were carpeted in a very plush Dresden blue. So was the hallway. The walls were covered with a lighter blue linen wallpaper, the moldings were white. Very classic. Lynn's bedroom echoed the color scheme. She was standing by her bed when I walked in.

"I guess you're awake after all," I observed.

"I don't sleep much anymore," she said as she tied the belt on her dark blue silk robe. It was one of those expensive pieces of lingerie, the kind that look like nothing but cost the earth. Her eyes were vacant. Her mouth was slack. She had given up whatever it was she had been holding on to.

"Don't you want to know why I'm here?" I asked.

She shrugged.

"I came to see how you are."

"I'm fine."

"You don't look fine."

"Well, I am."

I went over and put my hands on her shoulders. "Lynn, we need to talk about Brandon Douglas."

Lynn turned her head away. "I have nothing to say."

"Look, I don't care what you were doing with him. Remember me? I'm your friend. The one who lent you her house. I just need some information about this guy for myself."

She didn't answer. Instead she fiddled with her belt. Then she walked over to her dresser.

Its surface was cluttered with pieces of jewelry, bottles of perfume, and a variety of pictures of Lynn and her brother at different ages. She reached over, extracted a bottle of pills, opened it, tapped a Valium—how could I not recognize the stuff?—into her hand and swallowed it. "Doctor's orders," she told me even though I hadn't asked.

I followed her. "Tell me, did Gordon know about you and Brandon Douglas?"

She turned her back on me.

I spun her around. "Did you give Douglas something of your husband's?" I demanded. "A little token of your esteem, perhaps? Is that what you had to go down to Otisco Street to get?"

Lynn's eyes filmed over. "Don't you understand?" she cried. "I can't talk. I want to, but I can't." And she ran into the bathroom and locked the door.

I could have pounded on it. I could have made a scene.

But I didn't.

What would have been the point?

There was nothing I could do right now that was going to compel her to speak to me.

That much was obvious.

What I didn't know was why that should be the case.

On the way down the stairs I met Ken coming up. He had a big grin on his face.

"Dad wants you to call him immediately," he informed me. "He's very annoyed."

"Really?" I guess bursting in on his daughter wasn't in my job description. Oh well. I'd call him later. *Much* later. When he'd cooled down and I was in a better mood.

"Yes. Really. You're just lucky Gordon's at work," he added as he ran up the rest of the stairs to check on his sister, a woman I thought I knew but whom I was beginning to understand less and less.

I let myself out. As I walked to the car I had another idea. Maybe I should drive over to the plant and talk to Gordon. Maybe I could get some information about Brandon Douglas out of him. It seemed worth the ride to find out.

The shift at the plant must have been changing because there was more traffic on the two-lane road than I'd seen the last couple of times I'd been there. Both lanes were clogged and I had to inch my way along sandwiched in with all the other cars. It took me about ten minutes to get inside the lot and another five to find a space on the outer edge of the perimeter. It was beginning to heat up again, the early-morning coolness having vanished under the sun's hazy glare, and my face was damp with sweat by the time I got to the front office entrance. The blast of cold air that greeted me when I opened the door made me sneeze but there didn't seem to be anyone around to hear me.

The receptionist's cubicle was empty. I opened the door and went inside to the large area where the secretaries sat. The lights were on but the desks were deserted, the computers shut off. I looked at the clock on the wall. It said seven-thirty. Probably no one came in till eight-thirty. I walked through the brightly lit space and began threading my way through the maze of cubicles on the outskirts, looking for Gordon. I finally found him in the conference room. He was leaning over a polished mahogany table studying computer printouts, so engrossed in what he was doing that it took him a minute to realize someone was there. When he did he whirled around.

"Hello," I said. "Getting an early start?"

He looked confused. "I always do. What are you doing here?"

I lied and told him I was looking for his father-in-law. It seemed simpler than having to explain I'd just come from his house.

"He won't be in for another half hour or so," Gordon informed me.

"Then perhaps you can help me."

He glanced back down at the printouts on the table. "I'm really busy right now."

"This will just take a few minutes. It's about Brandon Douglas."

Gordon stiffened.

"I need some information."

"Why?"

"Well, Mr. Stanley asked me to help out with this situation. . . ."

"He did, did he?" he growled.

"Yes. Didn't he tell you?"

Gordon gave a bitter laugh. "He doesn't tell me lots of things."

I shifted my weight.

"I think he blames me for what happened."

"Why?"

Gordon pointed at himself. "Because I was the one who hired the guy to paint my house. He was looking for some extra work and I gave him Lynn's phone number and told him to call her up."

"It's not your fault. You didn't know."

"Try telling that to my father-in-law." Gordon rubbed his forehead. "Who would have thought that something that simple would lead to something like this?" He bit his lip and started fiddling with the computer printout pages on the table. "Evidently this Douglas went rummaging through the desk drawer in the study—I mean it was an easy enough thing to do. Nobody was keeping tabs on him—and took some cash.

"Lynn discovered it. But instead of calling the police or telling me, she decided to go down and get it. She thought that Douglas was just a messed-up kid. She didn't want to see him going to jail. But the bastard didn't want to give her the money. He was drunk. And then . . . he . . . I'm only sorry I didn't kill him myself . . . he tried to rape her. They struggled. And Lynn shot him." Gordon shook his head again. "I know this is trite, something everyone says. But he seemed like such a nice young man. So quiet. So polite. Who would have thought?"

"Who indeed," I replied.

Gordon had just given me Lynn's story.

The question was: did he believe it? Or was he just parroting it to cover his own ass?

"Did you ever get the money back?"

"The police haven't found it yet."

Probably because there wasn't any. I bit my fingernail. "Well one thing you can't take away from Douglas," I said to Gordon just to see what would happened. "He sure was a good-looking kid."

Gordon slammed the table with the palm of his hand. Computer printouts went flying. "He was garbage," he hissed. "He deserved to die."

Chapter
14

As I left I thought about what I'd learned from my interview with Gordon.

Not all that much.

Except that he hated Brandon Douglas.

Not that that was exactly surprising.

If I were him I'd probably feel the same way.

But did he hate him because he knew he was sleeping with his wife or because he held Brandon responsible for Lynn's present situation?

And if he knew about Brandon and Lynn did he know before or after Douglas was killed?

Because if he knew before that would constitute a definite motive for him killing Douglas. Wounded pride. Jealousy. Here was his wife fucking some twenty-one-year-old kid who worked on the assembly line. Some nobody who lived in the slums. The ultimate insult. I didn't see Gordon taking that well.

But then again Gordon might really not know.

Lynn might not have told him.

And the police might not have picked up on the relationship.

It hadn't made the papers.

And stuff like that usually did.

Maybe that's why Mr. Stanley had hired me.

To get his son-in-law.

Which was why Lynn didn't want to talk to me.

Because she was protecting Gordon.

But why should she be protecting Gordon? She didn't like him all that much.

God. This whole thing was getting way too confusing. I did a mental checklist of what I knew.

Brandon and Lynn were having an affair.

And Brandon either took or was given something out of Lynn's house. Something she had to get back.

What?

And then I wondered where the item—whatever it was—had gone?

Perhaps it was still at the house on Otisco Street.

It might even be worth going back and having another glance around. In the daylight the place wouldn't be as spooky. I'd be able to see what I was looking at. Always important.

But not now.

I'd done enough for one morning. I'd go later. Sometime in the afternoon. After all I still had a business to run and phone calls to make.

What I figured I'd do as I got into my cab was swing by my house, pick up Zsa Zsa who had probably peed over the kitchen floor by now, stop at McDee's and get an Egg McMuffin and some coffee, and then head out to the store.

Along with everything else we had some scorpions and hissing cockroaches arriving by air freight and I wanted to make sure I was there to help Tim get them out of the box.

Sure enough Zsa Zsa hadn't waited. Or rather she waited until I walked in the door before she let loose. I mopped the floor, then locked up the house and stopped at McDee's and picked up an Egg McMuffin, a large Coke, and two coffees because my caffeine level had fallen to dangerously low levels, before proceeding to the store. Julio was waiting for me.

"Here," he said walking toward me as I got out of the car. "A present." And he shoved a large Mason jar full of flies at me. "For the lizards. To make up for yesterday."

I thanked him and we went up to the store together. As I walked I decided I was definitely doing something wrong here. Most women get a rose to demonstrate contriteness. I got bugs. But the geckos and skinks would love them.

"I caught most of them in our kitchen," Julio explained as I unlocked the shop.

"I bet your mom was happy."

"Yeah. She keeps saying she's gonna get these fly traps, but every time she goes to the store she forgets. You have to sneak up on the suckers and then you whip a bag over them and put 'em in the jar. It's easier when they're screwing 'cause then they ain't paying attention."

"I think that's true of most species," I remarked as I opened the door to the store and stepped inside. Pickles quickly sniffed my leg and ran away before Zsa Zsa could lick her. I guess friendship only goes so far.

Julio giggled. "Can I see Martha?"

"Sure. Just keep her in the back."

He started off in the direction of the storeroom, then stopped.

"Yes?" I set the McDee's bag on the counter.

"It's about A.J.," he told me, a worried look on his face.

"What about him?" I unwrapped my sandwich and took a bite while Zsa Zsa clawed at my leg to let me know she wanted some.

"He told me he's coming over here today."

"Just what we need," I said as I broke off a small piece of sandwich and gave it to the puppy. She grabbed it and ran away. "Did he happen to say why?"

Julio shook his head. He had the jar of buzzing flies clasped to his chest like some bizarre talisman.

"Well, I guess we'll find out when he gets here. Who knows? Maybe he's decided to buy some tropical fish."

"I don't think so."

I didn't either, but I could always hope. I shooed Julio into the back room, reached for the phone and called the anthro department and asked for Howie Kaplan. But he wasn't teaching this summer session. The secretary gave me his number and told me to try him at home. Which I did. I got lucky and caught him just as he was leaving for a picnic. I told him who I was and what I wanted and he was intrigued enough to ask me to come out to his house in Manlius around nine that evening so we could talk. I thanked him, hung up, and got down to work.

The morning turned out to be great business-wise. In the first half hour I sold two tortoises, a six-foot corn snake, and a hundred dollars' worth of salt water fish. Then when Tim came in, I told him I was going out to Hancock and pick up my order from Delta air freight office. As I was leaving, Maria walked in to play with Zsa Zsa, something she'd been doing almost every day since Gomez had disappeared.

"She likes me," she said, her eyes lighting up as Zsa Zsa licked her fingers.

"Of course she does," I replied.

She took a dog biscuit out of her shorts pocket. "Come on, Zsa Zsa, I have a treat for you."

Zsa Zsa stood up on her hind legs.

Maria giggled and ran toward the back room with Zsa Zsa hot on her heels.

"Are you going to give her Zsa Zsa if Gomez doesn't show up?" Tim asked. He'd just come out of the back. "They like each other a lot."

"So I noticed."

"It would be a nice thing to do."

"Actually, I'm thinking of buying her another cocker spaniel puppy."

Tim gave me an incredulous look. "But, Robin, that's three hundred bucks!"

I shrugged. "I'll take it out of Mr. Stanley's money." And I left.

By the time I got back to the store, an hour and a half later, Maria was gone and Zsa Zsa was sleeping the sleep of exhausted puppies. I lit a cigarette and put the box I'd gotten from the airport on the counter. Then I called Tim over, slit the tape, and opened the flaps. Each item was tied up in a separate cloth bag. And each bag was surrounded by a nest of crumbled newspaper. Twelve in all. Seven scorpions and five hissing cockroaches.

"Here goes," I said as I lifted a bag out, untied the knot, and shook it into one of the small clear plastic containers I had waiting.

The cages, twelve inches by nine inches, had desert scenes painted on their floors, cacti stenciled on one of their sides, and escape-proof tops. The scorpion shot out into it, tail curved up, looking to sting. I clamped the lid on and studied what I bought. Ordering is one thing, getting what you pay for is something else. Most of the firms I dealt with were reputable, but every once in a while someone tried to slip a sick reptile or insect by.

But this scorpion looked okay. It was between three and four inches long, jet black and shiny. Its claws were bulbous and he was waving them back and forth to show that he wasn't happy.

"Ugly fucker, isn't he?" Tim said as he reached for the second bag. "Why'd you buy them?"

"They're hot right now and I got a good deal," I explained while I began emptying the third scorpion into its plastic case.

But I guess I wasn't paying enough attention, because instead of going straight in the scorpion grabbed onto the plastic sides of the cage and scrambled onto the counter.

"Shit," I cursed as he scurried toward the cash register.

I hurriedly took one of the cages and put it over him. Then I took another cage and put it under the counter lip and moved the first cage toward it. A few seconds later the scorpion had fallen into the second cage and I put the lid on.

"Well, I guess that was our excitement for the day," Tim observed. Then he reached into the box again.

"Not quite." I nodded toward the front door.

A.J. sauntered in. "What's that you got?" he demanded, pointing at the little cages lined up on the counter as he crossed the floor.

This was someone who didn't waste time with commonplace pleasantries. "Scorpions," I replied.

"Hey, I seen those things on the nature show. They live in the desert, right?"

"Right."

"And they're poisonous?"

"Venomous. Some of them."

"How come you're selling 'em, when you wouldn't sell me the snake I wanted?"

"Snakes are different."

"They seem like the same sort of thing to me."

"Trust me. They're not."

A.J. tapped one of the cages with his finger. The scorpion curled his tail.

A.J. smiled. "He looks mean as fuck."

"He is."

A.J. tapped the cage again. The scorpion's tail went higher. "I like these little mothers. How much you getting for him?"

"Forty." I'd been going to charge twenty-five, but I figured A.J. could afford the difference.

"I was coming here to make you order me a diamond-back, but I'm gonna take him instead. In fact," he said, looking at the counter, "I'll take those two, too. Can you get me any more?"

I pointed to the carton. "I have four more in here. Fresh off the plane."

"Good." He reached in his pocket, took out a thick roll of bills and handed it to me. "Take what you need out of this."

"I will as soon as you tell me what that guy you and Julio saw looked like."

A.J. chuckled. "You know you got balls."

"Not the last time I looked I didn't."

He laughed harder. "Okay. The truth is I don't know."

"What do you mean you don't know?" I demanded. "You saw him, didn't you?"

"Yeah, but he was moving real fast."

"You must have seen something."

"I was stoned off my ass. On opiated hash. I wasn't exactly paying attention if you know what I mean."

I did. I'd smoked that stuff myself. This guy could probably have curtsied in front of A.J. and he still wouldn't have been able to describe him. So that was that. Another dead end. It was discouraging. Tim and A.J. started joking around and I turned my attention back to the scorpions. It took another half an hour to get them all caged and packed up.

"I can't believe you sold those to him," Tim told me the moment A.J. was out the door, shopping bags in hand.

"Why not?" I asked as I put the two hundred ninety-nine dollars and fifty cents I'd taken off A.J. in the drawer. "After all, money is money."

"What do you mean, why not? Why didn't you want to sell him a rattler? The man's completely irresponsible. God knows what he's going to do with them."

"You know what he's going to do with them. He's going to use them to guard his stash."

"What if he does something else—like put one down someone's back?"

"So?" I picked up Zsa Zsa who was now nibbling on the heel of my sandal.

"How can you say 'so'?"

"The worst that can happen is that somebody gets stung."

"And dies."

I laughed. "You're thinking about the little red ones. And then that would only happen if the person who got stung was a very small child or someone with a heart condition and even then the probabilities of something like that happening are slim. The ones I bought look ugly as sin but they're harmless."

"Oh." Tim looked sheepish. "I didn't know."

"You should study your arachnids a little more carefully."

"I thought scorpions were beetles."

"I rest my case. Tell me, did you really think I'd get something in here that's dangerous? Especially after what happened to John last year?"

"No," he conceded. "I guess not." Then another thought crossed his mind. "But A.J. thinks they're really bad."

I smiled. "I know."

"What happens when he finds out he paid nearly three hundred dollars for nothing?"

"He won't find out."

"But if he does?" Tim insisted.

"Hey, I told him not all scorpions are venomous. It's not my fault he heard what he wanted to instead of what I said."

Tim shook his head. "I think you're making a mistake."

"What's another in a cast of thousands?" I asked before turning my attention to the hissing cockroaches.

Chapter
15

It was four o'clock in the afternoon by the time I walked out of the store. Two kids were squirting each other with water cannons near the parking lot. One hit my leg by mistake and they both sprinted away, giggling as they went. But I didn't mind. I wouldn't have yelled at them. The cold water felt good in the heat. As I opened the door of my cab a cat scooted out from underneath. It had been resting in the shade. I slid in and drove down to Otisco.

As I pulled up to the house I reflected that it didn't look any better the third time I visited it than it had the first and second times. The yellow police tape fluttering across the grass and the red brick path up to the steps was just another piece of litter in an already plentiful supply. As I stepped on the tape I couldn't help but remember how Lynn had looked as she sashayed up the steps in her white suit and how she'd looked coming down on the stretcher. And then

I thought about the noise Manuel and I had heard in the dark the other night.

Instinctively I slipped my hand in my pants pocket and touched the knife Manuel had given me. Even though I hadn't wanted it when he'd made the offer, now I was glad I'd accepted. The metal felt reassuring under my fingers. It told me I could take care of whatever came up. Or at least I had a chance to. At that moment I began to understand the attraction of guns. And I almost wished I had one.

I took a quick look around and slipped inside. As the door closed behind me I spent a few seconds thinking about running home and popping a Valium and maybe having a shot or two of Scotch just to take the edge off my nerves. But then I decided that was a very bad idea. Since Murphy's death and the shooting I'd been getting entirely too dependent on chemical solutions for my own good. If I wasn't careful I was going to find myself spending thirty days drying out in a private institution somewhere. Instead, I lit a cigarette—my drug of choice—and looked around.

The place had been stuffy the last time I'd been here. It was still stuffy, but now it was a mess. Books and clothes were scattered all over the floor, courtesy no doubt of a police search and a little freelance prospecting by the local neighborhood inhabitants. I walked into the small room on the left. The cartons that had been neatly stacked against the wall had been upended and the windows and blinds, which had been dirty to begin with, were now covered with a dusting of opaque white powder—a residue of the powder the police used to dust for fingerprints.

I studied the stuff on the floor. It would have helped if I knew what I was looking for but since I didn't I'd just have to go through everything and see what I could come up with. Fifteen minutes later I was pretty sure that there was nothing here from Lynn's house, at least nothing of significance, in the room. The clothes were mostly old and worn and anonymous—the kind of jeans and T-shirts you could find at any mall in America. The books were all sci-fi, mystery, and horror.

A good half of them were titles I'd always wanted to read, but hadn't been able to find. Brandon Douglas had evidently spent a great deal of time and money assembling his collection. I started thumbing through them. About a third of them had Matt Lipsyle's name written on the inside cover, another instance of proof that Douglas didn't believe Lipsyle had killed his sister. Otherwise, he wouldn't have had them around.

But who had killed her?

Who was he tracking?

I looked at the copy of *Do Androids Dream of Electric Sheep?* I was holding. Too bad it couldn't answer that question.

I tossed it back in the carton with the others and was heading toward the door when I impulsively turned around, picked up the carton and carried it to the front door so I could get it on the way out. It was a shame to let them go unread.

The next room, the one with the weight-lifting equipment, was now practically bare. The bench was gone. So were the bar and the weights. The only thing left was the water bottle with the Atilla's logo. I picked it up and turned the plastic bottle over in my hand while I thought. Atilla's was a small storefront gym over on the North Side for serious bodybuilders only. It might pay me to speak to some of the guys there. Maybe Brandon Douglas had talked to them. Maybe he had even said something I might find interesting. It was worth a gamble. I added it to my mental list of things to do, put the bottle back down on the floor and moved on to the dining room.

Except for the sofa and the upturned orange crates the room was now empty. No more stereo. No CD player. No television. No Oriental rug. Manuel and his friend Rabbit had done a good job. The only thing left was the sofa. I wondered if they'd taken the weight equipment, too, or if that had been someone else as I knelt down and ran my hands under the sofa cushions looking for God-knows-what. But there was nothing there except lint and dust. I wiped my hands on the back of my pants and got up slowly. My leg was stiffening up from all the kneeling down I'd been doing. Maybe missing three weeks of physical therapy wasn't such a good idea after all. Even if it was boring and unpleasant. Maybe I should call up and make an appointment and go back.

As I continued on into the kitchen I thought I heard barking upstairs. Then the sound died and I decided the noise must have come from somewhere outside. I took a look around. Of all the rooms this seemed to have fared the best. Maybe it was the smell of rotten garbage that had kept everyone out. Besides the carton I'd taken the other night, everything else seemed to be in place. Since my last cigarette had gone out I lit another one to mask the odors. Then I began opening and closing drawers and cabinet doors. But the only things I found were a metal spatula, two paring knives, six or seven odd pieces of silverware, a frying pan, a saucepan, and several cans of protein powder, boxes of bran cereal, and a case of Evian.

By now the smell was beginning to get to me and rather than wasting time looking for the source I carried the remaining two cartons into what had been the dining room and set them down on the floor. I lifted the first one onto the sofa and looked inside. It was all Brandon Douglas's old sporting gear. I tossed the baseball in the air a couple of times before putting it back in the box wondering as I did if there was any family to claim this boy's things. Somehow it seemed like such a pity to throw them out.

I sighed and went on to the second box. It was full of *National Geographics*, but down on the bottom, pushed in a corner, was a small crumpled brown paper sandwich bag. I pulled it out, opened it up, and dumped the contents out on the sofa. It was old jewelry. Nothing that looked too good. Mostly keepsakes. At a guess I'd say the pieces had belonged to Brandon's mother and sister. There was an old square watch set with colored stones, a small pink and white cameo in a silver setting, a knot of gold chains that had become hopelessly tangled together, a silver thistle pin with a purplish stone in the middle, and a wide, thin embossed wedding band.

I gathered everything up and put it back in the bag and started on the third carton. By now I was feeling more than a little discouraged. Because while it was true that the things I'd found had helped me get a better picture of Brandon Douglas, there was nothing I'd seen that I recognized as having come from Lynn's house.

Nothing.

Maybe the police had taken it.

Or Gordon.

Or some kid.

Or the killer.

Or maybe it didn't even exist except in my imagination.

Maybe Lynn had been lying about having to get something that Brandon had taken back.

Now that I thought of it that wouldn't surprise me.

After all, God knows Lynn had lied about everything else.

Even though I didn't want to I was beginning to think that she might have killed Brandon Douglas after all.

I pushed the thought aside and started up the stairs. I doubted anything was up there, but it would be foolish to leave without taking a look. It was hotter on the second floor than the first. I wiped the sweat off my forehead with the back of my hand. The barking I'd heard downstairs had gotten louder, more frantic. It almost sounded like it was coming from the backyard. But I didn't pay much attention because by now I was standing in front of the room in which Brandon Douglas had been killed.

I'd been drawn there almost against my will. I didn't want to go in. But I forced myself to anyway. I don't know why. I knew there'd be nothing to see. The police would have taken everything in it. And I was right. The room looked exactly the same. Except of course now it was empty. No Brandon. No Lynn. Nothing except smears and rivulets of dried blood on the floor. And a chalk outline where Brandon had lain.

I shivered. Suddenly I didn't want to be there anymore. I backed out hurriedly and went through the next five rooms as quickly as possible, looking over my shoulder all the time, because even though I knew it was stupid I couldn't shake the feeling that someone was watching me. By the time I got downstairs I had my knife out and in my hand. I grabbed the carton of books and headed for the door.

It was cooler outside and I stood on the porch for a few seconds enjoying the feel of the slight breeze on my arms and face and watching a big puffy white cloud drift across the sky and thinking about what a total jerk I was. I hate it when my mind gets away from me like that. When I was through beating myself up I headed down the stairs toward the car. Then I heard the damned dogs again. Only this time they were whining. The sound bothered me. It was like children crying. And then I thought about Gomez. After all, he had been lost in this area. I put the carton down on the grass and went around the house to the backyard.

At first I didn't see anything but weed trees and over-grown laurels. Then I saw a small opening in the bushes. I walked over and stepped in. I mean, what the hell, right? 'In for a penny, in for a pound,' as my grandmother used to say. I'd come this far. I might as well finish the job. Leaves brushed at my hands and face. A wasp buzzed around my nose. I brushed it away and continued on. The fit was tight but somebody had definitely been through this way not too long ago, maybe even the guy Julio and A.J. had seen the afternoon Brandon had died. Brandon.

I shook my head at myself. After going through his stuff I felt as if we were on a first-name basis. A minute later I came out into somebody else's backyard, whose I didn't know. Portions of the paint on the back wall of the house had peeled away, leaving bare wood visible. A rain gutter dan-gled from the second floor. Clusters of milkweed, saw grass, and dandelions were sprouting in the clayey soil. A pyramid of tires stood over in one corner. In another was a red metal storage shed. The sound of barking and whining was louder now. It held an excited tone. The closer I got to the shed, the stronger the smell of excrement became. I opened the door.

Four puppies stared up at me from the gloom. There was a cocker, a scottie, a golden, and a little dog with rough brown fur, white paws, and a star on his chest.

"Gomez," I cried. Maria was going to be so happy.

He started dragging himself toward me. From the angle of his paw and the way he was holding it, it looked like it was broken. The other puppies looked on, their tongues lolling out of their mouths, too weak to move. When I reached inside the shed to take them out, the heat was overwhelming. There was no water, no food. The floor was covered with piss and shit. I held my breath as I leaned in and scooped the puppies out. As I carried them to the laurel hedge I looked up at the house.

No one was looking out the window.

I didn't see any lights. Any movement.

It looked like no one was home.

If they had been, they would have been out here already.

Which was good.

Because I didn't want to meet whoever was inside and argue with them about what I was doing.

Let the police deal with them.

I glanced back down at the puppies lying on the grass. They were panting, their sides were heaving. They were suffering from heat prostration. They needed to cool down—and fast. I spotted a hose curled by the side of the house, ran over, and turned on the tap. A stream of water shot out of the hose nozzle. I pulled the hose across the yard and sprayed the pups. None of them even yelped. I dribbled water in their mouths. Their tongues moved to get every drip. A few minutes later they were up on their feet. I cupped my hands and gave them a little more. Then I walked back and shut the water off. Too much at once would make them puke. I was heading back toward the pups when I heard a noise.

I turned around.

Joe Davis was coming around the corner of the house. When he reached the hose, he looked up and saw me. Then he saw the open shed door. His eyes narrowed. His hands balled up into fists.

Instinctively my hand moved to the pocket my knife was in.

Chapter
16

"What are you doing here?" he snarled.

"Is this your place?"

"Fuck you."

"You know you really are a scumbag. How could you do something like that?" And I pointed at the puppies lying in the shade of the hedge. I was too angry to be afraid.

"I'm not doing anything. You're the one that's trespassing. You're the one that's stealing dogs."

"So they're not yours?"

He stepped closer. "I should call the police on you and have you arrested."

"That's a laugh."

He took another step toward me.

"Stop."

"Why?" And he giggled. "Don't you want to become better acquainted?"

I reached in my pocket and took out my knife and

depressed the lever. There was a satisfying click as the blade sprang out. "Maybe you want to become acquainted with this?"

"Big blade. Very impressive. I like big things." Davis licked his lips. "Think you got the guts to use it?"

"Why don't you come closer and find out, asshole?"

"Oh, I'll come closer all right," he hissed. "Real close. Close enough to trim those ears of yours."

"Maybe I'll be the one to do it to *you.*"

"I don't think so." And he took another step toward me.

As I watched him advance, watched the gleam in his eye I realized that he wasn't going to leave. He wasn't going to go away. He was coming for me. Here. In the daylight. And he'd get me. He was stronger and faster and meaner. And there was no one around to help. Even if I screamed it wouldn't matter. By the time somebody got here it would be too late. Unless I did something first. My hand closed over the knife shaft.

Davis took his time as he came toward me. He wasn't in any hurry to finish this. He was enjoying himself too much. I stood there waiting for him with my heart pounding and the blood roaring in my ears. Then when he got close enough I reached out and slashed. He jumped back. But not fast enough. A red line appeared across his upper arm. He put his hand over it. Blood seeped through his fingers. He looked down and then looked back at me in surprise.

"Just get out of here," I said.

He smiled. "Not bad."

"Leave." My God, I thought, he's coming after me again. But he didn't. Instead he turned to go. He took two steps and stopped. His eyes were cold. The pupils were dilated

"That was fun. We'll play again."

"I doubt it." The blood was still roaring in my ears.

He leered. "You're going to dream about me tonight. Hot dreams. The kind that burn you up." And he walked away.

I shivered despite the heat. Jesus, had Davis thrown the Molotov cocktail through my window? I certainly wasn't going to ask him. George could do that. I gathered up the puppies and ran for the car before Davis could come back. By the time I reached the shop, they had recovered enough to create total pandemonium. When I came through the door with them Zsa Zsa took one look and dove into the dog pack while Pickles jumped on top of the counter.

"Gomez?" Tim asked, pointing to the mutt limping toward him.

"Gomez," I answered as I picked the pup up. "Listen, call Maria and tell her her dog is here and then call the dispatcher and have him patch you through to George. Tell him I think I found some of his stolen puppies. Meanwhile, I'm going to take these guys in the back and feed them."

Tim nodded and reached for the phone. I had just finished filling up the last dish with kibble when Maria came running through the door.

"Gomez!" she cried, scooping the little dog up. She scrunched her face as the puppy licked her from forehead to chin.

"Watch out for her paw," I warned. "I think it's broken."

"Broken?" Maria repeated, a panicked look creeping over her face.

"Don't worry," I assured her. "We'll get it fixed up. She'll be fine. I promise."

Maria smiled. Then she sat down on the floor, cradled Gomez in her arms, and rocked her from side to side. When I left she was feeding Gomez out of her hand.

George arrived fifteen minutes later. "Where'd you find them?" he asked as we walked to the back room. Maria looked up when we came in, then went back to playing with her dog.

After careful consideration, I gave George an edited version of my story. I told him I'd been passing by when I'd heard barking and gone to investigate. George gave me a funny look, but he didn't say anything. Which was good. Because I really didn't want to have to explain about being inside the house on Otisco Street. Especially since the yellow tape was still up.

"Tell me again about Davis," he ordered.

And I did.

"How bad do you think you cut him?" he asked when I came to the end.

"Not that bad really."

"Enough for stitches?"

I thought it over. "Probably not."

George chewed on the inside of his cheek. "Okay," he said after a moment. "Here's what's going to happen. I'm going to drive over to that house, take a look around, and talk to the neighbors. Then I'll pick Davis up and bring him downtown."

"You think you can find him?"

"You'd better believe I will."

"Why do you think he's doing this?"

"Because he's a low-life scumbag son of a bitch," George spat out. He was about to say something else but Maria looked up and George stopped. "Let's go out front," he suggested.

"Good idea."

Tim stopped dusting when we walked out into the main room. "What about the pups?" he asked.

"What about them?" George replied.

"What's going to happen to them."

"I'll call the ASPCA. They can stay there till I contact their owners."

Tim and I exchanged glances.

"They can stay here," I said. "They've been through enough."

"You sure?" George asked.

I nodded. "As long as it isn't more than a couple of days." Pickles would not be pleased, but it couldn't be helped.

Tim rubbed his head. "Sometimes I really don't like our species very much."

"Me, either," George agreed. "Especially these days." He straightened up. "I think it's time I took Maria home, got a statement from her mother, and then went out there and started catching the bad guys."

I made him promise to call when he knew what was going on.

After George left, Tim and I spent the rest of the afternoon and evening playing with the puppies. By the time we closed up Tim had fallen in love with the golden, named her Annabel, and decided to take her home with him for the night. I only hoped he wouldn't be too unhappy when her owner showed up.

It was a little before nine when I locked up the store, but somehow it felt more like twelve. For a few minutes I considered calling Howie Kaplan and changing our appointment, but then I realized I was probably tired because I hadn't eaten yet so on the way out to Manlius I stopped at Burger King and got two Whoppers, an order of fries, and a Coke. By the time I finished them I felt almost human again. Then I lit a cigarette, turned on the radio, and started reading street signs.

Manlius is one of those small towns where the streets are tree lined and curvy, the houses are old and picturesque,

and its very easy to get lost in the dark. It took me longer
then I expected to find Howie Kaplan's house. Even though
it was on the main road the front was almost completely
obscured by overgrown hedges. I was just getting out of the
car—Zsa Zsa was sleeping in the front seat—when a motor-
cycle roared up beside me and stopped.

"Robin Light?" the speaker asked lifting up the faceplate
of his helmet.

"Yes?"

"Howie Kaplan. Call me Howie." He extended a hand and
we shook. "Why don't you follow me inside? You'll have to
excuse the mess," he said as we entered the hallway. "My
wife's been away at a workshop out West for the past three
weeks and I'm not very good at cleaning. That's the trouble
with these old farmhouses," he continued as he put his helmet on what looked like an Early American cherry wood
dresser. "They have all these nooks and crannies you have
to dust." He ran his hand distractedly through his tousled
blond hair and I thought that with his wild hair, full beard,
grizzled arms, and large size he looked like an amiable teddy
bear. "Give me a modern house any day, but my wife fell in
love with this one—so what you are you going to do, right?"
He grinned and I fell in lust. "Come on, let's see what we
have in the fridge," he added, beckoning for me to follow.

When I walked into the kitchen I could see why his wife
had fallen in love with the place. Even I might be moved to
cook in a space like this. The room was at least twenty feet by
twenty feet. There were wood beams on the ceiling and a
brick fireplace on one wall. The other wall was lined with
shelves filled with dishes and cookbooks. A collection of
antique rolling pins and cookie cutters decorated a little
alcove. A professional stove sat next to a tile countertop. In
the middle was a scrubbed pine table. While I was still gawk-

ing, Howie opened the refrigerator and started rummaging around.

"Here we go." He produced two Dos Equis, handed me one, and motioned for me to sit. "The Janet Tyler murder," he said as he twisted the top off his beer. "Now that was an interesting case." And he took a swallow. "After you called I went upstairs, dug out my old notes and reread them."

"You were the first one they called, weren't you?"

"To look at the bones? Yes. Yes, I was. The interesting thing to me was the fracture on her leg." Howard leaned forward intent on explaining. "You see, I think it happened when the murderer flung the skeleton into the swamp."

"Flung?"

"Flung. As in tossed. The skeleton looked like a rag doll. The killer was obviously in a big hurry to get rid of the corpse and get the hell out of there." Howie took another sip of beer. "You see, the coloration of the bone inside the break was brownish."

"Yes," I said, not seeing at all.

"That means it could have absorbed its color from the soil after it broke on impact with the ground. Of course it could have also been sustained before. There's really no way to tell." He leaned back. "What about the sand?" I prompted, remembering the article I'd read.

"What sand?"

"The sand they found on her bandanna."

"Oh that." Howie's eyes lit up. "Now that was fascinating." He stroked his beard. "You see, Montezuma has clayey soil, but the Feds found traces of sandy soil clinging to Janet Tyler's bandanna."

"So that's how they knew the body had been moved?"

Howie nodded. "Sometimes, when they want to, the Feds

do good work. Of course they do have great lab facilities."
And he gave a little sigh of longing.

"And the soil came from a place called Pearson's?"

He nodded.

"Exactly where is Pearson's located?"

"About midway between Weedsport and Syracuse. It's a
big place. Pulls in lots of locals and college boys for summer
jobs." Howie fingered his beard again. "Now don't quote me
on this but I remember hearing the Feds were getting ready
to subpoena the company employment rolls so they could
go through them."

"What happened?"

"Nothing. Lipsyle confessed before they got around to it
and that was the end of that." Howie began spinning the
bottle cap around.

"Do you think he did it?"

"He confessed, didn't he?"

"That's not what I asked."

"I'm aware of that." He paused and spun the cap around
again. "The truth is, I really don't know. Have you ever
thought about guilt?" he asked suddenly.

"I'm not unfamiliar with the concept," I replied cau-
tiously, wondering where the conversation was going.

"You know guilt is really a social construct. I mean, think
about it. An act is committed that breaches society's fabric.
That breach needs to be healed. That is accomplished by
some sort of sacrifice. Sometimes society makes amends.
Sometimes the individual does. The important thing is that
the tear is closed and life goes on."

"So you don't believe in justice?"

"Justice, as you mean it, is a Western concept."

"We are Western."

"You're right." Howie laughed. "You'll have to forgive me.

I'm teaching a class called Law In Society in the fall and since cultural isn't my field I've been boning up, doing a lot of reading about other societies' concept of justice and I suppose it's gone to my head. Well, no matter." He waved his hand around. "Let's talk about something else, shall we?"

That was fine with me. I wasn't exhausted, but I wasn't in the mood for philosophical discourses, either.

Chapter
17

Zsa Zsa and I were sitting at the bar at R.J.'s drinking beer and eating peanuts when George walked in. I waved and he headed toward us.

"I was hoping to find you here," he told me after he ordered a draft from Connie. Then he lapsed into a brooding silence.

"So what happened?" I finally prompted after a moment had gone by.

George drummed his fingers on the bar. "The backyard you found the shed in?"

"Yes?"

"Forget it. The house is owned by an eighty-year-old lady who's been in the hospital for the last six months."

I cursed silently. "Is anyone living there?"

George shook his head. "Not as far as the neighbors know. And believe me I asked them all."

"You know Davis lives across the way."

"I'm aware of that. Unfortunately it doesn't help."

"Here." Connie put a mug in front of George.

Foam dripped over the side. Zsa Zsa leaned over and licked it up.

George shook a finger at her. "Didn't your mother tell you that beer isn't good for dogs?"

She ignored him and went on licking.

"Obedient, too." He moved his glass and faced me again. "I picked up Davis and took him down to the PSB."

"How was his arm?"

"He had a bandage. I asked him what happened."

"And?"

"He claimed he cut himself on a wire fence."

"Right. What else did he say?"

"That he was just walking along, heard a noise, and came back to check and see if everything was all right."

I wanted to kill the guy. "Remind me to vomit."

"I know. But I've got nothing to hold him on. I had to let him go."

"So we're back where we started?"

"Except we have some live puppies instead of some dead ones." George raised his mug and took a big swallow.

"What about that comment he made to me about hot dreams?"

"He claimed he never said it. He claimed you made it up. Said you had the hots for him."

"Bastard," I said with more vehemence than I'd intended. Connie shot me a quick look and went back to shelving glasses.

George took another big gulp. Then he sighed. His shoulders slumped.

"Tired?" I asked.

"You could say that," George replied and began tracing a curlicue on the bar top with his finger.

"Why don't you go home and get some sleep then?" I suggested.

"I'm not that kind of tired."

"Then what kind of tired are you?" I inquired as Zsa Zsa turned around and stuck her rump up. I began rubbing it.

George stopped tracing and looked up at me. "The fed-up kind of tired."

"With Joe Davis?"

He slammed the counter with his palm. "With him and everyone like him. With not being able to do anything about people like him. With having to get up every morning and wade through shit."

Zsa Zsa righted herself and sat down. "That's what being a cop is, isn't it?" I asked as I stroked the top of her head.

George took a peanut and held it out to the puppy. "And that's why I'm thinking of doing something else," he said as she gobbled it down.

"As in . . . ?" It was hard imagining George as anything else.

"Going back to school."

"For what?"

"Medieval History."

"Come again?" I blinked in astonishment.

"I said Medieval History," George repeated belligerently.

"You're kidding." The words slipped out before I could stop them, but try as I might I just couldn't see George as a scholar.

"What's the matter?" he demanded, his feelings clearly hurt. "Don't you think I can do it?"

"I'm sure you can," I stammered. "It's just that I never pictured . . ."

"Me studying something like that," George said finishing my sentence for me.

"Well, you have to admit . . ."

"You think I should become a teacher or a social worker, don't you?"

"I think you should do whatever you want."

"You know what my major was in college? History."

"Good."

"You don't think I'm going to do well on my GREs, do you?"

I rubbed my forehead. "Jesus, George, give me a break."

"Fine." And he threw a five on the bar and stalked off.

"What's the matter with him?" Connie asked as she collected the money.

"At a guess I'd say an extreme case of frustration." And I paid and left.

Okay, so George was frustrated and angry about Davis. Well, so was I. But he didn't have to take his bad mood out on me. I got into my cab, slammed the door shut and drove home. At least I wouldn't have to listen to anybody rant there. The house was quiet. In fact, it was too quiet. I thumbed through the day's mail, gave the newspaper a quick glance, then got a chocolate bar out of the fridge, went into the living room, and turned on the TV. An old vampire movie was on. I started watching it. And that was the last thing I remember.

I woke the next morning around seven to Zsa Zsa sitting on my face and licking my ears. I spit dog hair out of my mouth, rolled off the couch, and took Zsa Zsa out for her morning pee. I was too lazy to make coffee so I finished off the rest of a bottle of flat, warm Coca-Cola—which was truly disgusting—and went upstairs to get dressed. But I ended up lying down on my bed instead. Just five minutes, I told myself as Zsa Zsa snuggled up next to me. I had just closed my eyes when the phone started ringing. I fumbled around for it.

It was Lynn's father. Damn. Damn. Damn. I knew what he was going to say and I didn't want to hear it. Which was why I hadn't answered the messages he'd left on my machine. All five of them.

"I've been trying to get hold of you," he said. "Don't you return your calls?"

"Sorry. I've been busy. What can I do for you?" I asked even though I really didn't want to hear the answer.

"My son is very upset with you. He feels your intrusion was completely unwarranted."

"Have you ever thought that he might be a little overprotective toward his sister?"

"I'm not paying you to barge into my daughter's household or to comment on familial relationships," Stanley snapped.

I pulled the phone toward me. "Then what are you paying me to do?"

"To find out what happened."

"I'm trying."

"Then talk to her friends like I asked you to do in the first place."

"I don't think they're going to tell me much." Lynn wasn't big in the confidence department. Witness me. I was supposed to be one of her best friends and look what she'd told me. Zero.

"Talk to them anyway."

"Is that an order?"

"Yes."

I hung up.

Fatuous asshole.

The phone started ringing.

Yeah. Yeah. Yeah. I disconnected the thing. Let Stanley stew. The last thing I was going to have was him breathing down my back, telling me what I should and shouldn't do. I wasn't playing puppet for him. He hadn't paid me enough for that. But when I calmed down a little I had to admit that he did have a point.

Maybe I should go and talk to Lynn's friends.

Maybe she *had* told them something.

And it wasn't as if I had to waste time trying to find them.

From what I knew of Lynn and her pals, I had a pretty good idea of where they'd be on a hot summer's day.

It was one o'clock by the time I got out to the Mount Tolen Golf Club. The curved driveway going up to the club-house bisected the club's golf course. But no one was playing on the greens. It was too hot. They were probably all inside the clubhouse having lunch. The clubhouse itself was fake Tudor with lots of beams going this way and that. The topiary around the walls—a head here, a dog and a cat there—gave the place a surreal air. I parked in the lot and followed a flagstone path around the clubhouse to the pool.

It was Olympic size. The water lapped against the diamond-shaped tiles. The white lounge chairs were arranged in rows of threes. Toward the back tables with umbrellas offered a modicum of shade. A few children were running about, while their mothers read or chatted with their friends. Two lifeguards were conferring off in a corner, while a third sat in a chair by the pool looking bored. An air of serenity hung over the scene, the kind of serenity only money and power could buy.

I put my hand over my eyes to shade them from the sun's glare and looked around. It took a minute but I finally spotted Lynn's friends sitting at one of the back tables. It was like triple vision. The three of them were all blonde, all tan, all in their late thirties, with the well-exercised bodies, gold jewelry, and the unlined faces and regular facial features that visits to the plastic surgeon confer. As I approached the three surveyed me, blank expressions on their faces. I'd met them several times when I was still going to Lynn's parties, but they obviously didn't remember, so I introduced myself again.

"Of course," Jan, the oldest one, said as the light of recognition dawned. "Why don't you sit down?"

I pulled up a chair.

"Such a shame about Lynn," Jan said turning her gold bracelet around. "Isn't it Marge?"

"Dreadful," Marge remarked as she whipped out a compact and began to reapply powder to her nose.

"When I heard it on the radio I just didn't believe it," Bree, the youngest, told me. "Just didn't believe it at all. What could she have been thinking about?"

I stepped into the opening. "That," I replied, "was what I was hoping you could tell me."

"She never said anything to me about anything like that," Bree assured me.

The other two nodded in agreement.

"Would you mind telling me what you did talk about over the last few months?"

"The usual." Marge snapped her compact shut.

I waved a dragonfly away. "What's the usual?"

"Clothes, trips, decorators—she was in the middle of redoing the guest bedroom." Nothing new there. Lynn was always in the middle of redoing something.

"Do you know if something was bothering her?"

"She seemed okay." Jan squeezed some suntan lotion out of the tube lying on the table and began rubbing it on her chest and arms. "But she wouldn't have told us if she wasn't," she added. "She wasn't like that."

"Though I did hear that she and her husband had a big argument last month," Marge said.

"What else is new?" Bree cracked as she reached for the suntan lotion. "They always fought."

"Do you know what it was about?" I asked.

Bree yawned. "The usual, I assume."

"Which is?"

"Gordon's tootsies."

"Bimbos would be a better word," Marge said. "If they weren't under twenty-five and stacked out to here"—she cupped her hands and held them in front of her chest—"he wasn't interested. He got them all out of the typing pool."

I leaned forward slightly. Now this was new. Lynn had never talked about Gordon screwing around. "Excuse me, but I'm confused here. Isn't Gordon the one who is jealous?"

"Absolutely," Bree assured me.

"Classic male," Marge put in. "You know. He can, she can't. Very possessive. I was at the club when he punched one of the guys for looking at her the wrong way. Glen was going to press charges, but Lynn's brother stepped in and calmed everyone down."

"Thank God for Ken." Jan flicked a ladybug away. "I don't know what Lynn would do without him. He's always there for her. He's just a nice guy. I wonder why he never got married?"

"Maybe he's gay," Bree suggested.

"Don't be ridiculous," Jan snapped.

"Well, how do you know?"

"Because Louise had an affair with him."

"That doesn't mean anything these days."

"So did Ellen." Jan smiled triumphantly. "And Amy."

"I wouldn't mind going to bed with him myself," Marge added. "I like his ass."

"Oh, brother." Jan rolled her eyes.

"I think we should get back to Lynn," Bree said.

"Good idea," Marge agreed. "We don't want Robin to go away with a terrible opinion of us."

I laughed and assured everyone I wouldn't. Then I asked them if Lynn had ever said anything about seeing Brandon Douglas.

Bree scratched under her gold charm bracelet with a crimson nail. "Wasn't that the man she confessed to killing?"

"That's right."

Marge wrinkled her forehead. "Didn't she have a fight with him?" she asked her friends.

"No," Bree corrected. "That was Joe Davis."

Chapter
18

"What?" I couldn't believe what I was hearing. Jan obligingly repeated it for me. "Are you sure?"

"Positive," Bree said. "I picked her up for lunch that day."

"You mean you saw him? He was at her house?"

"He might have been earlier, but he wasn't there when I dropped by."

"Then how do you know she had a fight with him?"

"Because she looked really angry when she got in the car, so I asked her what the matter was."

"And she said?"

"She said, 'Joe Davis can rot in hell.' Then she caught herself and changed the subject."

"And she didn't say anything else?"

Bree shook her head.

"What did you talk about after she said that?"

Bree tilted her head slightly while she thought. "Whether or not I should get new chairs for the dining room."

"And Joe Davis's name didn't come up again?"

"Not that I heard," Bree said.

The two other women agreed.

"Didn't you ask?"

"No," Bree replied. "I didn't. It wasn't any of my business."

But it was *mine*.

Despite yesterday's experience and Mr. Stanley's warning about bothering Lynn, I called her the moment I walked in the store. But no one was home. I didn't even bother leaving a message. I just hung up. I'd drive out and talk to her again later. Eventually she was going to break down and tell me what I needed to know. And if Mr. Stanley didn't like it, too bad. He could fire me.

Tim smiled. "Notice anything?" he asked as he walked out of the back room.

I thought. "It's quiet." There were no yips, no barks.

"Right you are."

"Where are the puppies?"

"Their owners came over and picked them up. George made the phone calls this morning."

"Except for Annabel."

Tim looked startled. "How did you know?"

"You wouldn't be smiling if she was gone."

Tim rubbed his head. "I don't know why I like her as much as I do."

"Where is she now?"

"In the back. She and Zsa Zsa are taking a nap."

"What did Merle think of her?" Merle was Tim's Great Dane.

"Not much. Not much at all."

"Well, James isn't real fond of Zsa Zsa at the moment,

either," I said as I went over to the fish tanks and started checking their Ph balance. When I was done with that I got busy sweeping the floor. But even though I was working, I couldn't stop thinking about why Lynn had argued with Davis.

To argue meant you had to have a connection and I couldn't see what possible connection those two people could have.

They belonged in different universes.

No.

In different galaxies.

What was it that had drawn them together?

I speculated on the answer while I fed crickets to the tokay gecko and chopped up fruit for the iguanas, but nothing I could conceive of made any sense. I was still thinking about it when Manuel walked in. He was holding a brown paper bag out in front of him.

"I heard Joe Davis got pulled in," he said. The paper around the bottom of the bag began moving in and out. Something was definitely in there.

"George took him down to the PSB," I explained as I eyed the sack. "He had a few questions he wanted to ask him."

"Is that why he's so pissed?"

"I guess so."

"He telling people he's going to teach you a lesson."

"Not if I see him first."

"Just watch your ass."

"I don't think that's a biological possibility, but I intend to do the best I can."

Manuel groaned. "You still have the knife I gave you?"

"Right here." I patted my back pocket. "Never leave home without it."

"Good."

"Now, are you going to tell me what's in there?" And I pointed to the bag.

"A snake."

"Snake?" Tim asked as he joined us. He'd just been straightening out the leashes. "What kind of snake?"

Manuel shrugged. "I don't know. It's got some long weird-sounding name."

"And why are you bringing it to us?" Tim asked him.

"I was hoping you guys could give me some money for it."

"How'd you get it?" Buying stolen merchandise was not something I liked to do.

"Well, this guy . . ."

"This guy?"

"Yeah, this guy . . ."

"Does 'this guy' have a name?"

"Everyone has a name."

"You want to tell me what it is?"

"Why do you care?"

"Because I like to know where my merchandise comes from." First rule of teenage conversation, I thought as I answered him. Never give an answer when you can ask a question.

Manuel put his hands on his hips. "You think this thing is hot, don't you?"

"Given your history the possibility did cross my mind."

"Well, it's not."

"Good. Then you wouldn't mind telling me how you got it."

"What if I don't want to?"

"Then I won't buy it." Buying illegal merchandise was bad for several reasons. You could get hit with whopping fines from the Feds if they found out. It was bad for the environment. And you ended up supporting unscrupulous dealers who sold dying animals and didn't care what kind of havoc they wreaked getting them.

Manuel scowled. "Oh, all right. I was supposed to get this guy something . . ."

"Something?" I let the guy's name go for the moment. I'd get back to it later.

"Yeah, something, but he didn't have the money to pay me so he gave me the snake instead, satisfied?"

I allowed as how I was because stealing snakes actually wasn't Manuel's style. He and his friends tended more toward car stereos and radar detectors.

"He said he paid two hundred for it," Manuel continued. "I figured maybe you could give me a hundred."

"That depends on what it is and what condition it's in," I answered.

"Why don't we take a look?" Tim suggested.

"Fine by me," Manuel said and upended the bag.

The snake crawled out and slithered along the counter. I took one look and I had to put my hand over my face to hide my smile.

Manuel rocked back and forth on the balls of his feet. "So what do you think?" he asked after several seconds of silence had elapsed.

Tim rubbed his shaved head and sucked his cheeks in to keep from laughing. "You got scammed," he finally announced when he'd gotten sufficient control of himself.

"What do you mean?"

"It's just a garter snake. You find them all over the place."

"But A.J. said it came from Africa," Manuel blurted. "He said one of his friends smuggled it in for him and that it was on the endangered something . . ." Manuel's voice faltered.

"Species?" I supplied.

"Yeah. That's it. The Endangered Species List."

"Well, A.J. lied."

"That fucking son of a bitch," Manuel cursed. "That fucking son of a bitch. I'm going to wring his fuckin' neck." Then he strode across the floor and out of the store, slamming the door behind him.

Tim picked up the snake. Its tongue flicked in and out as it slithered up his arm. "So what do you want to do with it?" he asked me.

"Put it back in the woods."

"Poor Manuel," Tim said.

"Yeah," I agreed.

"He definitely got screwed."

"It'll do him good for a change. Let him know how the other half lives." And we both looked at each other and laughed.

Tim and I spent the next couple of hours cleaning the tropical fish tanks and restocking the shelves. Pickles accompanied us. We'd finally had to lure her out from the stack of cartons she'd been hiding behind with a cat treat. I guess she'd just wanted to make absolutely certain that all the puppies were actually gone. We had a flurry of business around three, after which I cleaned up some of the paperwork on my desk and talked to my accountant and bank manager. At five I decided to take a break and drive over to Atilla's to see if I could find someone to talk to me about Brandon Douglas. So I left Tim in charge and fought the traffic over to the North Side. After circling Oak Street three times, I finally parked in the No-Parking zone in front of the place and went inside.

Atilla's was housed in what had once been a small store. The place was your basic body shop, a training ground for wanna-be Incredible Hunks. The men were all wearing tank tops, cutoff jeans, and work boots. Everywhere I looked muscles bulged and flexed and rippled. It was enough to make me long for a man with a potbelly and a book.

Because there was no air-conditioning the door was propped open. Three fans were blowing, their whirring lost among the clank of metal plates. But it didn't help. The place still reeked of sweat. As I walked in I became aware that there wasn't a Nautilus machine or a lick of spandex in sight. A couple of the guys gave me appraising looks, but most studiously ignored me.

I suddenly realized I was the only female in the place and I began to feel like I'd wandered into the men's locker room. It was interesting but uncomfortable and I had to fight an urge to leave. Instead, I asked the guy standing next to me where the owner was. By way of an answer he jerked his thumb over to the far side of the room, told me Atilla was over there, then went back to studying the iron bar on the floor.

Atilla, hunh? I wondered what his mother had really named him. I wondered what they called him for short: Tilly, maybe? I was still wondering when he started walking toward me. As I watched him I had to admit the name he'd chosen for himself fit. His head was shaved and he had high cheekbones, eyes that seemed to slant ever so slightly, and a cruel red mouth.

"What do you want?" he asked when he was about five feet away.

I almost laughed at the incongruity of the reedy voice coming out of the big body. It was like seeing a Great Dane and listening to a miniature poodle. Instead, I whipped out one of the business cards I'd had printed up on the way over and pressed it into his hand.

"You a reporter with the paper?" he asked, reading it. Lois Lane, girl reporter, was on the job.

"No. I'm freelance. I'm doing a magazine piece on Brandon Douglas and I was wondering if you could help me out?"

He nodded toward the center of the room. "You want to speak to Little Frankie."

"Thanks."

He shrugged and left.

As I threaded my way through the grunting men, the stacks of weights, the bars, and the benches, over to the man the owner had pointed out I was yet again amazed at how trusting people were. Show them a card and they believed you were whoever you told them you were. It never seemed to occur to them that anyone could walk into a shop and have a couple of hundred printed up for about twenty bucks.

"Yeah?" Now that I was standing next to him I could see that Little Frankie was average height, but he was so pumped up that he looked shorter. Even his fingertips were developed. "What do you want?" he asked.

I repeated the spiel I'd given the owner and handed him a card. He gave it back without even pretending to read it, took a blue towel off the weight rack and began drying his chest and arms off with it. "What about Brandon?"

"Did you know him well?"

"He used to spot me once in a while." Little Frankie folded the towel and put it on a stack of weights. "Let's talk outside. I'm ready to take a break." I followed him back out through the maze. The fresh air felt good on my face. I brushed a hank of hair out of my eyes. Frankie leaned against the door frame and surveyed the street. Besides a couple of kids leaning against a wall and passing a bottle of Pepsi around no one was out. "He was a nice kid," Frankie continued. "It's too bad what happened to him."

"Did you know him long?"

"About eight months."

"Is that when he came down from Weedsport?"

"I don't know. That's when he started coming to the gym."

"How often did he come here?"

"Three, four times a week. But he was about to up it to five."

"How come?"

" 'Cause he was going into training. He was getting ready to compete—like me. I think he could have won himself a couple of trophies. Maybe gone on to the New York State finals. I was helping him with his diet and his exercises."

"Did he ever talk about anything personal with you?"

"Sometimes. Like he wanted to know what he should do about this older broad he was seeing. She was always pestering him."

Lynn. I swallowed. It couldn't be anyone else.

"I told him to drop her. Especially if he was gonna start coming here five days a week. He just wasn't going to have the time."

"And did he?"

"I don't know." Little Frankie shifted his weight from one leg to another. "He didn't say and I didn't ask."

"Did he ever say anything about his sister?"

"He used to talk about her all the time. It's a shame what happened to her."

"It certainly is."

"That's why he came here, you know. To find his sister's killer."

"And did he?" I leaned forward.

"Yeah." Yes! I wanted to do a dance. "But he wouldn't tell

me who it was." My shoulders slumped. This was like being on a roller coaster.

"Did he say anything, anything at all?"

"Only that the person he was after was connected with Stanley Pharmaceuticals and he was going to bring him down."

Only of course things hadn't worked out quite that way.

Chapter
19

Little Frankie had given me plenty to think about.

I drove away from the gym feeling like I had a cyclone whirling inside my head.

What had Brandon found that made him believe he'd located his sister's killer at Stanley Pharmaceuticals?

God, I'd give anything to know, but of course God wasn't going to tell me.

And then I thought about Lynn and wondered if Brandon had broken off his relationship with her?

How had she taken it?

Not well, I would imagine.

Nevertheless, she'd gone back down to Otisco Street to see him.

So maybe he hadn't said anything to her.

Or maybe what she had to get back was so important that she couldn't not go.

But what could that possibly be? I still didn't know the

answer to that question, either. I sighed and reached inside my pocket for a cigarette. The pack was empty.

Great.

I definitely needed one.

Now.

I started looking around for a grocery. Two blocks later I spotted a little mom and pop hole-in-the-wall on the corner. I went inside. The store was jammed from top to bottom with merchandise. A stooped, sour-faced man was working an ancient register. Two people were standing in line waiting to be cashed out. I automatically picked up a copy of the *Herald* and took my place behind them. The front page had a story about the current mayoralty race, another about revitalizing the neighborhoods, and then, down on the bottom, was another story about the problems the SUNY health center was having dealing with prisoners who had AIDS.

"Hey." I looked up. The guy behind the counter was glaring at me. "You're holding up the line. What do you want?"

"A pack of Camels."

"Don't you know smoking is bad for you?"

"Ask me if I care," I retorted as I tossed the money for the cigarettes and the paper on the counter.

"It's people like you that are running up our health bill," he grumbled as he picked up the dollar bills.

"If you feel that strongly don't sell them," I snapped and left.

I hate people like that. Always pointing out other people's flaws and never attending to their own.

I got back in the cab, opened the pack, and lit one. Then I finished reading the article I'd started in the store. The gist of it was that the state was spending lots of money on guards for these patients. It used Matt Lipsyle as an example.

Matt Lipsyle.

Janet Tyler's supposed killer.

He hadn't wanted to talk to me five or was it six years ago.

I wondered if he'd be willing to now.

Sometimes being that sick changes your disposition.

And he was here. In Syracuse.

On the fifth floor. According to the paper.

I folded the *Herald* up and put it on the seat.

Maybe, Lipsyle knew something.

It certainly wouldn't hurt to ask.

Of course what I should do was call Attica and get permission.

But that would take a long time.

And sometimes, I'd learned over the years, if you just presented yourself things had a way of working out.

And if they didn't, so what?

The worst that could happen was that the guard would tell me to get lost.

I started to hum.

I had to go around twice before I found a parking space in the lot across from the hospital. The air felt thick as I crossed the street. The few people out were walking slowly, as if they'd been pounded down by the humidity. I opened one of Upstate's heavy glass doors and went inside. The lobby smelled faintly of chemicals and disinfectants, but it was cool and that was what counted now. I crossed the lobby quickly and stood by the elevator bank.

Except for a man mopping the floor and a woman at the concession stand the place was deserted. Maybe illness was taking its summer vacation. I automatically reached for a cigarette, then remembered where I was and stopped. Hospitals had always made me queasy. They brought back too many bad memories and after my recent stay in the burn unit that was especially true. It was a visceral, but irrational response. I took a couple of deep breaths to quell my nervousness. Then the elevator doors opened and I got on and rode up to the fifth floor.

The ward was quiet. A few patients were doing the hospital shuffle around the halls, IVs in tow, getting their daily quota of exercise. I'd taken about five steps when I heard a bloodcurdling screech. No one at the nurses station even glanced up. They continued doing their paperwork and chatting with each other. The patients kept walking. I guess the scream must be a regular occurrence. As I was walking past the station I noticed a guard talking with a blond nurse. They were standing toward the back, away from everyone else. Given the looks they were exchanging, the tilt of their heads, their proximity, and the way they were touching it was clear that they were fascinated with each other. I only hoped the guard was Lipsyle's and that the fascination held. Who knew? Maybe I'd even get lucky. Maybe those two would find an empty room and spend the next half hour screwing.

I walked down the hall quickly and stopped in front of room 5116. There was a chair outside, for the guard no doubt, but it was empty. So far so good. I read the name plate on the door. Matt Lipsyle. I'd come to the right place. I took a deep breath and stepped inside. From the entranceway I could see that Matt Lipsyle's eyes were fastened on the overhead TV. His lips were parted. They were the only fleshy thing on his face, everything else was skeletal, stripped away.

If the man weighed ninety pounds he weighed a lot. It was as if AIDS was literally eating him alive. His arms, or what I could see of them, were mere ropes covered with large purplish bruises. His bed was in the center of several machines that beeped and chugged. He was attached to them by gobs of tubing that sprouted out of his body in every direction. A heavy metal shackle ran from his ankle to the frame of the bed. Like the man was really going to go somewhere, I thought as he turned to look at me. This guy would be lucky if he could make it to the bathroom by himself.

"Who are you?" he asked when I was almost by his bed.

The words came out in painful, jagged gasps, as if he had had to force each syllable out into the air.

"I'm Robin Light."

"Light. I like that. I'm getting pretty light, too." And he started to laugh and ended up in a coughing spasm that doubled him over. I went to help, but he held up his hand indicating he wanted me to stay where I was so I stood and waited for the spasm to subside. "How come you're not wearing a mask?" he asked when he'd gotten his breath back enough to be able to talk. "You're not hospital, are you?"

"No, I'm not." And I explained why I'd come.

"I've got nothing to say," he told me when I was done.

"I don't think you understand."

"Oh, I understand all right," Lipsyle said before I could continue. His eyes drifted back to the TV. He wet his dry, cracked lips with his tongue. "So Douglas was killed? So what? People die all the time." His voice was flat and hard. "Shot. Stabbed. Hung. Overdose. AIDS. TB. It don't make no difference. In the end everyone goes in the ground anyway. Just look at me."

"What about justice?" It was a stupid thing to say and he didn't even bother turning his head when he answered.

"Justice? That's just some fancy word rich folks invented to make 'em feel better when they screw us poor people."

"My friend, the one who confessed to killing Brandon Douglas, is rich."

Lipsyle scratched around his IV. "I know. I seen her on TV. What's your point?"

I couldn't answer because I didn't know.

"Don't worry, they'll send her someplace nice," Lipsyle continued. "Not like the place they sent me. She'll probably even get her own room. Her daddy will see to that."

"I'm not sure she did it." The word here was 'sure.' For a fleeting moment I thought how ironic it was that my efforts to clear her had only made me doubt her innocence. But I shoved that thought aside. I wasn't ready to deal with the consequences yet.

"She confessed," Lipsyle replied. "They read it right on Channel Nine News."

"Like they read your confession?"

Lipsyle reached for the remote and changed the channel. "I told you I ain't got nothing to say."

"Who murdered Janet Tyler?"

He clicked the remote again. "It don't make no difference anymore," he whispered.

"Yes, it does."

"No one cares."

"You're wrong. Brandon Douglas's killer cares. A lot."

"I'll tell you what matters." And Lipsyle turned toward me. For a few seconds his face glowed with passion. "My kids. My kids and my wife. They matter. And that is all that counts. You can stick everything else in the garbage as far as I'm concerned."

Then he closed his eyes. His jaw dropped. For a few awful seconds I thought he was dead, but then I realized he'd just fallen asleep. I stood there staring down at Matt Lipsyle while his chest laboriously rose and fell, wondering why a man who so passionately cared about his family would confess to something that would take him away so far from them?

Could Brandon Douglas have been wrong?

Had Lipsyle actually killed Janet Tyler?

No.

At least not according to Little Frankie.

According to him, Brandon Douglas knew who his sister's killer was.

And it wasn't the man lying in bed in front of me.

It was someone who worked at Stanley Pharmaceuticals.

But then why had Lipsyle confessed?

As I thought back to what he'd just said, I realized he'd never actually told me he'd killed Janet Tyler. He'd just said it didn't matter anymore.

Why didn't it matter?

Why would he want his children to live with the knowledge that their father was a murderer?

What could the trade-off possibly be?

I couldn't imagine an answer and I certainly wasn't going to get one from Lipsyle.

Even if he were awake.

I stood staring at him for a moment, willing him to wake up and tell me, but he kept sleeping and I finally tiptoed out. I was walking down the hall when I saw Matt's wife, Norma Lipsyle, coming toward me. I recognized her instantly from Zeke's but I could tell from the expression on her face that she hadn't made a similar connection.

She'd made an effort to spruce herself up. She was wearing pink lipstick and blue eyeliner and she'd combed her lank blond hair off her face and pinned it back, but that just seemed to call attention to the rash on her face and the circles under her eyes. Then I noticed she was carrying a Tupperware container in her hand—she was bringing food to her husband. I felt an overwhelming rush of pity. Poor lady. Trying to put on a cheerful face for her dying husband. It had been bad enough to find Murphy dead, I couldn't imagine what it would have been like to have to watch him die. For a moment I wanted to reach out and tell her that I understood. But then I stopped myself. She probably wouldn't want a stranger coming up to her and saying something like that. I know I wouldn't.

As she went by me I realized I'd seen the dress she was wearing before. It was an off-the-shoulder full-length flowered summer frock that was fitted on top and then swept out into a tulip skirt. On Lynn it had looked good, on Norma Lipsyle it just hung. Still the dress had cost a hundred and fifty dollars. I knew because Lynn had been boasting about what a bargain she'd gotten. But a hundred and fifty dollars wasn't a bargain for someone in Norma Lipsyle's situation. It was an unimaginable luxury. Then I recalled the station wagon she'd driven away from Zeke's in. It had been a Saab. A new one. Something definitely didn't fit. Where was this woman getting her money from?

It certainly wasn't from welfare. Maybe she had a rich family? But if she had a rich family why would she be on welfare? At least that's what the girl at Zeke's had told me. Maybe she'd been wrong. I almost turned and followed her, but then I saw the guard coming back down the hall and decided I'd better leave well enough alone. I could always find her house and talk to her there. And then I remembered something else, something I'd forgotten. Mrs. Z. had told me she had come from Weedsport. I wondered if she'd known these people? She probably had. After all Weedsport was a small enough place. I cursed my own stupidity as I drove over to her house.

Luckily for me, Mrs. Z. was delighted to see me and

delighted to talk. She got me a glass of iced tea and sat me down on a rocker next to hers on the porch. First we chatted about her birds and about whether or not a raven was a good bird to keep as a pet and when we decided it was, we discussed how Mrs. Z. could acquire one. That took about twenty minutes. Then I introduced the subject of Weed-sport.

"I never did really like that place," Mrs. Z. confessed as she fanned herself with a piece of paper. "Too many people minding everyone's business but their own. Too many people related to one another. That's why I moved here when my husband died. To get away. One of my cousins had a florist shop on Teall and said she'd give me a job. I said yes and it was the best decision I ever made." She paused to take a sip of tea.

"Did you know Norma and Matt Lipsyle?"

"Of course. Poor Norma. She was offered a scholarship, don't you know, to some Downstate school, but she refused it. Said she was in love. Didn't want to leave Matt Lipsyle. Oh, was she sweet on him! And then of course she got sick."

"Sick?"

"Yes, with something women get. It has some Latin name. I forget what. But Matt didn't care." Mrs. Z. threw up her hands at the memory. "He was a nice young man. Don't let anyone tell you different. Used to be my paperboy. But he was a dreamer. I could tell right off he was one of those people who never get anything done. Just sit around and think about doing it." Mrs. Z. gave her rocker an emphatic rock. "And look what happened to him."

I refrained from saying that he'd definitely done something—not a good something—but a something neverthe-less.

She sniffed. "I don't believe for a minute he killed Janet Tyler. Neither did anyone else. 'Cause Petros didn't care."

Petros had been the DA who tried the case.

"He was just in a hurry to get the case wrapped up so he could go on his honeymoon with that young wife of his. If you ask me somebody should have taken him out and shot him for accepting that boy's confession. And I know there were lots of other folks who felt the same way. Why Matt didn't have a mean bone in his body. And anyway he was head over heels in love with Norma. Didn't have eyes for anyone else. Ever. Of course his family hated her. Just loathed the ground she walked on for causing so much trouble. They thought she was nothing but poor white trash. And sickly to boot. Now, I'm not talking about Matt's mom and pop you understand. They were killed in a crash when he was six. Terrible thing." She shook her head in remembrance. "No. It's his cousins I'm referring to."

She took another sip of tea. "They passed him around all over the place—from house to house—like he was an old dishrag. I can't see as how that's any way to raise a child. No wonder he got away from them the first chance he got. Didn't want to have anything to do with them. Didn't even want to work in the family business. I heard they even offered to make him a foreman, but he wasn't having any. Too bad he ended up the way he did. And now I hear he's dying. So young, too." She tsked tsked. "There's just no way to tell how things are going to work out." Then she glanced down at her watch. "Oh, dear." Her hand flew to her mouth. "I didn't realize it was so late."

I checked the time on mine. It was seven.

She started to get up. I went to help her, but she waved me off. "I'm afraid I'm going to have to go inside now and start getting ready for bed. I know it's early for you young folk, but when you get to be my age it takes a long time." She smiled ruefully. "Of course everything takes me longer than it used to." She reached out, took one of my hands in hers, and patted it. Her skin felt like parchment. "Now you be sure to find out about that raven for me."

I promised I would and left.

Chapter
20

As I drove to Noah's Ark I thought about what I'd learned from Mrs. Z. and Matt Lipsyle and tried to figure out what the information I'd gathered meant. By the time I reached the store I had a glimmering of an idea. I was still thinking about it when I walked inside. Then Zsa Zsa came running over to greet me and I put those thoughts aside and knelt down to pet her. She was wagging her tail so hard that she was almost walking sideways.

"She went in the storeroom," Tim informed me as I lifted the puppy up, "so you don't have to bother taking her out."

"You do that?" I crooned to her before I caught myself. No use making more of a fool of myself than I usually did.

After all we didn't share any DNA.

Really.

She answered by giving my nose a lick.

I scratched Zsa Zsa under her chin. Then Pickles came

out from behind the counter and Zsa Zsa squirmed out of my arms and ran after her.

"Anything exciting happen since I've been gone?" I asked Tim while I watched the two animals playing tag around the aquariums.

"Not really." Tim twisted one of his earrings absentmindedly as he spoke. "A.J. came by and wanted to know if that was really a garter snake. He looked pretty pissed when I told him it was." Tim chuckled at the memory. "Then a sales rep from Coddled Canines dropped off a brochure for organic dog food." I stifled a groan. This was the latest rage. All the companies were putting their own versions out. But it only sold in neighborhoods with cappuccino bars, not in places with Seven-Elevens. "Julio took Martha out for some fresh air," Tim continued.

"Where?"

"Burnet Park."

"That should be interesting." I was glad I wasn't there.

"And George called to say he went over his stolen dog sheets again and he still can't find a listing for the golden you found."

"That's good for you."

"I know. She's almost housebroken, too."

I groaned. Life was definitely unfair.

Tim laughed and we got back to work. After we closed up the store Tim fetched Annabel from his flat and the four of us, two dogs and two humans, went up to the field in back of Nottingham High School. Tim and I sat on the bleachers and watched the clouds scudding past a red moon while the puppies romped round the track. The wind was still blowing and every once in a while one of the puppies, a golden blur in the blackness, would pick up a scent and dash off for a few feet before coming to a dead stop.

"Looking forward to school in the fall?" I asked Tim. He'd just started Onondaga Community College last winter. This was his third semester going part-time.

"Yeah, it's like a whole new world out there."

"That's what I like about books. You open the cover and step into a different universe."

"I was thinking of the girls myself." The moon glinted on Tim's shaven head as he bowed it.

I laughed and Tim pulled his cigarettes out of his pants pocket, extracted two, lit them both, and handed one to me.

"I thought you quit," I said as I took a puff.

"I did. And now I'm starting again. I mean everyone has to die of something, right?"

"Right."

He took a puff and exhaled. "So, you seeing any one interesting?"

"Not at the moment."

"Are you seeing someone uninteresting?"

"I'm not seeing anyone," I said in a burst of irritation. For the past six months, everyone I knew had been pushing me to go out. Only I didn't want to. I wasn't ready yet. The idea of dating, let alone sleeping with someone made my stomach knot with anxiety. I knew feeling that way was stupid, but it didn't help. I still felt it just the same.

"It has been a year," Tim reminded me.

"Believe me I know how long it's been."

"Right." Tim licked his lips. "You know you shouldn't let what happened with Murphy . . ."

"Influence me?" I could hear a bitter edge in my voice that I didn't like. I'd been hearing it a lot lately and I didn't know what to do about it. "Now why should I do something like that?"

"What are you planning to do: live like a nun?"

"I don't think convents take Jews."

I could see Tim's eyebrows rise. "You're Jewish?"

I laughed at his surprise. "I even went to Hebrew school."

"What happened?"

"I don't know." I twirled a lock of hair around my finger as I thought about it. "I guess it became less and less important and then I met Murphy and he didn't believe in religion and I just drifted away from it."

"Maybe you should drift back."

"I've been thinking about it."

There didn't seem to be much more to say so I changed the subject and Tim and I spent the next half hour talking about Joe Davis and the stolen dogs and about whom he had been intending to sell them to.

That night I dreamt about Murphy. Maybe my conversation with Tim summoned him up. My grandmother always said that's why you never called the dead by name. Because if you did they'd appear. He was leaning against a palm tree down in a little cove we'd discovered in Isla Mujeres. He was smiling and holding out a coconut to show me. I ran toward him and we kissed. I could feel the sand under my feet, I could smell his skin. Then I heard a buzzing and he was gone. I was awake. Tears were rolling down my cheeks. All I wanted to do was crawl back into my dream.

Instead, I turned off the alarm and got out of bed because I had to be at the physical therapist's office at eight o'clock. I'd finally made the appointment and now I had to go to it. God, I hated this, I thought as I wiped away my tears with the back of my hand while I ran outside with Zsa Zsa. I hated feeling this way. Murphy was dead. The man had turned out to be a total creep. He'd lied to me. He'd cheated on me. He'd almost gotten me killed. It was time to let him go. But I couldn't. I still wanted him so badly it hurt. God knows why. I'd never thought of myself as a masochist, but maybe I was.

"Never again," I vowed as Zsa Zsa and I went back inside the house. "Never again will I let someone do that to me. You hear that?" I asked her.

She wagged her tail to show she understood and went over to the kitchen cabinet where I stored her dog food, sat down, and fixed me with her big brown eyes.

"From now on its just us girls."

She barked her agreement and I fed her, threw on some clothes, and ran out of the house.

Movement Associates was housed in a squat, rectangular building on the corner of East Genesee and Crouse. Nothing decorative or frivolous marred its gray concrete surface. In fact it reminded me of my physical therapist. Hilda Dunlap was a small, merciless woman with eyebrows that ran across her brow like a bridge and hands that could have torn a steel girder apart. She clucked as she tested the mobility in my leg and then proceeded to put me through an hour of sheer hell. By the time I left, despite the air-conditioning, I was covered with a film of sweat. On the way home I resolved to do my exercises no matter what.

I gave Zsa Zsa a piece of toast while I ate a Snickers bar and an Oreo cookie sandwich. Then I took a shower and put on a pair of baggy jeans, a black T-shirt and my clogs, brushed my hair, and headed for the store. It was still muggy outside, the rain hadn't come yet, and my cab seat felt unpleasantly clammy. As I drove down East Fayette I caught the occasional smell of rotting garbage. Then as I was turning onto Ashton the person in the car ahead of me stopped short to talk to someone across the street and I almost plowed into them.

Cursing, I put my foot on the accelerator and shot around

the stopped Ford, narrowly missing an oncoming car. I was still in a foul mood when Tim walked in the store an hour later, but when he showed me the box from Dunkin' Donuts my mood brightened. Especially when I saw he'd included a couple of chocolate peanut ones in his selection. After my second one I got to work. But I couldn't seem to concentrate. I kept thinking about what Little Frankie had told me and trying to decide what to do.

Finally I went into my office and called Lynn. Unfortunately, according to the housekeeper she was asleep. Great. I got out the phone book and looked up Joe Davis's number. Just for the hell of it. Surprisingly it was listed. Somehow I hadn't expected that. I dialed. He wasn't in, either. Probably at work, I thought. I threw my pencil across the desk in disgust and started pacing. I felt too restless to stay in the store so I decided to take another trip out to Stanley Pharmaceuticals. After all, Lynn's father *had* said I could talk to the personnel guy when he'd hired me. Maybe there'd be something in Brandon Douglas's file I could use. And maybe while I was out there I could take a peek at Joe Davis's file as well. After all, he did work at the plant. He did live next to Brandon. Maybe there would be something that would connect the two.

It was twelve by the time I got out to the factory, mostly because I'd stopped at home to change into a respectable outfit: straight skirt, jacket with padded shoulders, and heels. I also put on makeup and jewelry. Over the years, I've found that people are more apt to respond to you if you look the part you're trying to play. And I looked different enough so that at first glance the receptionist didn't even recognize me when I asked her where the personnel office was. Located among a maze of rooms that ran along the left side of the building, it took me awhile to find it, even with her instructions.

"Come in, come in," the man sitting behind the desk said when I knocked. He had his lunch, a sandwich, an apple, and a banana spread out in front of him.

I was surprised his food wasn't beige. Everything else in the office was: beige carpeting, beige wallpaper, beige file cabinets. He was even wearing a light tan suit. Between the color and the hiss from the air-conditioning I was beginning to feel as if I'd wandered into a sensory deprivation tank.

I looked at the name plaque on the desk as I approached. Ripley. I wondered if he'd believe me or not?

"Yes?" he asked when I was standing in front of his desk.

I introduced myself.

"So what can I do for you?"

I gave him a big smile. "I need you to get me Brandon Douglas's personnel file. Mr. Stanley has authorized me to look at it."

"I don't know." Ripley fingered his bow tie worriedly.

"Call Mr. Stanley and check," I said daring him to, but really praying that he wouldn't. Maybe hanging up on Stanley hadn't been such a good idea after all. I had a feeling he might throw me out of the factory rather than grant my request.

"Well." Ripley sighed. "I suppose it will be all right. Especially since he's no longer working for us." Now that was certainly an interesting way of referring to Douglas's death. "But if you want to look at anyone else's file, I'll need written authorization."

"Fine." Damn, I thought as I watched Ripley get up and go over to the file cabinet. How the hell was I going to get to see Joe Davis's. But I'd just have to worry about that later.

A moment later Ripley handed me a tan folder. The letters on the side said: BRANDON DOUGLAS.

"This is very irregular." Ripley pulled at his bowtie again.

"I know and I appreciate it." I opened the file and started reading.

"There's confidential information in there."

I glanced up. Ripley's Adam's apple was bobbing up and down in indignation. I made a soothing noise and went back to reading. If there was anything in there that wasn't in the public domain I certainly didn't see it. The kid been born in Weedsport, gone to school there. He'd graduated from high school with a C average and then worked at Zeke's, Burger King, and a number of other dead-end jobs. After which . . . I looked up.

"Douglas worked at Pearson Construction?" I asked, struggling to keep the excitement out of my voice.

Chapter
21

"Why?" Ripley scrunched his face in concern. "Is there a problem?"

"No. None at all," I assured him. "Just the opposite, actually."

According to Howie Kaplan that was where Janet Tyler had been buried before her killer had dug her up and flung her in the Montezuma Wildlife Reserve.

Ripley unfolded his hands. "A lot of our people out on the line have worked there."

"Really?" I put Brandon Douglas's folder down. "Do you know what he did?"

"Doesn't it say on his application?"

"Not really." Brandon had written something about doing general construction work. That meant he could have done anything. "Didn't you ask?"

Ripley harrumped. "Are you suggesting that I didn't check his references?"

Sensitive, wasn't he? I bet he hadn't. And I bet Stanley had come down on him for it.

"Because," he continued, "I called up and asked if his work had been satisfactory. I was told that it was and that was all I needed to know. After all, the man wasn't applying for a position in R and D."

"Of course." I reached for a cigarette, but Ripley pointed at the No Smoking sign and I reluctantly put it away. As I did I wondered if it was something that Brandon Douglas had seen or heard at Pearson Construction that made him come here to Syracuse? Or was it just coincidence? No. From what I knew of Brandon Douglas, he had gone there to search for clues to his sister's killer. I'd bet anything on it. And he'd found something. Something that had led him here to this company. Something that had eventually gotten him killed.

But what?

The murder was over ten years old.

What had surfaced?

Had he talked to someone?

Had he managed to go through the company records?

And then I thought of Joe Davis. No matter where I turned his name kept coming up. Had he worked at Pearson Construction ten years ago? He looked in his late twenties, early thirties. It was possible. I had to get hold of his employment file and find out.

But I couldn't ask Stanley.

And Ripley had just told me I needed written authorization.

My eyes roved over the room and fastened on the file cabinets standing by the far wall. Ripley had taken Douglas's folder out of the second drawer. Douglas. Davis. All I needed was a couple of minutes with Ripley out of his office.

I sat up straighter. Suddenly I knew what I was going to do.

Ripley coughed. "If there's nothing else," he said looking at his sandwich with longing.

"Just one more thing." I could almost hear Ripley groan. He surreptitiously glanced down at his watch. "A little thing," I reassured him. He looked slightly relieved, but only slightly. More than anything else he wanted me out of here. "If you could just make me a copy of Mr. Douglas's file."

Ripley's eyes widened. "Well, I don't know. I need writ ten . . ."

"Authorization." I finished the sentence for him.

"That's right," Ripley said. "I do."

"Then why don't you call and get it."

"I will." And Ripley reached for the phone.

"Of course if it were me I wouldn't want to interrupt Mr. Stanley's meeting," I continued, dropping my nugget of information with a slightly superior air.

Ripley stayed his hand. "He's at a meeting?"

"That's what he told me." I put all my sincerity into my lie. "Something to do with European distribution rights." I did-n't know what I was talking about, but I had to admit it sounded impressive. "I think he's hoping to expand to the Common Market."

"Really?" Ripley pulled his hand back and started finger-ing his tie again. By this point it was starting to look like a daisy that needed water. "That's very interesting. I hadn't heard."

"I wouldn't have either," I confided. "Except I just hap-pened to be in his office when the call came through. Actu-ally"—I leaned forward and lowered my voice—"I don't think he wants anyone to know. The talks are just in the exploratory stage, the pre-exploratory stage. I probably shouldn't have told you . . ."

"I won't tell anyone," Ripley quickly assured me.

I put my hand over my heart. "That's a relief. I'd hate to have Mr. Stanley angry with me."

"Isn't that the truth," Ripley agreed. "The man really does have a ferocious temper."

"Yes. He has very little patience for interruptions." I made a show of glancing at my watch. "I'm afraid I have to be going soon and I really am going to need a copy of the Douglas file for my records," I added, praying as I said it that Ripley didn't ask what records I needed the copy for. I looked at the phone. "So if you're going to call Mr. Stanley I'd appreciate it if you could do it now." And I crossed my fingers and waited.

Ripley thought for a moment. "That won't be necessary," he finally said. "I'm sure he wouldn't mind. After all, he did say you could see the file."

"Are you positive?"

"Oh yes."

"Because I wouldn't want you to do anything you're not comfortable with."

"No. No." Ripley got up. "I'm sure it'll be fine." I suppressed a smile as he headed toward the door. "I'll just be about five minutes. The copy machine is on the other side of the building, near the typing pool."

Sounded good to me.

The moment he was gone I jumped up and headed for the file cabinet. Thank God the personnel office was at the end of the hallway. Hoping nobody came by, I opened the second drawer and ran my finger down the C file tabs. Cabineri. Cerro. Certs. Certs? Jesus, I pitied the person who was stuck with a name like that. I hurried on.

"Come on D," I muttered under my breath. "Where are you?"

Good. Here they were. In the middle of the drawer. I had a Dan. A Dante. Ah. Davis. I pulled the folder out a little. No this was a John Davis. Drats. Then came Dennis. Dennis? Where the hell was Joe Davis? I rechecked. Not there. Damn. Just my luck. The thing was probably misfiled. I went through the rest of the D's. Davis's file wasn't there. I closed the second drawer and opened the third.

Then I checked my watch. A minute had gone by. If I took two more that gave me a safety margin of two minutes. More than enough. I hoped. For a fleeting second I wondered if I should stop now when I was ahead. But I didn't. It was a lesson I'd never seemed to learn. I don't know why. My mother used to say it was because I had no common sense and maybe she was right. Heart pounding, I went through the third drawer at light speed and found nothing. Then I did the third file cabinet. Joe Davis's file wasn't there. I glanced at my watch. One minute left to do the last cabinet. I took a deep breath, opened the top drawer and started searching. I could feel my heart beating as I ran my finger down the folders. Finally I was done. But I still had nothing to show except a lot of paper cuts on my fingertips.

Davis's file wasn't here.

Or if it was, I had missed it. Which I doubted.

So where the hell was it?

The desk.

I ran over to it. I had my hand on one of the drawers when I heard footsteps. Ripley. I quickly took a cigarette out of my pocket and lit it as he came through the door.

I smiled. "Sorry, but I couldn't wait anymore. Isn't there an ashtray around here?"

Ripley scowled while he came around and took one out of his middle drawer. "Filthy habit," he reproved as he gave it to me.

"You're right. It is." And I ground my cigarette out. "Do you have it?"

"Of course." He placed a copy of Douglas's employment application in my hand. "Sorry for the delay, but there was a line."

Thank God for small favors I thought as I indicated the files. "This must be a big responsibility."

"Oh yes."

"You're like the guardian of everyone's secrets."

"Well, I wouldn't go that far. Gordon . . . I mean Mr. Marshall keeps some of the folders, too."

"I thought he was head of sales."

"He is."

"Then why are personnel files kept in his office?"

Ripley shrugged and sat down. "I just do what I'm told." He reached for his sandwich and bit down on it with obvious relish. "After all, this is a family business and if I've learned one thing over the years its that family businesses do things their own way."

You could say that again, I thought sourly as I went back down the hall. Why the hell was Davis's file in Gordon's office? Why wasn't it with the other ones? What made Joe Davis so special? That's what I wanted to know I decided as I fell in behind two secretaries who were chattering away about their weekends, their boyfriends, and their bosses. I was still engrossed in my own thoughts, when I heard them talking about Gordon. Suddenly I began to listen more carefully.

"The man is never here," the woman dressed in pink from her shoes up to her earrings complained. This was obviously someone who took color coordination seriously. "He just puts all his stuff on his Dictaphone and leaves. I have questions and I can never find him. Like today," she huffed. "I have a ten-page memo I have to type for him. But he didn't tell me how he wants it set up and I can't get hold of him to ask."

"Where is he?" the one wearing a tight black mini-skirt, a black blouse, and white sneakers with bobby socks asked. "Maybe you can give him a call?"

"Who the hell knows," Ms. Pink replied. "Probably out racing around somewhere in that car of his. I tell you if he weren't the boss's son-in-law he'd be out on his ass."

"He does come in early."

"Yeah, but he's usually gone by the time I get here."

"Just do the best you can."

"That's easy for you to say, but if something goes wrong I'll be the one to get the blame. I'll be the one who'll get fired, not him."

"I know. Life sucks, doesn't it?"

"Speaking of which," Ms. Pink squared her shoulders, "did I tell you my ex's latest?"

But before I could hear what it was the lady in black opened the door on her right and went inside. Her friend followed. The door closed and the hallway was quiet again. As I continued walking, I kept glancing at the copy of Douglas's file that Ripley had given me, and wondering if the idea that had been forming in my mind would work. It should. From what I'd just heard Gordon was definitely out of the building, let alone his office. I could just walk into it. If somebody stopped me I could always say I was dropping off Douglas's file. They wouldn't know I wasn't. If I ran into Mr. Stanley—God forbid—I could always say I wanted to talk to Gordon. And if I ran into Gordon . . . if I ran into Gordon . . . well hopefully something would occur to me by then.

After all, I was here.

And it did seem a pity to go away without having my question answered.

What I was contemplating doing was definitely worth the risk. And actually there really wasn't much of that. The worst thing that could happen was that I'd get thrown out of the building. I kept walking. By now I was beginning to get the feel of the place so instead of retracing my steps and having to deal with the receptionist again, I cut through the main office. Most of the desks and cubicles were occupied with women who were either typing on word processors or talking on the phone. No one even glanced up as I threaded my way through to the corridor on the other side.

I walked a little farther, passing the sales room where I'd seen Gordon the other morning. The man's office had to be coming up soon. I started reading the names on the doors as I went by. Barker. Highsmith. Cahill. Ken Stanley. I paused for a minute. In contrast to the other doors, which had had their names and titles painted on in sober black, Ken's had a brass nameplate. His name and title were etched in Helvetica. The crown prince. He acted the part, too.

For the first time I wondered what everyone thought of him. Did they resent him? especially since his father seemed to be cutting him slack he didn't cut other people. And then as I contemplated the plain block letters that spelled out Gordon Marshall's name and title I wondered how he felt. Was he jealous? Resentful at the favoritism being shown? After all, at least Gordon was evidently at the plant every morning. Which was more than you could say for Ken. I had yet to see him in here. Everytime I'd been at Lynn's house, Ken had been there not here. Maybe he worked at night? Maybe he'd stopped working when Lynn started having problems? It would be interesting to find out. Then I decided who cared? What difference did it make? I knocked on Gordon Marshall's door. No one answered. I glanced up and down the hall. It was empty. So far so good. I opened the door and slipped inside.

Chapter
22

I must be nuts, I thought as the door clicked shut behind me.

Or obsessed.

Obsessed. Yes. Definitely that.

Over the past couple of weeks, Brandon Douglas's murder had become the proverbial pebble in my shoe.

It bothered me. I kept thinking about it. Even when I didn't want to. I couldn't seem to get his face out of my mind. Or the look on Lynn's when I'd found her that afternoon cradling Douglas's lifeless body.

Maybe I kept thinking about it because I couldn't reconcile what I'd seen with Lynn's confession.

Or maybe it was simply that since Murphy I'd grown allergic to lies and liars.

But still.

Two illegal acts in one hour.

For Manuel or Julio that was nothing.

For me it was a new personal best.

Although George probably wouldn't be impressed.

Oh, well.

But then if I were lucky he wouldn't know.

I took a deep breath and glanced around. Unlike his father-in-law's work space Gordon Marshall's was small, maybe fifteen feet by twenty at the most, and unassuming. The walls were white, the lights were fluorescent, and the furniture was basic office-modern issue. Despite what the secretary in pink had said to her friend about Gordon, his office was obviously a place where work got done.

He might not be here all that much, but when he was it looked like he produced. His desk was cluttered with papers. Both his In and Out boxes were overflowing. So was his trash basket. There was a bunch of letters waiting to be signed resting on top of a pile of magazines. The two far walls were covered with flow charts and sales projections. Books were stacked on the floor. On top of those were a few *Wall Street Journals*. But I didn't see any file cabinets. Anywhere.

Had Ripley been lying?

No.

Why should he?

He had no reason to.

Gordon probably kept the files in one of his drawers. A lot of people did that. But just to make sure they weren't somewhere else, I took a quick look through his papers. They weren't there. Then I walked around the desk and tried the top drawer. But it turned out to be locked. Damn. I tried the other three. They were locked, too. Now that was interesting. I wondered what was in there that needed to be locked away as I studied the desk a little more carefully. It had four drawers, two on each side, and was probably made of some sort of particle board and covered with a wood veneer. Then I squatted down and took a look at the lock on the top right-hand drawer.

Even with my meager experience I could see it didn't look like anything that couldn't be picked with a minimum amount of effort. First I took a paper clip off of Marshall's desk, straightened it out and tried to spring the lock with that. But it didn't work. Okay. I reached in my pocket, extracted my wallet and took out my Visa card. Maybe I could 'loid' the lock. I hadn't watched TV for nothing. I was just about to slip it in when I heard footsteps coming down the hall.

I froze. My heart was hammering. I waited as whoever it was passed by Gordon Marshall's office and kept going. The footsteps trailed away. I let out the breath I didn't know I'd been holding and slipped my credit card in the opening between the drawer lip and the wood and felt around for the lock. When I found it I tried to work the card in while pressing down. But nothing happened. The card wasn't stiff enough to depress the locking mechanism. Then I thought of Manuel's knife.

I slipped my card back in my wallet, got the knife out, and clicked it open. I licked my lips in concentration as I inserted the blade and jiggled it around. I felt something give. I pressed down. The drawer slid open. I felt a tremendous sense of triumph. Until I looked inside. The only things there were five golf balls, a couple of tees, and a pair of golf gloves. I almost laughed. So much for my fantasies about Gordon's secrets. I went on to the next drawer.

It contained two opened bags of miniature Nestlé Crunch bars, three Snickers bars, and a half-eaten package of Ho Ho's. As I ate a Nestlé Crunch I thought that the man had at least one redeeming feature after all. I didn't do any better with the two drawers on the other side. The top one contained several issues of *Playboy* and a well-thumbed copy of *Jugs*. Gordon was obviously a man of high-class tastes. The last drawer was empty. Except for three paper clips and a scrap of tannish paper caught in the crack between the bottom and side.

I picked up the piece of paper. It was manila, the kind of manila they make office folders from. One side of it was rounded, while the other side was ragged. It must have gotten stuck when the files were moved. I clicked my tongue against the roof of my mouth.

Well, the files *had* been here.

Ripley had been right about that.

But they weren't here now.

Not anymore.

Someone had moved them.

So where had they gone? And when? And most importantly why?

What made them so special?

Why had they been singled out for this treatment?

And then I wondered about Joe Davis.

After all, according to Stanley, Davis was just some poor snook who worked on the production line.

But the way his file was being treated certainly didn't support that contention.

Unless, of course, it really was misplaced and I was making a big deal about nothing. Not an unknown possibility for me I had to admit.

Damn. All this for nothing. I shut all the drawers and pulled on them to make sure they were locked. Well not exactly nothing. I now knew that Gordon Marshall had a fondness for mass-market candy and girlie magazines and played golf. Certainly not criminal activities I decided as I closed the knife and slipped it back into my pocket. I glanced at the clock on the wall. I had been in here for over five minutes already. It was time to go. Even I had to admit I'd pushed my luck far enough.

I was turning to leave when my eyes fell on Gordon's engagement calendar. Quickly, I flipped back to July 22nd, the date Brandon Douglas had been killed. According to his calendar, Gordon had been at work that morning. But from two to six he'd been busy attending a conference entitled, "How to Motivate Your Sales Staff" on Salina Street. Salina Street wasn't that far away from Otisco Street—a matter of ten minutes by car at the most. If there was traffic.

I tapped my fingers on my thigh while I thought. The conferences I'd covered for the paper had usually been fairly big affairs. There'd always been lots of people at them. Lots of different activities taking place at once. A lot of people milling around in the hallways drinking coffee, eating Danish, and talking. I'd always found it easy to slip in and out. No one ever paid any attention. I wondered if that's what Gordon Marshall had done. Slipped out, killed Douglas, then slipped back in. He could have. If he had preplanned everything.

He could have called Brandon Douglas and set up a meeting. He would have had the gun in his car. Maybe he even had a set of coveralls so he wouldn't get his clothes dirty. I closed my eyes and tried to visualize the scene. He'd parked around the corner, come in through the back door, gone upstairs, and shot Douglas. Or maybe he hadn't planned it. Maybe something had set him off, and he'd gone running over to talk to Douglas, and they'd started to fight, and Brandon had had a gun and it had gone off. Then Lynn had walked in. He'd panicked, run upstairs to the attic, climbed onto the roof, shimmied down the drainpipe, run through

A.J.'s backyard, and driven off. I opened my eyes. No. I couldn't picture Gordon doing that. Manuel, yes. Gordon no.

On the other hand the man wasn't noted for his self-control.

He was possessive as hell.

And Lynn had been sleeping with Brandon Douglas.

According to A.J., she'd been going to Douglas's house two, three, four times a week.

Maybe Gordon was having her followed and had found out.

Maybe Lynn had told him in a fit of pique.

And he flipped out. And killed Douglas.

Which would explain why Lynn had confessed to something she hadn't done. She would see the murder as her fault.

It was plausible.

It fit Lynn's and Gordon's personalities.

Except, and it was a big except, the explanation I'd come up with didn't tie in with the Janet Tyler murder. And I couldn't help thinking that Douglas's death was linked to his investigation of his sister's death. Everything pointed in that direction.

Still it would be interesting to find out if Connelly had gone to the trouble of alibiing Gordon Marshall. Connelly certainly wouldn't tell me, but maybe I could get George to find out. It would certainly be worth a shot. I gave the desk a last quick glance, but there was nothing else of interest on it. It was definitely time to leave. As I closed the door, I was surprised at how exhilarated I felt and I began to understand how the rush from doing something like this could be almost addictive.

I turned and started back down the way I came. I'd taken

about three steps when I heard Mr. Stanley's voice booming down the corridor. My euphoria vanished. I didn't want to talk to him just now. I didn't want to have to explain to him what I was doing, why I was doing it, or what I was thinking. At least not yet. I looked around. The hall ahead of me dead ended.

I couldn't go forward. And if I went back I'd meet Mr. Stanley. I was just about to resign myself to that eventuality when I realized that maybe there was another way out after all. I walked toward the door at the end of the corridor. It didn't have anything printed on it so the odds were high that it wasn't somebody's office. In fact, as I listened to the noises coming from the other side of the wall and worked out the mental geography of the place, I was pretty sure that the door I was now standing in front of led to the manufac- turing plant, in which case I could just go in, scoot around to the back door, go out, and find myself in the parking lot.

I ducked inside and found myself standing in the middle of a lab. So much for my sense of direction. The room was about twenty by fifteen. Two doors, both closed, led off to who knew where. A long counter with a double sink in the middle bisected the area. Along the far wall there was a large, double refrigerator with metal doors, some counter space, another sink, and a hood. Racks of test tubes and retorts stood on another counter.

"Yes?" A woman, the only person in the place, looked up from the microscope she had been peering into. "What do you want?"

When I didn't answer immediately she hopped off of the stool she'd been sitting on and came over to where I was standing. As she came toward me I could see that she was one of those small, thin women with childlike bodies who look like they never made it through puberty. But her face didn't match. It was lined and hard with a pinched mouth, narrow eyes, and a nose job bad enough to make me wonder what it had looked like before.

"This area is off limits."

"I didn't realize," I said looking around.

She compressed her lips into a thin line and crossed her arms over her chest. "I've told your boss a thousand times I can't have people traipsing through contaminating things." She pointed to the door. "If you want to get to the factory, you'll have to go out and around like everybody else."

"You're doing biogenetic research here, aren't you?" I said, suddenly understanding what I'd stumbled into.

"Yes I am and I'd get a lot more of it done if people didn't keep barging through my work space. So if you wouldn't mind . . ."

But I didn't hear the last part of her sentence because just then the door on the far right opened and Joe Davis came in.

"Hey, Doc," he said.

Then he saw me.

Chapter
23

"So how's your arm?" I asked Davis. Miss Concerned, that was me. "Healing nicely?"

He let out a strangled growl.

The woman moved between us quickly.

"Look," she told both Davis and me in a tone of voice that left no doubt as to the depths of her irritation. "I don't know what's going on and I don't care. What I do care about is that I am in the middle of running an important experiment, one that I do not want to have to repeat, and I don't have any more time to waste on this kind of nonsense. I want both of you out of here now." And she pointed to the other door, the one Davis hadn't come through. "Or else I'm calling security."

"Yes, ma'am," he snarled, drawing out the "ma'am."

Then he left.

"Does he work for you?" I asked as he slammed the door shut behind him.

She lifted up the phone. "I'm dialing security now."

"Right." And I followed Davis through the door on the left.

I would have preferred to leave the way I'd come in, but I didn't want to take a chance on meeting up with Mr. Stanley.

On the other hand I wasn't real hot to meet up with Davis, either.

But I didn't think he'd start anything with me.

Not when there were people around.

Nevertheless I went through the door with my heart pounding.

Davis wasn't in sight.

He wasn't in the loading bay. The place was empty. No trucks. No people. The big double doors were open. The sun was streaming in on the concrete floor. I peered back inside the plant. From where I was standing I could see men taking cartons off of a conveyor belt and loading them onto a hand truck.

I thought for a moment.

Maybe he'd gone back into the plant.

Or maybe he was waiting for me in the parking lot.

That thought didn't make me feel real happy.

I took my knife out of my pocketbook and held it as I hopped down from the concrete bay and starting walking through the lot.

But Davis wasn't there. Just row after row of parked cars getting hot in the sun and an occasional sparrow taking a dirt bath. Either Davis had left or he was inside working. I really didn't care as long as he wasn't near me. I didn't pocket my knife till I was in my car and out of the parking lot. As I drove back to the store I wondered why Davis had walked into the lab and what could be happening on Monday at 12 o'clock that could possibly involve Ms. Science and Joe Davis. One thing about the man, I decided as I parked and went inside Noah's Ark. He had a propensity for hooking up with unlikely people. First the fight with Lynn, then this thing with Ms. Science. It was all very odd.

Tim, Manuel, and Julio were clustered around the front counter when I walked in. A bag from Taco Bell stood nearby. Pickles was batting at a crumpled-up food wrapper that had fallen to the ground while Zsa Zsa was munching on a tortilla.

"We saved you a couple of burritos," Tim said looking up.

"Thanks." Until I'd seen the bag I hadn't realized how hungry I was. I took the first burrito out, dispatched it in three gulps, and went on to the second.

"So what's going on?" he asked as I wiped some hot sauce off of my shirt. Why was I such a slob? I couldn't seem to eat anything without leaving a portion of it somewhere on my clothing.

I gave him an edited version of my morning while I dabbed at the spot.

"Ah so," he said, giving a bad imitation of Charlie Chan.

Manuel smirked. "I know what happened."

"What?"

"Davis and that lady are probably getting it on. They was just setting up another time to do it since your comin' there messed things up."

"That's not even a remote possibility," I said after I'd swallowed the last of the second burrito.

"How do *you* know?" Manuel demanded.

"Because I do." Good answer, Robin. But the idea was too ridiculous to even think about. I wiped my hands with the napkin that had come in the Taco Bell bag and threw everything in the trash.

Julio nudged Manuel in the ribs. "Boy, you got sex on the brain. What's a matter? Ain't you getting any?"

Manuel drew himself up. "I'm getting more than you. That's for sure."

"Says who?"

"Says Raymona."

"That bitch?"

"I thought she was your bitch."

"Like I'd ever have anything to do with her sorry ass."

"That's not what I hear."

"Well, you hear wrong," Julio stated glaring at Manuel.

"Yeah, man, whatever," Manuel muttered and started fiddling with one of the fake mice in the box next to the cash register.

Julio turned back to Tim and me. "You know what I think we should do? I think we should stake this guy out and find out what's happening."

Manuel put the mouse down. "Do you know who you're talkin' about?"

"Yeah, I know who I'm talkin about," Julio shot back. "Davis don't scare me. I think he's just got everyone punked."

"And what you goin' to do?" Manuel demanded. "Run after him?"

"No. We'll use a car."

"Whose?" jeered Manuel. "Your cousin's?"

Julio drew himself up. "She'd give me it if I asked her."

Manuel snorted. "Yeah. Just like she did when she called the police after you borrowed it to take us to the mall."

"That was different," Julio insisted.

"You ain't even got a driver's license."

Julio grinned. "So what? I can still drive pretty good."

Manuel prodded Julio's shoulder with a finger. "Don't you ever learn nothing?"

"You calling me dumb?" Julio challenged.

I could see where this was going.

"All right." I clapped my hands before things got out of control. I felt like a teacher in a home for juvenile delinquents. "Let's get one thing straight. Nobody is doing anything. Nobody."

"Hey, talk to Julio." Manuel indicated his friend. "I don't want to get near Joe Davis. Ain't I told you that?"

"Yes, you did," I conceded, wishing that Julio and Manuel would both go away. I liked them. Most of the time. Even though they were a pain in the ass. But not now. I had too many other things on my mind. "What do you guys want anyway?"

"Oh. I forgot." And Julio whipped a battered copy of *Charlotte's Web* out of his back jean's pocket and waved it under my nose. "I came to show you I read ten more pages."

"Good for you." I clapped him on the back.

"I'm going to see Martha now."

"Go ahead."

Zsa Zsa suddenly appeared next to my leg. I picked her up and rubbed her belly. She gave a small groan of pleasure and licked my ear.

"You want to say hello?" Julio asked.

"Maybe later. I'm a little busy now."

Julio shrugged and walked into the back. "Okay. But if she doesn't get to know you, she's never going to like you."

Before I could answer the phone rang. Tim reached over and picked it up.

"For you," he said, handing me the receiver. "Mister Stanley," he mouthed. "And he doesn't sound happy."

He wasn't.

"So?" Tim asked when I hung up a few minutes later. "What did he want?"

"He fired me."

"Why?"

"He said and I quote, 'I didn't do what I was told and that I was more trouble than I was worth.' "

Tim chuckled. "Anyone could have told him that."

"Who fired you?" George asked from the open doorway, filling the frame with his bulk.

"Mister Stanley," I replied, once again amazed at how a man that big could move that quietly. "Lynn's father. And close the door. You're letting all the cool air out."

"Sorry." George shut it and crossed the floor. "I didn't know he'd hired you."

"He did."

"To do what?"

"Is this a cop question or a personal-information question?"

"Would you answer if it was a cop question?"

"No.

"Then it's a personal-information question."

"Okay." I stroked Zsa Zsa's ears. They felt soft under my fingers. "He paid me to find out what really happened on Otisco Street."

"Dumb move," George said.

"Are you saying he was really stupid to hire me?" I demanded.

"No, I'm saying you were really stupid to take the money."

"I know," I admitted reluctantly.

"What you did is illegal. You need a license. If he filed a complaint you could be charged."

The puppy started to wiggle. As I put her down I thought

about how Stanley's hiring me had stunk from the beginning. Only I hadn't wanted to admit it.

"You know," I said slowly. "I've always had the feeling he was using me, trying to steer me toward one thing and away from another."

George leaned forward. "Toward what?"

"That's the problem. I don't know."

"But you have an idea, right? I can read it on your face."

"Maybe an inkling of one," I conceded. "How'd you like to do me a favor?"

"I'm listening."

"Could you find out if Connelly alibied Gordon Marshall?"

I expected George to scream, but all he said was. "Okay."

I was shocked. So was Tim.

"You mean you're not going to give me a big song and dance about how you can't do that?"

"No."

I threw my hands up in the air. "I'll never understand you."

"It's simple. You're going to do this with me or without me and I've decided that I'd rather you do this with me. That's what I came here to tell you."

"I don't believe it." I was truly amazed.

"Now that I'm leaving the force I don't care anymore."

"You're leaving?" Tim's jaw dropped.

"One way or another by next January I plan to be out of my blues."

"Why? What are you going to do?"

"I'm going back to school and getting a Ph.D. in Medieval History," George told Tim. His jaw was jutting out. His tone challenged Tim to make a crack.

Remembering the other night in R.J.'s, I steeled myself. But Tim just said "cool, man" and I relaxed.

George must have noticed me tensing up because he said, "I guess I got a little out of line the other evening."

"Just a little."

He studied the leashes on the opposite wall for a moment. "Yeah. Well. I was just having a bad day."

"Everybody has them," I replied magnanimously. I could be gracious when apologized to and I knew this was the most apologetic George was going to get.

"So what are you going to do for money?" Tim asked abruptly.

George shrugged. "I don't know. I hope I can get an assistantship but till then I'll temp, work security, maybe open my own detective agency."

"If you're going to do that kind of thing, then why don't you stay where you are?"

"Because," George told him, "when I'm on the force I can't pick and choose what I respond to. I get the call and I go. You go back to the same family two or three times in one night for a DD. . . ."

"DD?" I asked.

"Domestic disturbance," he explained. "And you start thinking, 'Hey, who cares? They want to kill themselves? Let them. Just do it off of my shift so I don't have to fill in the paperwork.' " He cracked a knuckle. "And then there are the people I'd truly love to get. Like Davis." He cracked another knuckle. "I just spent half an hour with three hysterical children and their mom. Nice lady. Somebody took the family pet, a six-month-old yellow lab, right out of their yard. I'm sure Davis grabbed the pup, but I can't prove anything. So I'll file a report with CID and it'll just sit on Abbott's desk along with the others. And even if Abbott

wanted to do something about it he can't do much except
maybe go out and ask a few questions. He'd never get a sur-
veillance authorization for Davis. Too much money."

"I'll do it," I volunteered, hoping as I said it that Manuel
and Julio hadn't heard me.

"You'll do what?"

"Follow him around."

"The hell you will."

In the end George and I compromised. We decided to do
it together.

It was definitely going to be an interesting evening.

Chapter
24

I got back to my house a little after nine that night. It had been a slow evening at the store. Nobody had come in since six when the rain had swept into Syracuse with gusting winds, a clap of thunder, and a streak of lightning. Somewhere around seven the lights started flickering and I thought the power was going to go out. But it didn't and I spent the next two hours cleaning up, placing orders, and filling out my quarterly New York State Estimated Tax Return—always a favorite occupation. By the time I closed up shop the wind had died down and the rain had eased up. I'd just walked in my door and was looking at the mail when George rang the bell.

"Ready?" he asked when I answered.

I nodded and went out the front door, leaving Zsa Zsa asleep on the living-room sofa. I knew I should put her in her kennel but she looked so adorable that I didn't have the heart to disturb her, an action I hoped I wouldn't regret later on.

"I've got some soda, a few peanut butter and jelly sandwiches, and a couple of Kevlar vests in the backseat," George informed me as I got into his '89 Chevy Celebrity.

We'd both agreed that his car was better than mine for what we were about to do.

"Kevlar vests?" I looked around the Chevy's interior. There was nothing here that shouldn't belong. No old coffee cups. No candy wrappers. No loose change. Nothing. I wondered if his house was this neat. And then I realized that in all the years I'd known George I'd never been inside it. But then George had really been Murphy's friend not mine. "What the hell do we need those for?"

"Just in case." George put his foot on the gas and we shot down the street.

"Just in case what?" I asked as he came to a stop at the corner of Westcott and East Genesee.

"Anything happens."

And we took off again before I could find out exactly what it was that George thought was going to happen.

"Do you always drive this way?" I inquired while we sped through the intersection at Fayette and Cherry.

He chuckled. "That's why I became a cop, so I could drive fast. It's one of the perks of the job. Why?" He gave me a sideways glance. "Do you want me to slow down? Am I going too fast for you?" And he smirked.

"No, it's fine," I lied. No way was I going to admit I couldn't take what he was dishing out.

"Good." And he went even faster.

It was like being in the Grand Prix I decided as George swooped around another curve. By the time we got to the street Joe Davis lived on I'd come to like it. It was exciting.

But when I told George that I couldn't tell if he was happy or disappointed.

"How do you know if Davis is in?" I asked as we parked about four houses down. "How do you know he isn't working? He might have pulled a double shift."

"He didn't." George slumped down in the seat to make himself less visible. I did the same. "Wagner said he saw him go inside his house at eight-twenty. He didn't see him go out again."

"Wagner?"

"A friend of mine."

"A cop friend?"

"Yeah. He owes me a favor. You want something to eat?"

"Sure."

George leaned back and got the sandwiches out of the bag on the backseat. "Fresh ground peanut butter, with apple butter, on bakery bread," he told me, handing one to me and taking another for himself.

"Sounds good," I replied.

And it was. The truth is I like good food. I even like food that's good for you. At one time I even ate vegetables, although most people that know me now would find that as difficult to believe as a Marine wearing a garter belt. In the past year I've just been too tired or too distracted to make the effort. It's easier to grab a candy bar and swallow a vitamin pill. But I'm always happy to be fed.

"By the way," George said as I took a bite, "Gordon was at that meeting. People saw him there. But they weren't positive about the times."

"So he could have slipped out?"

"That's what I gather," George said and then he started to eat.

After we finished the sandwiches, George and I

exchanged Murphy stories. Then he began telling me about his ex-wife, a wife I hadn't even known he'd had. Maybe that was because he'd been married at eighteen, been a father at nineteen, and been deserted at nineteen and a half. George a father? Now that was a thought!

"Aren't you at least curious about the kid?"

"Of course, I'm curious," George said quietly, staring straight ahead, watching the rain fall on the windshield. "I've tried to find Doreen and William from time to time, but I've never had any luck."

"Did you ask her mother?"

"Doreen's mother died when she was sixteen. She was shot in a holdup outside of a convenience store. And her daddy moved away to Florida. Never came back. Forgot, I guess. No. I just came home one day and she was gone. The car was gone. All her clothes. All the baby's things."

"What did you do?"

"What do you think I did?" He snorted. "I went fuckin' nuts." Suddenly he pointed at Joe Davis's house. "Look. There he goes."

"I see." I leaned forward to get a better look.

Davis hurried down the block, head lowered, shoulders hunched up against the slanting rain.

"I wonder where he'd be going?"

"At a guess I'd say somewhere where he's not going to have to be outside a lot," George replied.

A moment later, as we watched, Davis walked around to a rusted red van that was parked under a streetlight, opened the door, and got in. The engine hiccupped, then coughed.

"Come on, come on," I said, leaning forward. "Start."

"He should get that car to a garage," George observed while the van sputtered. "It needs a tune-up. Bad."

Finally it turned over and Davis pulled out. I let out a sigh of relief and leaned back in my seat. When Davis was almost down to the corner George went after him.

"At least the van will be easy to follow," he murmured as Davis hung a right onto Bellevue.

There weren't that many cars out, weekday nights in Syracuse most people stay home, and George took care to try and stay at least a quarter of a block behind Davis. A few minutes later he turned into Grant and pulled into the parking lot of The River Styx, a rundown bar mostly patronized by wanna-be punks and skinheads, and parked. George glided to a stop across the street and killed the Celebrity's motor.

I moved forward. "I wonder if he's meeting someone in there?"

The bar's windows were blackened out making it impossible to see in. But the door was propped open. I realized if I strolled by it I could glance in. Then I realized I didn't even have to do that. I could probably catch a glimpse inside the bar from the street.

"Be back in a second," I said and stepped out into the rain.

George rolled down his window. "Where are you going?" he whispered fiercely.

I put a finger across my lips and pointed. He shook his head. I put up a finger indicating I'd just be a second and walked down a little ways. I'd been right. From where I was standing I could see inside The River Styx. It was like looking at a stage setting with the night framing the lit interior. I took a quick peek. Davis was standing in the middle of the bar drinking a beer and watching TV. I tiptoed back to the car.

"That was stupid," George grumbled when I got inside.

I sneezed.

"What would have happened if he had seen you? You could have blown our cover."

"Sorry." I wiped a drop of rain out of my eye. "But he didn't. See me, that is. I just wanted to find out if he was talking to anyone."

"And?"

"He's not. You wouldn't happen to have a towel or an old shirt you're not using around by any chance?"

"Here." George reached across to the glove compartment and took a couple of paper towels out and handed them to me. "Use these."

"You know," I said while I dried my face and arms and started blotting my hair. "I think we picked a lousy night to do this."

"I've been thinking the same thing."

"It's too nasty. People don't leave their dogs out when it's raining like this."

"So you want to quit?"

"No." Actually I was having fun.

"Me neither. And anyway if there's one thing I've learned over the years it's that you can never tell what somebody is going to do." He twisted around and reached in back for a soda. "You want one?"

"No thanks. I wonder who Davis is selling the dogs to?"

"Probably a dealer."

"A dealer?"

"Yeah, someone with a license to sell animals. You can get one from the Ag Department easy. Then he goes to the labs at the universities, hospitals, whatever and takes orders. You know, 'we need twenty cats for college biology, ten large dogs for cardiovascular experiments,' that kind of thing. Then he calls up someone like Davis, in the trade he'd be called a jobber, who goes out and fills the order. The universities, the labs, they don't look too close at what gets brought in. They don't ask too many questions."

"I wonder what he was going to do with the puppies I found?"

George took a gulp of soda. "Probably sell them to someone who'd use them to train pit bulls with. I'm told they sell puppies and kittens by the pound."

For a second I saw Zsa Zsa being torn apart, heard her terrified squealing, the laugh of the pit bull's trainer and felt a flash of white-hot rage course through my body. "He really is a disgusting excuse for a human being," I spat out. "Someone should remove him from the planet."

"Getting a little hot, aren't we?" George said dryly. "Lots of people are disgusting. Too damned many. Just be glad you don't do what I do and see what I see." He took another sip of soda. "That's why I like history. It's neat, it's clean, and it happened a long time ago."

I was about to reply when Davis stepped out of the bar.

"Here we go," George said, slinking back down in his seat.

Davis got in his car and made a U-turn. George and I slid down even farther. We held our breaths as he drove by. If he had turned his head even a fraction of an inch and glanced over he would have seen us, but he didn't, he just stared straight ahead. His mouth was compressed, his eyes narrowed against the glare of the streetlights on the rain-slicked street. He looked like a man in a hurry.

George waited for a second, then followed. Davis went back onto Bellvue. A couple of blocks later he made a turn onto Castle Avenue.

"I bet he's heading for Eighty-one," I said as George followed Davis onto Oak Street.

"He could be going onto Park," George countered, readjusting the speed on the Celebrity's wipers.

The rain was coming down harder again, making it difficult to see. Everything seemed to blur under the onslaught of the downpour. At Oak and Otisco Davis took a left. So did we. Fortunately there were enough cars still out on the road so that we weren't too conspicuous. George started whistling. A few minutes later Davis turned onto the route 81 on-ramp.

"It looks like I was right," I said as we followed Davis's tail-lights up it.

George nodded, his faced scrunched in concentration. He had stopped whistling when we hit the highway. Davis was traveling fast now, weaving in and out of the other cars, making it difficult to keep up and remain inconspicuous.

"He's certainly in a rush," George observed, his eyes glued on the red van.

"Maybe he's got a hot date."

George grunted, too busy to answer. About ten minutes later we followed Davis off at the Dewitt exit. He made a right on East Genesee, then a minute later made an illegal left onto Highbridge Avenue, a narrow, two-lane road that ran in back of Shoppingtown Mall.

"Where is this guy going?" George muttered as he killed the Celebrity's lights and glided after him.

It was eerie driving blind, using Davis's high beams as our only source of light. But George couldn't click on our brights because we were now the only two cars on the road. If he had turned them on Davis would have spotted us in two seconds. Suddenly the car lurched.

"Sorry," George said as he brought it back under control. "I think we hit a small rock."

I instinctively reached for my seat belt and fastened it. Something I should have done before. I'd spent enough time in the hospital for a while. I wasn't going to spend any more if I could help it.

A few minutes later Davis made a right turn onto Cedar Lane.

"I bet he's going to Cedar Park," I whispered as Davis flew on ahead of us.

George cursed under his breath.

I knew why he was cursing. Cedar Park was located on the Erie Canal. It consisted of a large open space for cars, a playground, a bridge over the canal and more open space, interspersed with lots of trees and brush. And the place was well lit. We couldn't follow Davis in, not even with the Celebrity's lights off. He'd see us. And if by some miracle he didn't see us, he'd hear the tires on the gravel. No. We were going to have to park on the grassy verge along the road and walk in.

And that's what we did. The ground was soggy, my feet squished every time I took a step. Even though the rain had lightened up, it was still falling steadily and George and I were both soaked in the four minutes it took us to reach the park.

"He better be here," George muttered as he reached a hand up and wiped the rain out of his eyes.

"He is," I whispered, indicating the van. It was parked in the far corner of the parking lot.

"So's somebody else." George pointed to the black Saab parked next to it. "It looks like we might have hit pay dirt."

"I certainly hope so." I stifled a sneeze. I'd hate to think that we had done all of this for nothing.

We crept forward keeping to the cover of the trees. The two cars sat there. I didn't see Davis or the person he was meeting.

"They're probably talking in one of them," I suggested.

"Probably. Can you make out the Saab's license plate."

"TNJ 324."

"Good. That's what I read, too." He turned around. "Now let's get out of here."

"Don't you want to stay?"

"Why?" He looked at me as if I were crazy. "We got what we came for. I'll run a make on the plate and see what comes up."

"And then what?"

"And then we'll go from there."

"Yeah, but I want to see who's in the Saab now."

George was just about to reply, when we heard a car coming.

"Fuck," I cursed.

George and I dropped down and hugged the ground.

A branch poked into my ribs.

Dirt tickled my nose.

A bug crawled over my cheek. I flicked it away.

Just go away, I willed whoever it was.

But they didn't.

An arc of light played over us.

I flattened myself out even more.

And prayed.

Davis's friends didn't seem like people I'd want to meet.

Especially out here like this.

Alone.

In the dark.

And then I wondered if George had brought his gun.

I hoped so.

I was just about to ask him when a voice boomed out, "Freeze. This is the Dewitt police."

Chapter
25

"Oh, shit," George said as he scrambled up.

I came out after him.

We walked toward the high beams with our hands up. The lights were so bright I had to look down at the ground to keep from being blinded.

George started talking. In ten minutes he and the Dewitt blues were laughing. In twenty minutes we were free to go, apologies all around. Of course by that time Davis and his friend were long gone.

"They probably went out the back way the minute they saw the lights," I said as the Dewitt cops drove away.

"Probably," George agreed as he brushed mud and grass off his pants and shirt.

I did the same. Then we got back in the car. The inside was definitely going to need to be cleaned.

"At least we got the license number." George paused to start the Celebrity. "I'll run it tomorrow."

"Can't you run it now?"

"Not from here. I don't have a computer in the car."

"We could go down to the PSB . . ." I suggested.

"You mean *I* could go down to the PSB."

"Yes. That's what I meant."

"You're right. I could. But since I'm not supposed to be doing this, if it's all the same to you, I'd rather run the request through on my regular shift."

I allowed as how I could see that.

"So how long do you think it's going to take before we get an answer?" I asked.

George shrugged. He still had smudges of mud on his cheek and jaw, light on dark brown. "We're supposed to get an immediate response. Usually we do. Unless the computer is down. Which has been happening a lot lately. Then it can take forever. I'll call you when I get something."

I leaned back in my seat and closed my eyes. Suddenly I was very tired. I couldn't wait to get home.

The next thing I knew George was saying, "we're here."

My eyes flew open. For a moment I didn't know where I was. Then I saw the porch and realized we were parked in front of my house. I mumbled a good night and stumbled inside the house. Zsa Zsa came to greet me as I went up the stairs. I went straight to the bathroom, stripped, and stepped into the shower. I stood there watching the mud come off my hands and arms and swirl down the drain. Then I toweled myself off and crawled into bed. God, it felt good to stretch out. And that was the last thought I had.

I awoke to Zsa Zsa sitting on my chest and licking my ear. I groaned and looked over at the clock. It was six-fifteen.

"Go away," I begged.

Zsa Zsa kept licking. Hey, I guess when you gotta pee you gotta pee.

"Okay, okay," I told her as I got up and slipped on the sweats lying on the floor next to the bed. Then I headed down the stairs and walked into the backyard.

The sky was a bright blue. A few cumulus clouds drifted overhead. The grass felt cool under my feet. A squirrel chittered in the pine tree a couple of feet away. It was a Norman Rockwell day, a day to be out in the country, I decided as I walked back inside the kitchen. I lit the gas under the tea kettle. As I measured the ground coffee out into the filter I thought about last night's events and wondered who the Saab would turn out to belong to? But for an answer to that question I'd just have to wait and see what George came up with. For a second I was tempted to call him and then I decided he was probably still asleep. After all, it was only a quarter to seven in the morning.

I gave Zsa Zsa a little milk mixed in with her Puppy Chow for breakfast, swallowed a vitamin pill, got a chocolate bar out of the fridge, and ate it while I poured the now boiling water through the grounds. I still couldn't get over the fact that whoever had met Davis was driving a Saab. In my head I'd pictured them driving a van or a pickup truck or a junker. Something cheap and sleazy. Which just goes to show how much I know I thought as I put some sugar in my mug, then poured in the coffee and added some milk. I was still thinking about the Saab and who could be in it as I went back outside.

Then as I sat down on the deck and watched Zsa Zsa stalk a dandelion my mind leapfrogged to another Saab, Norma Lipsyle's '93 station wagon, and I began wondering about her and how she got to driving a car like that, especially when, according to Mrs. Z., Norma's family was poor white trash and her husband's family, which was wealthy, hated their daughter-in-law's guts. The whole setup was definitely strange. Something didn't fit. And then I remembered something else, something I'd forgotten. I hurried inside, dug up Brandon Douglas's clippings on his sister's murder and flipped through them. Midway through the book I found the one I was looking for. I ran my finger down the article till I got to the fourth paragraph.

"Norma Lipsyle denies that she ever said that she saw Janet Tyler getting into a dark green MG TA the night before she was killed."

Dark green MG TA. Once again I thought about the specific car reference. I put my coffee cup down. Norma Lipsyle's car was beginning to make a little more sense. So was the dress, I'd seen in the hospital.

Had someone paid her off to change her story?

Were they still paying her off? After all, the Saab was brand new.

And what about her husband?

How did he fit in to this?

I decided that, if only to satisfy my own curiosity, I was going to have to drive out to Selic Road and have a chat with Norma Lipsyle and see what I could pry out of her. Only this time I'd buy a map.

But as it turned out I had to do something about my car first. Because when I got in my cab to go to work and turned the ignition key nothing happened. The damned thing wouldn't turn over. A fact that really pissed me off. Especially since I'd just had the starter replaced four weeks ago. I got back out, marched into the house, and called Victor.

He and his brother were at my house an hour later with their tow truck.

"Can you lend me a car?" I asked Victor as he hooked the cab up.

He ran his hand through his frizzy red hair.

"After all," I persisted. "You were supposed to fix this the first time around."

The two men exchanged glances.

"We got a Blazer sitting around," Victor's brother said.

Victor thought it over. "Okay," he finally said. Then he motioned for me and Zsa Zsa to get in the truck. "I guess it'll be all right."

The Blazer was black and had a big dent on its left side, but it ran and that was the important thing. I thanked Victor and sped away to the store. Tim was already there. Evidently George hadn't called yet. I'd just have to wait. I spent the next couple of hours helping Tim put away bags of dog and cat food and kitty litter. Then we scrubbed down the bird room and I left for Weedsport. As I headed toward the Thruway I thought about how nice it was to be outside. And how different it was from last night. The day was still picture-perfect, not too hot, not too cold and I enjoyed the feel of the sun on my arm and the breeze on my face.

I started thinking of my first sports car, an old MG B I'd named Sadie for reasons I don't remember. I'd gotten her in April and spent every spare minute I wasn't working racing around. Until September. When Murphy had totaled her out at Montauk Point. After I'd reluctantly given him the keys to the car. He'd walked away without a scratch, but the car had had to be junked.

But did I learn anything?

No.

On days like this I still miss her.

Him, too, for that matter.

But she'd been the better investment.

As I collected a ticket at the toll booth I switched mental gears and tried to think of what I was going to say to Norma Lipsyle when I got to her house. After all, you can't just barge in on someone and say, "where'd you get that money for that car? Who's paying you off to keep your mouth shut?"—at least not if you're not the cops you can't—and not get thrown out on your ass. For a brief moment, I thought about stopping off somewhere and printing up some cards saying I was with the IRS or the Social Services Department, but then I decided why risk doing something that could put you in jail when you didn't have to. Especially since my original story, the one I'd given the girl at Zeke's about being a magazine reporter, would do just as well.

Right before I turned off for Weedsport I slowed down to watch a hawk flying above me. It hovered, almost motionless, in the air, then swooped down and soared off again. I got on the exit ramp wondering what it would be like to own a bird like that. I'd heard there was a falconry club forming in the Syracuse area. It might be interesting to join. I'd learn something and it certainly couldn't hurt business. Then I put those thoughts away and started concentrating on where I was going. If last time was any clue I was definitely going to have to pay attention. But it wasn't. This time I didn't get lost. I managed to find Norma Lipsyle's house without any problem at all.

It was a small, pale green colonial, set back about three hundred yards from the road. The mailbox was in the shape of a duck and had Lipsyle printed on it in big, black letters. A couple of bikes lay across the path leading up to the front door. A plaster deer looked out from the lawn over to the woods. To its left a dwarf talked to three pink bunnies. The flower beds on either side were edged with white tiles. A large oak shaded the house. A tire had been attached to one of the lower limbs by a length of rope. A boy somewhere between the ages of nine and twelve was sitting in it.

When he saw my car, he jumped off and ran inside his

house. I pulled the car over onto the grass and cut the engine and got out. As I drew closer I could see the Saab station wagon parked next to the back door. If I remembered rightly they cost about twenty-five thousand dollars. The hatch was opened. Five bags of groceries were visible. Norma Lipsyle must have just come back from shopping.

A moment later she came out the door and headed toward me. The boy followed on her heels. She wasn't wearing any makeup, her blond hair was pushed back, her shirt and shorts were frayed and faded. The butterfly rash on her face was even redder. She looked fragile, as if the least little thing would break her apart. But she sure didn't act that way.

"Yes?" She stopped about ten feet away from me and crossed her arms over her chest. "What do you want? Because whatever it is you're selling I'm not buying."

I took one of my old cards out of my wallet and handed it to her. She looked at it suspiciously. "So?" she said when she handed it back.

"Can we go inside and talk?"

"Anything you have to say you can say out here."

This was not going well.

"You see I'm doing an article . . ."

"Article? What article?"

"I bet it's about Dad," the boy put in.

"Sshh," Norma instructed.

"He's right," I replied.

Norma drew herself up straighter. "Well, I ain't got nothing to say. Not to you or to anyone else."

I continued anyway. "I read about the car you said you saw the night before Janet Tyler died. The dark green MG TA."

Her cheek twitched, then stopped. "I made a mistake. Now, if you don't mind I got things to do."

"Yeah," her son said, his voice loud and defiant. "You heard her. We got things to do."

"It's okay." Norma put her arm around him and gave him a hug. "The lady was just going."

But I wasn't. At least not yet. "I've seen your husband at the hospital," I continued. "He didn't say much, either."

Norma looked down at her child. "Why don't you finish unloading the groceries?"

"But, Mom . . ." He gave me a hard stare.

"Go on now. The ice cream is going to melt."

"I . . ."

"I'll be fine. Really." And she smiled and shooed him away.

The kid left reluctantly, walking up to the car slowly, stopping every once in a while to make sure I wasn't hurting his mom.

"Nobody makes that kind of mistake. How much are you getting?" I asked as soon as he had taken a grocery bag into the house. "The car is worth at least thirty-five grand, your house is in pretty good shape. I bet if I walked inside I'd find a big TV and a VCR. Pretty good for someone who I understand isn't working."

Lipsyle's tic returned. "Go away."

"I don't understand." My eyes traveled to the station wagon. "Is that Saab worth more than your husband's freedom?"

Her rash flamed.

"Are you going to let him die in prison?"

Her eyes blazed. Her face came alive. "Just go away," she cried. "Go away now or I'll go in the house and get the shotgun."

I didn't think she would.

I didn't even think she had one in the house. She didn't strike me as the type.

I was just about to tell her that when a school bus came round the bend and stopped in front of the path leading to her house. The door opened and two children, a boy and a girl, bounded off and ran toward us. It was impossible to tell their ages. They could have been twelve or they could have been sixteen. Both were short and squat and had the wide faces and upturned eyes of Down's syndrome children. As I watched they raced over to Norma Lipsyle and hugged her so hard she almost toppled over.

"These," she said to me trying to put on a good show so they wouldn't get upset, "are Carey and Carl, my twins. Carey and Carl say hello."

They clapped and jumped up and down.

"Are you from Uncle . . . ?"

Norma hurriedly shushed them. "You two go in the house."

"But he always brings us candy," the boy said, his face crumbling in disappointment.

"If you go in the house your brother will get you some ice cream."

Both children smiled.

"With sprinkles?" the boy asked.

"And little silver balls?" the girl chimed in.

"Absolutely," Norma said.

"Goody, goody, goody." They began jumping up and down again.

"And after that we'll go out and hunt for four-leaf clovers."

They jumped harder. Norma watched them go up to the house.

"They're very sweet," I said when they'd gone inside.

"Yes, they are. And I love them very much."

"It must be difficult having to raise them by yourself."

"I manage."

"But then you do have Uncle . . . ?"

Norma glared at me. "Let me make this perfectly plain. My kids come first. I want them to have something when I'm gone. I want Carey and Carl to stay here in this house. Matt feels the same way and nobody is going to do anything to change that. Nobody. Do you understand?"

And I did.

Perfectly.

Chapter
26

As I drove back to Syracuse I tried to sort out what I'd just seen at Norma Lipsyle's.

Hypothesis: Somehow Norma and Matt Lipsyle knew who had murdered Janet Tyler.

But they didn't turn him in.

Instead, the murderer had made a deal with Matt: Go to jail in my place and I'll support your family.

But why would anyone do something like that?

I lit a cigarette and thought.

What would make me do something like that?

Good question. I took a puff and exhaled.

Well, I might if I found out I'd just tested HIV positive.

And we had twin Down's syndrome children.

And I wasn't trained to do anything that made any real money.

And my mother and father were dead.

And my relatives hated the woman I'd had four children with and kicked me out when I'd married her.

It might seem like an attractive option.

Very noble.

Self-sacrificing.

And it had the advantage of being peaceful.

Especially since there was no death penalty in New York State.

I wondered if Norma had agreed to the deal?

At a guess I'd say no.

Why would she?

She could go out and get a job and he could stay home.

And then I realized that she couldn't.

What was it Mrs. Z. had said about Norma being sick? That she'd had this disease with a funny-sounding name that women get.

And I thought of the butterfly rash on Norma Lipsyle's face.

The woman had lupus.

God.

She couldn't work. Not if she had a bad case of it. The disease wasn't fatal, but it could damage your heart or your lungs or your kidneys. It cycled in and out. Sometimes you were fine and other times you were so tired you couldn't get off the couch.

But maybe she hadn't wanted to take the deal anyway.

Or maybe she hadn't even known what her husband was going to do.

That's why she'd made that statement.

But then she'd retracted it.

Why?

Had she decided her husband knew best? Or had she been scared into doing it? After all, this guy *had* killed someone. Had he threatened to kill Norma if she didn't go along with the plan? Or had she just weighed the options and decided that this one made more sense?

I threw my cigarette out the window, changed lanes, and slowed down for the exit ramp. The more I thought about what I'd just conjured up the less sure I was. It was something I could see happening in India not America.

Still.

Norma Lipsyle was getting money from somewhere. Correction. From someone. From someone her kids called Uncle. From someone rich. Someone connected with Stanley Pharmaceuticals. The possibilities were definitely narrowing. To two people. But which? I didn't know. At least not yet. I glanced down at my watch. It was a little after one. I'd told Tim I'd be back between two and two-thirty. That left me an hour and a half.

Just enough time, I reckoned, to run down and talk to Pardos, the DA who had handled the Janet Tyler case. Especially since if my memory served me correctly he was now in private practice with offices down in the Bentley Settle Building, which was on the way—more or less—to the store. Who knew, maybe he'd have something interesting to say about Norma Lipsyle's statement and subsequent retraction. It was definitely worth a detour to find out.

Pardos's office was located on the second floor. It was large and airy, with brick walls, large windows, and wide, knotted-pine floors. Not corporate at all. In fact, the place would have made a nice apartment. The secretary was out, having lunch no doubt. Except for a vase containing two artfully arranged freesias and an engagement calendar her desk was empty. So were the chairs in the waiting room. It looked like Pardos wasn't exactly deluged with business.

He came out a moment later. He had a welcoming smile and a bouncy walk that seemed to go with his light gray bow tie, gray pants and shirt, and saddle shoes. I liked the saddle shoes.

"Hello," he said, extending his hand. "What can I do for you?"

I gave him my card. "I'm doing some research and I've got a few questions concerning one of your old cases that I'm hoping you can clear up for me."

Pardos resettled his wire-rimmed glasses on the bridge of his nose and looked around his waiting room with a half smile. "I can probably help you out. I seem to have some free time. You know, I think my mother was right. I think I should have gone into the family business," he said as I followed him inside. "Jewelry," he explained even though I hadn't asked. "My family owns Pardos Jewelry."

They were one of the biggest jewelry stores in town.

"Oh well." He sat down, propped his feet up on his desk, crossed his ankles, put his hands behind his head, and leaned back. "I guess I still could go in with my brother if I want to. But enough about me. Now tell me, what case are you interested in?"

"The Janet Tyler murder."

"Ah." He looked bemused. "That was a long time ago."

"Ten years."

"Are you doing an article for the paper? A book? A magazine article?"

"A magazine article," I said quickly. Who knew, I might even write one some day.

"What's the angle?"

Interesting question. "A possible wrongful verdict."

"There was no verdict," Pardos shot back. "The case never went to trial."

"Excuse me. Wrong term."

"You got that right." He untangled his hands and feet and sat up. "We had a confession and we went with it."

"Did you have doubts?"

"About the veracity of Lipsyle's statement? None whatsoever. If I had I wouldn't have gone with it. Despite what some people say I wasn't in a hurry to close the case."

"Would you mind telling me why you were so sure?"

"Not at all. Lipsyle knew all the details of the crime, things nobody but the murderer could have known."

"What about his wife's statement?"

"You mean the one about seeing Janet Tyler get into an MG TA outside of a bar the night before she was killed?"

"Yes."

"We couldn't find anyone else to substantiate the story. And believe me, we looked. And besides if my memory serves Mrs. Lipsyle recanted a short time later. The way I figured it was that she knew what her husband had done and she was trying to cover for him. Anyway, she was drunk."

"She still made a pretty specific identification."

"Her father used to have a car like that. When she was drunk she used to call anything that moved an MG TA."

I leaned forward. "What would you say if I told you that Matt Lipsyle was paid to confess to the crime?"

"I would say that you've been watching too many late-night movies."

"You know his wife has a real expensive car."

"So?"

"Where did she get the money for it?"

Pardos shrugged. "Maybe she's running numbers, investing in the options market, maybe she won the lottery. Who the hell knows? It could be anything."

"But . . ." I protested.

"No." He cut me off. "What you've done is take some facts and make some conjectures. And that's all you have—conjectures unsupported by any evidence." The phone started ringing. Pardos picked it up. "Hey, John, how's it going?" he said into the receiver. "I already told him that." A moment of silence. "No. I don't think you're in a worse position if you decide to negotiate." Another moment of silence. "Hold on a minute, would you?" And he clapped his hand over the mouthpiece. "I'm sorry," he told me, "but I have to take this call."

I got up. "Thanks for your help."

He waved his hand dismissively. "Don't be silly. Call me if you've got any more questions. But listen. For what it's worth I really think you're barking up the wrong tree."

He would, I thought, as I walked down the stairs to the lobby.

Otherwise, he'd have to admit he'd sent an innocent man to prison.

But he was right about one thing—at this point all I had were conjectures and conjectures weren't worth anything.

I still needed proof. And I had absolutely no idea how to go about getting that. Norma Lipsyle certainly wasn't going to talk and neither was her husband. I sighed and walked to my car. A ticket was decorating my windshield. Number fifteen. Maybe I could get Pardos to work out a deal. It would definitely be worth it. I threw the citation in the glove compartment and took off.

That's why I hate coming downtown. There is never any place to park. And the meter maids come around every two hours, vultures circling in for the kill. And yet the mayor's

office keeps telling everyone he wants to revitalize downtown. So the city puts in new lights, plants some trees, and
fixes the sidewalks. Too bad they can't figure out where to
put the cars. I mean Syracuse isn't New York City. Except for
a few restaurants nothing downtown is so compelling that
you can't find it in the malls.

Oh well. I was still thinking about how to solve the parking
problem as I pulled up in front of the store. Zsa Zsa came
running out to greet me as soon as I opened the door. I
picked her up and she licked my face in a frenzy of happi-
ness. I laughed and took her outside. Tim was waiting for
me when I came back in.

He smiled nervously. "You want the good news or the bad
news?" he asked.

"The good news," I replied as I briefly considered whether
my choice indicated I was an optimist or a pessimist.

Tim looked relieved enough to make me wonder what the
bad news was but since he was already launched into his
spiel I let him go on.

"George called a little while ago. He said to tell you he got
the make on the license plate." Tim rubbed the top of his
head.

"Yes!" I clenched both fists, waved them over my head,
and did a little victory dance. Then I caught Tim's lady-you-
are-really-nuts look and stopped.

"From what he told me it sounds like you guys had an
exciting evening."

"Oh, we did. Did he tell you who the plate belonged to?"

"Stanley Pharmaceuticals."

"Really?" I could feel my eyes opening in amazement.

"It's a company car."

"Damn." My elation vanished.

If only the cops had come twenty minutes later I might

have been able to get a glimpse of who was behind the wheel of the Saab.

Who the hell was Davis meeting that he couldn't see during the day when he was at work?

There had to be a way of finding out who had access to the car. I was thinking about how to do that when Tim said, "George also told me to tell you to stay away from the factory for now. He said he'll call you when he gets off his shift."

"Anything else?" I asked as I automatically flipped through the mail on the counter and put it back. Just bills. They could wait to be opened.

"That's it."

"So what's the bad news?"

Tim gave a nervous tic of a laugh and held his hands up. "Now, I don't want you to get upset about this."

My heart sank. In my experience those words ranked only slightly below "trust me" as indications that something truly bad was about to happen. "Upset? Why should I get upset?"

Tim looked down at the floor. "Martha's escaped," he muttered.

Chapter
27

"She what?" I screeched.

"She's gone."

"Julio is going to die," I snarled through gritted teeth.

"It's not his fault."

"Then whose is it, The God of the Spiders?"

Tim pulled at his earring and studied the floor. "Mine," he mumbled. "I guess I didn't close the top to the cage securely enough. She must have managed to push it open."

"So now we have a tarantula that can leap ten feet and that eats birds running around our store?" Actually I knew she could only jump six feet, but what's accuracy at a time like this?

Tim gulped.

"How long has she been out?"

"I'm not sure. I just noticed she was gone about an hour ago."

"Does Julio know?"

"Yeah. He's coming right over."

"What did he say?"

"He was very upset."

"So am I," I muttered while I scanned the store.

The spider could be hiding anywhere. Behind the stacks of dog food. Between the dog beds. On top of the shelves. In one of the heating vents. Maybe it had found the lizard that had gotten out earlier this morning. Maybe they'd start a little colony. It didn't bear thinking about.

"Did you look in the bird room?" I asked Tim.

"That was the first thing I did."

"Maybe we should look again." After all, to a bird-eating Brazilian that room would be a smorgasbord.

Tim was just about to answer when Julio rushed in.

"My Martha is gone," he cried. For a moment I thought we were listening to the afternoon soaps. "How could this have happened?"

"Good question," I replied, shooting a venomous glance at Tim.

"We must find her."

"I couldn't agree more."

And we set to work. Tim and Julio checked the bird room, then they went on to the back of the store, while I looked up front. I nervously moved the mice and gerbil cages, I searched around the guinea pigs, I got down on my knees and swept under the fish tanks with a broom, I restacked every single bag of dog and cat food, I moved the flea products and the animal treats off of the shelves. The truth was much as I wanted her found I didn't want to be the one to do it. I was just about to start on the leashes when Tim and Julio marched in from the back.

"Did you find her?" I asked hopefully. The idea of working with this thing running around my store, possibly even taking up residence there, was not something I wanted to consider.

"No," Tim said. "But we have a plan."

I straightened up. "I'm listening." At this point I was willing to entertain any suggestion regardless of the source.

"We set up a trap."

"Explain."

"We put a bird out on the counter and wait."

"A bird?"

"Yeah," Tim said nervously. "Like one of the parakeets."

"In a cage, right?"

"Of course," Tim said indignantly.

I thought it over. It might work. It was certainly worth a try. "Okay," I replied. "Let's do it."

Tim got a little blue parakeet out of the bird room, put it in a cage, and set it on the counter.

"I just hope the poor thing doesn't have a heart attack," I murmured as I dimmed the lights.

The bird's eyes were darting this way and that, trying to figure out what was going on. I felt bad for it, but I let it stay there because I felt worse for myself.

Julio hung the closed sign on the door and the three of us sat on the floor behind the cash register with our backs against the wall. Zsa Zsa came over and crawled into my lap. After a minute Pickles came around the counter and sat down next to Julio. I kept my eyes riveted on the counter. Nothing happened. We waited some more. Every minute seemed like an hour. My attention wandered. I began thinking about how Brandon Douglas and Lynn and Joe Davis and Stanley Pharmaceuticals all fit together. The answer was there in the back of my mind. Two more seconds and the dog would tell me what it was. Then I felt a nudge.

"You were asleep," Tim said.

"Was I?" I guess I was more tired than I thought. I rubbed my eyes. I definitely needed some coffee or a soda or a chocolate bar. Anything with caffeine and sugar would do. I glanced at my watch. It was nine. Time to close up. I stifled a yawn. My leg had stiffened up, my back was aching. "It's time to go," I whispered.

"We want to stay," Julio replied, also whispering.

"Fine," I mouthed back. As far as I was concerned they could camp out around the clock until that hairy eight-legged thing was found.

"I want my Martha back," Julio cried.

Tim shushed him.

"Believe me," I said standing up. "Nobody hopes you get her back more than I do."

When I left they were both still sitting there waiting for the spider to show. Zsa Zsa came bounding after me. We went outside. It was a beautiful dark velvet night. A light breeze was rustling the leaves. Someone had set up a grill on the lawn of the house across the street. The smell of cooking hot dogs and hamburgers filled the air. My mouth began to water.

I realized I hadn't had anything to eat all day. Maybe that was why I was so tired. I decided to stop at Burger King on my way home and grab a Whopper and a double order of fries. Then I'd stop and get an ice cream cone at Baskin-Robbins. Jamoca Almond Fudge. A double scoop. After which I'd go home and ring up George and find out why the hell he hadn't called me back yet, like he said he was going to.

But as I was traveling down Elm I saw Davis's van and my

plans changed. I started following him. I couldn't help myself. It was like a gift from God. And you don't say no to offers like that. Who knew, maybe Davis was going to meet the guy in the black Saab again? Maybe tonight I'd get to see who the hell was in it. It would sure save a lot of time if I could. After all, I reasoned, George had just said not to go near the factory, he hadn't said anything about following Davis.

Of course, if I was driving the cab I couldn't have done this. Davis would have spotted me in an instant. But since I was driving the Blazer it was okay. Even when Davis checked his rearview mirror the odds were he wouldn't see me. I grinned. Davis was mine. I followed him down Elm, onto West Geddes, then got onto route 81 and got off at the Almond Street Exit. As we drove past the SUNY Medical Center I thought he was heading for the university area. But then we took a left onto Comstock and I began to wonder.

There must have been something going on at Syracuse University because the street was clogged with cars and I had to do a little maneuvering to stay close enough not to lose Davis in the crowd. I was just lighting a cigarette when he turned onto Colvin. I followed. We traveled down that street for about ten blocks, him in the far lane, me five cars behind in the next lane over. Then suddenly Davis put on his blinker and made a sudden sharp turn into Oakwood Cemetery.

Fucking great, I thought as I edged into the far lane. The guy really had a flair for the dramatic, I'd say that for him. Why couldn't he just meet his contact in a bar like everyone else? Between the hills, the winding roads, the oaks, and the tombstones, you had to be careful riding around there in the day let alone at night. With a little fog, it would be a great horror movie set. After all it came complete with mausoleums and crypts. Lots of them. Old ones built of quarried gray stone.

And it didn't help that three or four people had been murdered here over the years. Or that a couple of gangs were reputed to roam the area at night looking for trouble. Or that the cops didn't patrol there that often anymore because they just didn't have the manpower. As I turned into the gate I briefly considered turning around and going home, but my curiosity was stronger than my good judgment so I continued driving up the main road.

I could see Davis's taillights off in the distance. I started to hurry, then slowed down. The last thing I needed to do was go off the road and get stuck. Driving around Oakwood at night was one thing. Having to walk out was another. Not that I was superstitious or anything. The road went straight up and I followed it. By now Davis's lights had disappeared. When I got to the top of the hill, I doused my brights and tried to spot his. At first the only thing I saw were the shapes of tombstones and crypts rearing out of the darkness and the slight swaying of tree branches.

Then over to the right and down, I saw the faint wink of a light. If I remembered rightly, that's where the old ruined chapel was. It was a good place to meet somebody, because the chapel was situated among three hills. Once you parked down there you'd be hidden from view. You'd also have a good view of anyone coming in. Only I wasn't going to use that road. I was going to circle around and take the path that went up in back of the chapel. Then I'd park my car and scramble down the hill and come around.

"This should work," I said to Zsa Zsa. She picked up her head, yawned, and put her head back down. "You're never going to take over Rin Tin Tin's place at this rate," I told her as I started up the car.

Zsa Zsa didn't even cock an ear. It's nice to have an enthusiastic partner. I leaned over and flicked on the parking lights. They sent out a weak glow. Hopefully it would be enough to drive by, but not enough for Davis to be able to see me. I squinted. I could just make out the contour of the path I was about to take. If I concentrated very hard and went very slowly, I should be okay. I took a deep breath and tapped the gas. I inched forward. Okay. I was on my way. For a little while the path went straight, then it started up a hill. The incline was steep, almost forty-five degrees. For a moment I was scared the car wouldn't make it.

"Come on, baby," I urged, stepping down on the gas.

I cursed as the gravel crunched under the Blazer's wheels, then it shot forward. Suddenly I was at the top. An angel loomed in front of me, seemingly coming out of nowhere. My heart started hammering in my chest. She watched impassively, an indifferent expression on her concrete lips as I yanked the wheel to the left and stomped on the brakes. I stopped with a jerk. Zsa Zsa slid off the seat.

"Jesus."

I'd come about a quarter of an inch away from hitting the statue.

My hands were shaking.

My heart was still beating way too fast.

Zsa Zsa scrambled back up and put her chin on my lap.

I took a deep breath, rested my head on the wheel and closed my eyes hoping to calm myself down.

But when I opened them again the angel was still staring at me. A chill ran down my spine. The hairs on my arms stood up.

Which was ridiculous.

It was Davis I had to worry about, not some lousy piece of sand and mortar.

But I couldn't help it. I put the car in reverse and got on the road as fast as I could.

As I drove away, I willed myself not to look back.

I didn't want to see the angel's vacant eyes following me.

By the time I reached the far side of the next hill my breathing had almost returned to normal. So had my frame of mind. I parked, told Zsa Zsa I'd see her soon, locked the doors to the car, said a silent prayer and scrambled down the hill. I should have been wearing sneakers I realized as I skidded over tree roots and rocks. I would have had better traction. The only good thing about this spot I decided as I tripped on a fallen tombstone and nearly fell was that hopefully the noise of the cars from the Thruway hid the noise I was making.

The back of the chapel rose in front of me. Built in 1879, the building was a two-story gothic that would have been at home on the Scottish heath. From where I was standing I could almost lean over and touch the square of plywood someone had attempted to patch a hole in the roof with. I stopped and listened. I didn't hear anything except the sound of traffic. I'd have to get closer. God, after all I'd gone through I hoped I hadn't made a mistake. Then I heard a muffled bark, one that was too deep to be Zsa Zsa's, and I knew I hadn't. I'd been right. The bastard was here and he had some dogs in the back of the truck. Now I wasn't afraid anymore; I was just angry.

The hill the chapel was built against sloped down on either side. I chose the right-hand side because it offered more cover. I inched my way down slowly careful not to make a sound. Finally I reached the asphalt. There was a big parking area in the front of the chapel that led off onto the main road. Davis had probably parked his van there. Scarcely daring to breathe, I hugged the wall of the chapel and took one tiny step at a time. I was just at the side door when a hand reached out and grabbed my arm.

"I've been waiting for you," a voice whispered in my ear.

Chapter
28

It was Davis.

For a few seconds I couldn't move. I couldn't breathe.

In a dreadful flash I realized he must have heard me coming.

And waited.

And here I was: A sheep to the slaughter.

Davis was leering as he stepped out into the light. He wet his lips.

I struggled to break free from his grip, but he grabbed my shoulders and dug his fingers in as hard as he could. They were like steel. I couldn't twist away.

"Find what you were looking for?" he asked and laughed, a high-pitched whinny that erupted from his throat, then abruptly died. He brought his face closer to mine. I tried to lean back, but he pulled me nearer. "Remember what I said to you the last time we met?" He whinnied again. "About how little girls who hear too much need to have their ears trimmed? You know what? Yours are a little too big. They need to be cut down to size. And I don't even need a knife." And he made a clacking sound with his teeth.

The sound filled the darkness.

I could smell his sour breath.

I could hear the jagged pant of his breathing.

And the intake of my breath.

He leaned even closer, pulling me toward him. I could feel his hair brush against my jaw. I was paralyzed with terror. I couldn't move. The noise from the cars on the highway washed over me. I caught a whiff of newly mown grass and wondered if someone had cut it earlier in the evening.

Then Davis's teeth raked my left earlobe. The pain broke the spell. A flash of adrenaline shot through my body. I brought my foot up and jammed it down as hard as I could on Davis's instep. He gasped and reflexively eased his grip. Those few seconds were all I needed to slip out of his grasp.

I started to run.

"I don't think so," Davis said and tackled me.

He grabbed me by the waist and spun me around. I kicked for his balls, but missed and hit his thigh.

"Bitch," Davis hissed. "I'll make sure you'll never forget this night. Ever. My face will be the last you'll ever see."

Despite the heat, I felt a chill. The hairs on my arms stood up. But I pushed my fear aside and summoned up all the rage I could.

"Fuck you, geek," I yelled as I reached in my back pocket and whipped out Manuel's knife. Davis laughed as I clicked it open.

"You got lucky the last time, but you won't again. This time I'll pay a little more attention." Then he began to sing. "Three blind mice," he chanted as he circled around me. "See how they run."

I moved in and slashed. The knife caught Davis's arm. He cried out and moved away. I went in again. Out of the corner of my eye I saw Davis's fist coming. But it was too late. It connected with my jaw before I could move out of the way. The night exploded into stars. Then Davis punched me in the stomach. My breath left me. I doubled over. The knife went flying out of my hand. I heard it clink as it landed on the asphalt. I stumbled after it. But Davis was ahead of me. He bent down and scooped it up.

"Now," he said. "We're really going to have some fun."

I tried to run, but the sky was spinning. It was hard to focus. I took a step back. My foot hit something long and round and I went down on my back. As I fell I saw another angel watching me from the hill. I cried out to her but she didn't answer. Then Davis was on top of me, pinning me to the ground. I twisted and turned but I couldn't get him off.

Davis punched me again. His fist outlined under the streetlights loomed above me, blocking everything else out. My head snapped back under the punch's impact. Blood filled my mouth. I remember hoping he hadn't knocked out a tooth. If there's one thing I hate it's going to the dentist. Davis's face got closer and closer, an obscene white orb. I heard a strange, high-pitched keening moan and realized I was making it.

"Please, God," I prayed.

I could feel Davis's teeth on my earlobe. A parody of a lover. They pressed down. I screamed. Then I heard another scream. Davis.

"What the fuck is that?" he roared.

I looked down. Zsa Zsa was biting Davis's ankle, hanging onto it for dear life. But she was so tiny, she wouldn't be able to last for long. I gathered all my strength and threw Davis off. He went over on his back. I began to crawl away, but before I could get very far he had his hand on my ankle, dragging me back. Then I saw the metal pipe, the one I'd tripped over.

I grabbed it, turned around and jabbed at him with the long end. Davis's grip loosened. I jabbed harder. He let go. I scrambled up. Then I heard a squeal and saw Zsa Zsa go flying. I hoped she was all right but I didn't have time to go see because a second later Davis was up. Somehow he had my knife in his hand. We circled each other. He feinted. I hit at his hand with the pipe and missed. I took a deep breath and concentrated.

Suddenly there was nothing except Davis and me.

I watched him dance around me. He was crouched low, moving Manuel's knife from hand to hand. I grasped the bar in two hands and swung. I heard a crack. Davis dropped to the ground. He was rocking back and forth holding his knee to his chest.

"You broke it," he cried.

His skin looked green under the lights.

"And now I'll break the other one." I was someone else. Someone I didn't know.

"Don't," he mewed.

I liked the sound.

I took aim and swung. I watched the pipe arc down. I was almost at his other knee when I came to my senses. No matter how much I wanted to I just couldn't do it. I threw the pipe on the grass and stood there sweating and shaking in the warm night air.

Davis's face twisted with hatred at me for the humiliation I had made him suffer. "Fucking cunt animal lover."

I thought of what Zsa Zsa had looked like when I'd found her, I thought of the condition of the puppies I'd found in the shed and my rage returned. But this time it was cold. I walked over to him, pushed him down and sat on his chest. He was too weak to resist.

"What are you going to do?" He looked at me fearfully.

I bent over him and smiled, just like he'd done to me. "You know what you're famous for?"

His eyes opened wide. He jerked his head up and down, not wanting to believe what he was hearing.

I took both hands and pinned his head to the ground. "Well, I've decided to see if it's possible." And I leaned forward, put my mouth around his eye and sucked.

Davis fainted.

I laughed.

Quid pro quo.

I felt something tugging at the cuff of my jeans. I looked down. It was Zsa Zsa. She was fine. I crawled off Davis and picked her up and kissed her. She licked my nose and my cheek.

"I'll never say anything bad about you ever again," I promised as I rocked her back and forth.

I still couldn't believe that she'd jumped out of the car window, raced down the hill, and bit Joe Davis. It was an incredible feat for such a small animal.

The two of us sat on the ground listening to the cars roar by. The angel watched us. When my hands stopped trembling I took a cigarette out of my pocket and lit it. I didn't think the angel would mind.

For a while I thought about how lucky I'd been and then Davis moaned and I began to wonder what to do about him. I couldn't just leave him lying there while I went to call the police. He was hurt, but he could still crawl into the van and drive away if he came around. The van. I remembered the dogs. I hoisted myself up, walked over and opened the back.

Five golden retrievers, a Saint Bernard, a Newfoundland, and an Airedale terrier stared out at me with soulful eyes.

"Sorry, guys," I said as I quickly closed the door before they could run out. Here was all the proof the cops would need to charge Davis. I wasn't about to let them get away. "It's tough but you'll just have to hang on for another hour or two."

I thought about Davis again. What I needed was something to tie him up. But I didn't have any rope in my car. Then I realized I did have leashes. And they should work just fine. And then I realized that Davis might have something in the cab of his van. After all, he had needed something to attach to the dogs. I walked over there, opened the passenger-side door and looked in.

I was in luck. A length of white cord was lying on the seat. There wasn't a lot, but there was enough for what I wanted to do. I took it and went back to Davis. He was still out cold. Probably from the pain of his broken kneecap. For a brief second I felt guilty about how much I'd enjoyed hurting him, but then I remembered what he was going to do to me and my guilt vanished.

He'd gotten what he deserved.

No, the sadistic son of a bitch had gotten less than he deserved.

Maybe he'd had a terrible life. Maybe he'd been abused as a child. I didn't care. That still didn't give him the right to act the way he did. I turned him over, crossed his wrists, and tied them together as tightly as I could. Then I dragged him over to the van and fastened the other end of the rope around the wheel axle because I was afraid that if I tied it to the bumper, he might pull it off. I tested the rope. It seemed like it was going to hold. Zsa Zsa and I started back up the hill.

My jaw was beginning to throb. I touched it gingerly and winced. It was sore but it wasn't broken. Then I became aware of the taste of blood in my mouth. I ran my tongue over my teeth. They were all there. At least for that. I licked my lip. Blood. It must be cut. But that was okay. It would heal. My stomach hurt, too, and my legs felt like lead. By the time I reached the Blazer all I wanted to do was go home, get a Scotch, and lie down on the couch. I opened the door and put Zsa Zsa down next to me. Then I started the car.

I drove out slowly, making sure I didn't go off the gravel paths. When I got to the top of the hill I waved at the angel and apologized for any bad thoughts I'd had about her. Then I got back on the main road and drove out. I stopped at the first pay phone I came to and called the police and told them what had happened. They told me to stay where I was, but I told them to forget it and gave them my name and address instead. They could come and get me if they wanted to. I was just too tired to wait and give them a statement. I needed to go home. I got back in the car and drove there as fast as possible.

The first thing I did when I got inside my house was head for the kitchen and pour myself a big glass of Scotch and take a gulp. The liquor stung like hell when it touched the cut on my lip but I didn't care. Then I swallowed four Advil and went back in the living room and lay down on the sofa. Zsa Zsa jumped up and sat on my chest. Which was okay with me. As far as I was concerned she could sit anywhere she wanted. I took another swallow and another and watched the pine tree outside my window. I was too tired to even turn on the TV.

My mind felt numb.

Every inch of my body ached and throbbed.

I closed my eyes.

I didn't even want to look in the mirror and see what my face looked like.

I knew I should get some ice for my lip and jaw. It would keep the swelling down.

But I couldn't seem to summon up the energy to even do that.

Then I wondered if they'd picked Davis up yet.

I yawned.

I should call and find out.

It would be stupid not to.

Instead, I turned on my side and snuggled into the pillows.

I shut my eyes tighter.

It was so nice and clean and quiet and calm in here.

I really liked my house I decided as I drifted off to sleep.

The next thing I knew I heard a ringing. At first I thought it was the phone. Then I realized it was the doorbell.

"Okay, okay," I grumbled.

I glanced at my watch. It was almost three in the morning.

God. Couldn't the police have waited till eight or nine? What a bunch of assholes.

"I'm coming," I yelled as the ringing continued.

I groaned as I got off the sofa. If I'd been sore before I fell asleep that was nothing to what I felt now. I hobbled down the hall. Whoever was doing the ringing had a lead finger. He hadn't let up once.

I opened the door.

George was standing there. In uniform. "We have a lot to talk about," he said.

I let him in and closed the door behind us.

Chapter
29

George shook his head. "Davis really got you good," he said as he followed me down the hall.

"Do I look that bad?"

"In a word: Yes."

"I haven't had the heart to look in the mirror yet."

"Don't. You'll just get depressed." He pointed to my jaw. "Is it broken?"

"No. Just badly bruised."

"Are you sure?"

I moved it up and down. "See? I couldn't do that if it was fractured."

"You should ice it. If you don't and you think it hurts now just wait until tomorrow."

I headed back toward the living room. "I don't think I have the energy to even get the cubes out of the tray."

"I'll get them," George said. "You go lie back down. P.S. I

told Waldeman you'd be in first thing in the morning to make your statement."

"I can do that." And I began hobbling back into the living room.

"You'd better," George called after me. "Are you sure you don't want to go to the hospital and get checked out? I can run you down there."

"I'm positive. There's nothing wrong with me that three days in bed and a case of pancake makeup won't cure."

"Okay. You're the boss." And George went into the kitchen. He reappeared a few minutes later with a plastic bag filled with ice cubes in one hand and my bottle of Scotch and a glass in the other. "Of course if you went down there you could talk to your pal Davis."

"So you did get him?" I asked as I took the ice bag out of George's hand and held it up against my jaw.

"We got Davis, we got the van." George poured himself a shot of Scotch. "As a matter of fact I just came from the ER. What did you do to his knee?"

"I hit him with a pipe. How bad did I get him?"

"Let me just say that his running days are over. If you'd gotten his other knee, too, he'd be looking at the world out of a wheelchair." George took a sip of Scotch. "He got cut, too."

I didn't say anything.

"This time it was bad. It took fifteen stitches to close it up."

"What a pity."

"They found the stiletto that did it on the grass."

Damn. I'd forgotten all about it.

"For the record you wouldn't happen to know whose it was?"

"For the record?"

"Yes."

"It was Davis's," I lied. "He came after me with it."

"And you struggled and cut him accidentally."

"Exactly. Then he got it away from me and I picked up the pipe."

"I figured it was something like that." George gave me a long unfathomable glance. "You know those knives are illegal."

"I know." I was too tired to play games.

"And they're not much good in the protection department, either. Especially if you can't take someone by surprise. But you've already found that out." I didn't answer. "Here." He threw a small canister in my lap. I read the label. It was pepper gas. "Next time use this. It'll stop anyone who comes near you."

I picked it up. "Thanks." For some reason I could feel my eyes film over. I quickly changed the subject. George didn't need to see me lose it twice in two weeks. "So what happened to the dogs?"

"They still had their collars on so Waldeman called their owners. They've all been picked up. Much to Waldeman's relief. Especially since he was in charge of the shit patrol."

"Good. And Davis is going to be charged?"

"Absolutely." George took a sip of Scotch and set the glass down. Then he held up his right hand and proceeded to tick off the charges on his fingers. "We got him for assault. You'll testify to that."

"You'd better believe it."

"Then three of the dogs he stole cost over three hundred and fifty dollars apiece. The Newfoundland costs over five hundred. More felonies. He entered two people's houses to get the Airedale and one of the goldens. So we have breaking and entering. Then of course we have firebombing your house."

I readjusted the ice bag. My jaw was beginning to go numb. "So he did do that?"

"Yup." George looked incredibly pleased with himself. Somehow I had the idea that piece of information had not been freely given.

"Did he say why?"

"Yes, he did. It seems that when he saw you out in the parking lot at Stanley Pharmaceuticals he assumed you were trying to gather information on him. He was trying to warn you off."

"I don't get it," I said, lying back. I felt dizzy again. Zsa Zsa snuggled up next to me.

"It's simple. Davis was selling some of the dogs he stole to Stanley Pharmaceuticals. Not all of them, but some of them."

Suddenly I remembered the barking I'd heard when I'd gone out there. I thought the noise had been carried by the wind. But it hadn't. There had been kennels on the premises. Then I recalled the lab at the plant. When I'd walked in I'd seen two doors. Davis had come out of the far one. That's where the animals must have been housed.

Of course. I could have hit myself for not seeing it sooner. Stanley Pharmaceuticals was doing biogenetic research. According to the article I'd read in the *Herald* the company was on the verge of a big new breakthrough. Breakthroughs meant testing and testing meant animals. And if the medicine had something to do with the heart those animals would most likely be dogs, because their hearts were similar to human ones. I wondered if that's why I hadn't been able to find Davis's personnel file. If that's why it was some place separate? Because whoever was in charge of the animal procurement program didn't want the personnel guy to know what Davis was doing. Or who he was reporting to.

"Did he say who he was dealing with?" I asked as I shifted the ice pack to the side of my face.

"The woman who ran the lab."

"Is she going to be charged?"

"I doubt it. I'm sure the lab is fully licensed. She'll just disclaim all knowledge. Say she's sorry, that she didn't know. That kind of thing. At most she'll get a slap on the wrist."

"And Mr. Stanley?"

George snorted. "He's not even in the picture."

"Did Davis tell you who was in the black Saab?"

"Some lab tech. But he was lying. I could tell."

"So who do you think was in it?"

"I don't have a clue."

"What about the other people he's working for?"

George considered. "I think Davis is going to deal," he said after a moment. "He's got too many charges not to. Then we'll roll up the ring and cart them away."

"And everyone will live happily ever after."

"Not exactly. But it's the best we can do right now."

Suddenly I yawned. I couldn't help myself.

"Maybe you'd better go back to sleep," George said.

"No, I'm fine," I protested. "I want to hear more." But my eyelids felt as if they had grit under them. It hurt to keep them open. "I just need to rest my eyes for a minute."

"Sure," George replied.

"I hate it when you humor me," I retorted.

A second later I was sound asleep.

George said he left five minutes later.

It was almost ten when I woke up. I couldn't believe how badly I ached. I don't think there was a part of my body that didn't hurt. I felt like I'd been mangled. Somehow I managed to haul myself off the sofa and into the kitchen where I swallowed six Advil. Then I called Tim and told him I wouldn't be coming in, after which I called the PSB and told them I'd be there around two o'clock in the afternoon. If they wanted me any sooner, they could just come and get me. I tottered to the back and let Zsa Zsa out, never mind that she'd already gone. At least it had been in the kitchen instead of the rug.

It was another beautiful day, warm and bright, and I took it in greedily. Last night had made me especially appreciative of what I could have lost. Then I went back in, brewed some coffee and took it out on the patio along with a chocolate bar and just sat there and studied my neighbor's snapdragons. I could see them through the fence. Maybe next year I'd grow some myself. In fact, maybe next year I'd start a garden. Raise tomatoes. The Advil started to kick in. I could feel the throbbing in my jaw lessen. I closed my eyes again. Just for a minute I told myself. I woke up at twelve forty-five. Damn. I was going to have to hustle if I didn't want to be late. There was no use pissing Connelly off any more than I already had.

I hauled myself out of the chair and headed upstairs for the bathroom.

I walked in and looked in the mirror.

In a perverse way I was transfixed.

I leaned over and gently stroked my face with the tips of my fingers. I actually looked worse than I felt.

Which was hard to believe.

The skin over my jaw was yellow and purple—never my best colors. The jaw itself was swollen. Part of my lower lip had puffed out to three times its normal size. I had a bruise under my eye, and a nasty-looking cut on my cheek that I couldn't remember getting.

Well, there was one good thing I decided as I ran a bath. I looked so bad that Connelly would go easy on me. I'd just waltz in, give my statement, and go home.

Only that's not the way it went.

By some miracle I managed to get to the PSB on time.

But I might as well not have bothered.

Because he was late.

I just sat in his cubicle smoking one cigarette after another, staring at the wall, and thinking about how much I wanted to home and go to bed.

Midway through my fourth cigarette Connelly finally honored me with his presence. He was wearing a grease spot on his tie, a stain on his jacket, and an evil expression on his face.

"I should have you arrested," he growled as he walked through the door.

"For what?" I knew the man was an asshole, I just hadn't realized how big a one he was.

But he didn't answer. "What were you doing in Oakwood?" he asked instead.

"Taking a shortcut." If he wanted to play that way so could I.

"And you just happened to meet up with Davis."

"That's right."

Connelly's jaw tightened. I knew I was pissing him off by lying but I wasn't about to tell him the truth and get myself into even more trouble than I was already in. He threw the stiletto on the table in front of me. "Sampson tells me Davis attacked you with this."

I nodded.

"But according to Davis you followed him into the cemetery, you pulled the knife, and you went after him."

I pointed to my face. "And then I did this to myself?"

Connelly ignored my crack and went on. "Why were you following him?"

"Whose side are you on anyway?"

The detective's face colored. "I'm going to tell you one last time. Keep out of police business. We don't need your help. We don't want your help."

"At least now Davis is behind bars—no thanks to you," I spit out thoroughly enraged.

"Oh yeah?" Connelly's face was now in his purple phase. If the man didn't watch it he was going to check out one of these days. "Well, for your information we've spent two months setting up a sting to catch Davis and his pals. Your grandstanding nearly ruined the whole operation. Now give Mulroy your statement and get out of here before I do charge you with obstructing justice."

"With pleasure," I retorted as I stomped out of the room and down the hall.

Okay so maybe I should have left Davis alone.

Maybe I had gotten a little carried away.

But everything had turned out okay anyway.

Connelly didn't have to be such a jerk.

Chapter
30

I spent the next two days at home either lying on the sofa and watching TV or dozing out in the deck chair on the patio. George came by in the evenings bearing pizza, containers of ice cream, and videos, and we sat and ate and talked. Then around nine Tim would drop in and tell me what had happened at the store. Both evenings I fell asleep before he and George left.

By the third day, I no longer looked like the loser in a heavyweight title bout. Midweight maybe, but not heavyweight. I just looked bad. The swellings on my jaw and lip were down and the bruises on my face were turning greenish-yellow, a definite improvement over purple. I even felt better. The throbbing in my jaw was containable with two Advil every four hours instead of six and I could laugh without doubling over, so I decided to go into work the next day and give Tim a break. At least for the morning. I figured if I felt tired in the afternoon I could always go home and take a nap.

I got to the store about 9:00. At 9:40 the power went out. I called Ni Mo. When I finally got through, the woman on the other end of the line told me that a transformer had blown, that they had a crew on the way over, and that they were hoping to be back on line within five to six hours. Great. Just what I wanted. To be alone in a store with no lights and Martha crawling around. I hung up, called Tim and told him to swing by the store between three and four o'clock and open up if the electricity had come back on. That way we'd still get the evening crowd. After all, you can't make money if you're not there. Then I refilled the water and food dishes, changed the bedding in the cages that needed it, and dialed Victor. I was tired of driving the Blazer, I wanted my cab back and this seemed like the perfect time to get it. Victor's brother told me it was ready and I went to pick it up.

"What happened to you?" he asked when I walked into the garage.

"Nothing I want to talk about," I told him. Then I paid and left.

It felt good to be back in the cab as I drove out of Buckingham Plaza and headed down Meadowbrook. I'd missed it. But it did have a lot of miles on it. Maybe I should start thinking about getting something a little more reliable, something that wasn't in the shop on the average of once a month. Maybe I'd start shopping around in the fall I decided as I drove down Crawford. The street was peaceful. Everyone was at work. I parked in my driveway and followed Zsa Zsa inside my house, but I was restless, feeling the need for something to do. I remembered the carton with Brandon Douglas's books so I went outside, brought them in, and shelved them. That inspired me to tackle the cartons of books sitting in my living room. They'd been there for a little over a year. It might be nice to finally get them out of there.

I'd started sorting them before Murphy died and never finished the job. Since it was another nice day I dragged three of the cartons out to the patio. Then I sat down on one of the lawn chairs and started looking through them while Zsa Zsa tried to eat the pages. Most of the books were old novels, obscure reference books, and college texts, a testament to the problem I have throwing out books, any books. I was trying to decide what to do with them—I didn't even think the Rescue Mission would want them—when I came across an old favorite called, *Sports Cars* and opened it up.

It was a picture book, filled with page after page of sports cars made from the thirties to the fifties. I'd bought it at Barnes and Nobles a couple of months before I'd gotten my MG B and for a while I used to put myself to sleep at night looking at it.

I flipped through the pages. Yes. There she was. Sadie. She really had been nice. If it hadn't been for Murphy I'd still be driving her. I turned the page. A picture of the MG TA popped out. I studied the earlier model for a moment. The body was boxier than mine. The grills a little more pronounced. It had been made before "aerodynamic" had become the car industry catchword.

I continued turning. Ah. There was a Morgan. They still made them today. By hand. There was a long waiting list. I'd always wanted one, always loved the look of the leather strap across the hood. But unlike Lynn I'd never been able to afford something like that. The MG had been about as far as I could go moneywise and even then it had been a stretch. I stared at the picture. I could see why Lynn hadn't wanted to give hers away—even if she didn't drive it anymore—why she'd insisted on storing it in her garage. I know that's what I would have done. I yawned and put the book aside and reached for *Cats Of The World*.

"So," I said, showing a picture of a gray tabby to Zsa Zsa. "What do you think?"

Not much obviously from the way she tried to bite the cover. I was studying a Turkish Van when something occurred to me. I reached over and reopened the car book and flipped through the pages I'd been looking at.

Jesus. I put my hand up to my mouth. I couldn't believe I hadn't seen it sooner.

I turned to the MG TA and stared at it. This was the car Norma Lipsyle had said she saw Janet Tyler get into.

Then I turned to a picture of the Morgan. Lynn's car.

They looked alike.

If Norma had been drunk, which Pardos said she was, it would be easy to confuse a Morgan and an MG TA. Especially at night. After all they were both dark green. They both had the same body style, the same cut of the door. They were about the same size. It was an understandable mistake.

I shut the book and thought.

Up till now I'd always assumed the person that had picked Janet Tyler up had been a man.

It was, on the face of it, a natural assumption.

But what if that wasn't the case?

What if it were a woman with short hair, wearing a baseball hat and a jacket. In the dark, from a distance it might be possible to make that kind of identification mistake. Especially if you'd had one too many beers.

Was Lynn the person Brandon Douglas had come to find?

Had he made love to her so he could get in her house and find the evidence that would convict her of the murder of his sister?

Had Lynn killed Janet Tyler?

And then killed Brandon to protect herself?

Had George been right all along?

Had she been in shock because of what she'd done?

No.

This was ridiculous.

I didn't even know if Janet Tyler and Lynn knew each other.

Most likely they didn't.

They'd lived in different cities, belonged to different social classes, led totally dissimilar lives, were different ages.

Nothing linked them together.

Nothing.

And yet . . .

And yet I couldn't shake the feeling that they were connected.

I tapped my fingers on the side of the chair while I thought about who would be likely to have the information I needed. Who knew about life in Weedsport?

I went round and round. Then suddenly the answer dawned on me: Mrs. Z.

I put the book back in the carton and went inside and called her up.

"Did those two know each other?" she asked me over the phone. "Is that what you wanted to know?"

"Yes."

She chuckled at the obviousness of my question. "Why of course they did."

I gripped the phone a little tighter.

"They were distant cousins related on their mother's side."

"Did they get along?"

Mrs. Z. gave a wry laugh. "Do oil and water mix? Fortunately they didn't see each other all that much."

I did some math in my head. Janet had been eighteen when she was killed ten years ago. Lynn was now thirty-eight. Ten years ago she would have been twenty-eight. At that age a ten-year age span was a lot. What the hell was she doing hanging around with an eighteen-year-old?

"What on earth did they fight about?"

"For one thing Lynn was just jealous of Janet."

"Why?"

"Janet was a very pretty girl and it galled Lynn." There was a short pause. "She always liked to be the star, you know."

Yes. I could see that. Lynn did always want to be the center of attention. But still. You didn't go around murdering someone for a reason like that.

"Anything else?"

"Well, I probably shouldn't say this but if you want to know the truth, I think they were keeping company with the same man. At least that's what people said at the time," Mrs. Z. added.

"You don't happen to know who the man was, do you?"

"Gordon Marshall," Mrs. Z. replied promptly. "The man Lynn married."

My God. I couldn't believe this. "I didn't know he came from Weedsport. I thought he was brought up somewhere down in Rhode Island."

"He was. But in the summer he used to come up and visit his mother. She moved up to Weedsport after she married Jack Pearson."

"The guy that owns Pearson Construction?"

Mrs. Z. corrected me. "Well, actually he and his brother own it."

I thanked her, hung up the receiver, and leaned against the wall.

My head was pounding. It felt like it was going to explode. I couldn't sort it all out. I didn't know what to do.

My friend, someone I'd known for seven years, someone who spent most of her life shopping, a murderer?

I couldn't believe it.

I wouldn't believe it.

Her husband yes. Her no.

Or was that just what I wanted to think.

After all, she had killed someone when she was fifteen.

Even though it had been justifiable.

Or so I'd been told.

But maybe it wasn't.

Maybe the crime had just been hushed up and swept under the carpet.

Especially since she'd shot some redneck.

And her father was wealthy, an upstanding member of the community, a player in the political game.

I started pacing around the house.

I couldn't sit, I couldn't read, I couldn't watch TV. I took Zsa Zsa for a walk. That didn't help. Finally I decided I had to talk to Lynn and find out what was going on for once and for all.

Zsa Zsa was asleep on the sofa when I left the house. Outside the wind was picking up. The nice weather of the morning had vanished. The sky had turned gray, black clouds were massing in the west. The temperature was dropping. I rubbed my arms. For a moment I thought about running back in and getting a windbreaker but I was in too much of a hurry to bother.

I made the drive out to Lynn's in record time: Ten minutes flat. By then the wind was whipping the branches of the trees back and forth. I parked in back of Lynn's Jag. Good. She was home. As I got out I heard the rustle of pine needles being dragged across the garage roof.

I hadn't noticed how large the garage was before. You could probably get four cars in there easy. I tried the door, but since I didn't have an opener it wouldn't go up. I walked around to the side and peeked in the window. I could just get a glimpse of the Morgan in the back. For a few seconds I entertained the thought of trying to find a way in. But then I realized there wouldn't be any point. Even if Janet Tyler had been in it any evidence of that fact would have been erased a long time ago.

I walked back up the path to Lynn's house. A few drops of rain splashed on the ground. Soon the drops would turn into a downpour. I rang the bell. No one answered. After a few seconds I walked around to the side door. It hadn't been closed all the way. I pulled it open and called out. When nobody answered I went inside. Except for the sound of a radio playing somewhere upstairs, it was quiet in the house. I walked into the hallway and took a look into the living room. Lynn wasn't there. I checked the kitchen and the dining room. No luck. Maybe she was sleeping. I climbed the stairs to her bedroom two at a time. The carpet muffled the sound of my footsteps. She wasn't there, either. Maybe she was at the pool. I was turning to go when my eye caught sight of a gold thistle pin lying half buried under a scarf on top of Lynn's dresser.

Something made me pick it up.

I weighed it in my hand.

It looked so familiar.

I'd seen it before.

Then I remembered.

I'd seen its twin in the bag of jewelry I'd found among Brandon Douglas's things. Except Lynn's was gold and had a small ruby in the center, while the other one was made of silver.

But still they were very close.

Coincidence?

I was trying to decide when I heard voices. Lynn's and Ken's. A moment later they were at the door.

Chapter
31

I shrank back against the wall, but they didn't look inside. They were too involved with each other. They paused at the door and kissed. It was long and low and lingering. I managed not to gasp. Lynn closed her eyes. Ken ran his hands over her breasts and pulled down her bathing suit straps.

"So we're friends again?" he asked, caressing her nipples. They became erect.

Lynn nodded, her face contorted with pleasure.

He cupped his hands under her ass and drew her to him. "And there's never been anyone like me."

Lynn made a low gurgling noise.

"Go on," Ken ordered. "Say it."

"There's never been anyone like you," she repeated, her voice heavy with passion.

"Good." Ken bit her neck. "No one knows what you like the way I do." And he started to pull the rest of Lynn's suit off.

I couldn't have moved if I wanted to.

I was so shocked I was rooted to the spot.

Ken had Lynn's bathing suit down around her thighs when he looked up and saw me.

"Jesus Christ," he yelled.

Lynn opened her eyes and screamed.

"I'm so sorry, so sorry," I stammered.

She pulled her bathing suit up. She looked ashen, the way she had when I'd found her on Otisco Street.

I began edging toward the door.

"You're not going to tell anyone, are you?" she pleaded.

"No. No," I promised. All I wanted to do was get out of there.

"You have to understand he's the only one that's ever done it for me. Ever. It's been that way since I've been twelve. That's not so bad, is it?"

I swallowed.

"Is it?" she begged, wanting absolution.

"Of course not," I mumbled. I was almost at the door.

But before I could inch my way through Ken grabbed my arm. "What's this?" he demanded, holding up the hand I still had Lynn's pin clutched in. I hadn't realized I was still holding the piece of jewelry.

Lynn gasped. Her eyes widened in terror.

"I told you to get rid of it," Ken snarled. "Why don't you ever listen to me?"

"Because it was from you." Her voice was tremulous. "I tried to, but I just couldn't." And Lynn started to cry.

"Shut up and get the gun," he ordered as he wrenched the pin out of my hand.

I started to run, but he grabbed my hair and twisted it down forcing my head back.

"You're not going to hurt her, are you?" Lynn whispered.

"No," I managed to get out. "He's going to take me out on a date."

Ken let go of my hair. As I brought my head back up he slapped me across the face. I gasped with pain. I guess my bruises hadn't healed quite as much as I thought.

"Just do it," he told his sister and she scurried out of the room.

She was back a few minutes later with a .357 Magnum. I shivered. Douglas had been shot with a .357, too.

"Do you always do what he tells you to?" I asked as Lynn handed her brother the gun.

"She does if she know what's good for her," Ken snapped. He pointed the Magnum at me. The barrel looked big enough to crawl down. "Now what exactly are you doing up here?"

"I came to talk to Lynn."

"About what?"

"Going out for lunch."

He slapped me again. Lights exploded before my eyes.

"Do something," I begged Lynn. But I knew she wouldn't. She was cringing in the corner, biting her nails, avoiding my eyes.

"This is about Janet Tyler, isn't it?" Ken demanded.

Lynn slid down on the floor and hugged her knees.

"Do you want to tell me about it?" I asked her.

She rocked back and forth. A mewing noise came out of her mouth.

"She doesn't have anything to say," Ken said and he slapped me again, harder. I heard something snap.

"Don't," I heard Lynn cry as my head jerked back. Idly I wondered how many brain cells I'd lost in the last two days.

Ken waved the Magnum in my face. "On second thought let's finish this conversation somewhere else. Go on. Move."

Lynn wrung her hands together. "Where are you talking her?"

"Some where private, somewhere where we can talk."

"You don't believe that, do you?" I asked her.

"She believes what I tell her," Ken said.

"Call the police, please," I implored.

"I can't." The tears were streaming down her face. "I just can't."

It was pouring when we walked outside.

Very appropriate.

I felt as if I were in some gothic novel.

"You drive," Ken ordered as he motioned me over to the passenger side of the cab.

"Any particular place?"

"I'll tell you when I get inside. Now move."

I got in first and slid over. Then he followed. I put the key in the ignition and turned. I was hoping the cab would stall out, because it doesn't always like wet weather, but it started right up. Figures. When you want something to work it doesn't and when you don't want something to work it does.

"Okay. Let's go," he said.

I drove down the driveway. "Don't you think you're taking this protecting your sister bit a little too seriously?" Then I glanced at his face and saw the smirk and understood. "She didn't kill Douglas, you did."

"That's right." He smiled. "My sister hates the sight of blood. Has since she was six."

"What about that guy she shot? Oh." My voice trailed off. He'd been the story's source. "You made that up, didn't you?"

"I'd clap, if I wasn't holding this." And he jiggled the gun.

And he'd been so convincing, so sincere. The quiver in his voice, the trembling hands.

"I call myself a creative reweaver of reality," he said as I pulled out onto Maple Drive.

We drove along in silence for a little while, the only noise the flip-flop of the windshield wipers. The rain was coming down in sheets by now. I skidded a little and as I brought the cab back under control it occurred to me that perhaps I could run the cab off the road and make a break for it before Ken had time to shoot. I sped up.

"Slow down," he ordered. "I don't want you doing anything that will get us into an accident or call attention to the car."

I put my foot farther down on the gas anyway.

I heard the hammer click. "I mean it," he warned.

"Right." I eased up. Even if I jumped out of the cab while it was still going, he'd still manage to shoot me before I hit the door. And I wasn't ready to have that happen yet. "Which way do you want to go?" I asked when I got to the corner of Maple and East Genesee.

"Toward the city."

"So why did you kill her?" I asked as I made a left. I kept looking around for a patrol car, but I didn't spot any. Naturally.

"Janet Tyler?"

I nodded, wondering as I did if there were more victims.

"It was an accident."

"What kind of accident?"

"She liked to play rough and things just got out of hand. And then she was dead and I panicked. I figured the DA wouldn't understand what we were doing so I buried her in the gravel pit—which wasn't hard seeing as I worked there. When I heard they were going to start digging around there I had to dig her back up and get rid of her."

"So Norma did see you that night?"

"Yeah. I was driving Lynn's car. I saw her, too."

"And she went to the DA."

"Stupid bitch."

"And you went to her husband."

"Hey, just because I made a mistake doesn't mean I have to spend the rest of my life paying for it."

"Not when you can have someone else do it for you."

"What's the harm? It was a good deal. I supported his family better than he could. The guy was going to die anyway."

"How'd you know? I thought test results were supposed to be confidential."

"They are. His wife told her friend and her friend told her friend and her friend told me. Actually I was doing him a favor. Matt thought so, too. I mean this way he'd have something to give to his kids. They could have a few extras."

"You're really a prince among men." I was driving slowly now, trying to keep Ken talking so I could figure out what to do.

"Hey, some people got luck and some people don't. That's just the way it is. Norma understood once I explained it to her."

"And what did Lynn think of your little affair?"

"She was pissed, really pissed. Especially since Janet was sleeping with Gordon as well. That girl really got around."

"She must have been especially upset when she found out you'd given the same pin to her and Janet."

"I was young and stupid and anyway hers was gold and it had a ruby. She had the better one."

"You told her that?"

"Yes."

"And she believed you?"

"She kept it all these years, didn't she?"

Yes she had and for the life of me I couldn't figure out why. "Can I get a cigarette?"

"No. Forget it. Keep both hands on the wheel." And he took the pin out of his pocket and studied it in the dim light. For some reason I remembered my college room-mate's boyfriend. He'd given identical bracelets to four girls on campus. It seemed he'd gotten a bargain he couldn't pass up.

Suddenly I had an idea, a lousy idea, but at this point any idea was better than none at all. "I know where the other pin is," I said, hoping he'd want it.

Because while it was true the thistle was the only piece of evidence linking the Stanley family to Janet Tyler, it was also true that it really wasn't much of a link. There were lots of ways to explain it away. I was just hoping Ken was too upset to be thinking clearly.

His eyes narrowed. "Where is it?" he snarled.

I repressed a smile. "At Noah's Ark." Hopefully the lights would be on and Tim would be back at work.

"Go there."

"If I give it to you, will you let me go?"

"Sure," Ken said and smirked.

I shuddered. But at least now he had a reason to let me live a little bit longer.

"Is that why you went to kill Brandon Douglas? To get it back?"

"I didn't go to kill Brandon Douglas, I went to scare him into leaving my sister alone." Ken's face hardened. "She had no business fucking around with him—none."

"And you went to tell him that."

"No. I didn't go to tell him that," he repeated, mimicking my voice. "I went to beat the shit out of him. But when I came in and saw the pin out on the kitchen counter I knew.

He'd been using my sister. He'd been fucking her so he could get in our house and get to me. And that was even worse."

"So you shot him?"

"Damn right I did."

"And Lynn saw you."

"She was coming up as I was going out."

"You went over the roof."

"Exactly."

He was the guy A.J. had seen running past him.

"Leaving Lynn to deal with a dead body. You're just a regular knight in shining fucking armor, you know that?"

"It served her right for screwing around." And he jammed the gun into my upper arm and twisted the barrel around. It hurt like hell. "Just remember who's got the Magnum." As if I could forget. "Anyway, we agreed she'd stay. Especially since the whole thing was her fault. If Brandon hadn't been in her bedroom, he would never have seen the pin, and made the connection."

"And she took the gold one back, right?"

"Right. I told her to get rid of it and she told me she had."

"I guess she lied."

For a moment Ken seemed to be looking past me to a different time and place. "I don't expect you to understand. Lynn and I have a special relationship. We belong together. I knew that from the moment my mother brought her home from the hospital. We look the same. We think the same. I practically raised her."

"Isn't that supposed to be the parents job?"

"That's a laugh. Our mother," said Ken, giving the words a sardonic twist, "couldn't be bothered and Dad was always at work."

"Didn't he notice what was going on?" It was difficult to believe that he hadn't.

"Don't be stupid. The man was never home. He was always at the factory or the country club. And as for our mother—she was too busy with her pills and her booze and her parties and her friends. As long as we were quiet and stayed out of her way and didn't give the housekeeper a rough time everything was fine. You know when she walked out it took us a day to realize she was gone." Ken laughed bitterly. "What a waste of a human being she was."

I glanced over. "Lynn told me her mother died when she was eight," I said slowly.

Ken wiped his lips off with the back of his free hand. "Yeah, she did, she just did it in a motel room down in Vegas." He drummed his fingers on the dash. "Downers and alcohol will do it every time."

"I'm sorry," I murmured.

"Don't be," Ken barked. "Lynn and I have each other. There's nothing wrong with what I . . . with what we . . . did. We haven't hurt anyone."

"Really?" I turned toward him. "What about Brandon? What about me?" I demanded.

"Keep your eyes on the road," he ordered as I drifted toward the shoulder.

"Well," I said as I turned the steering wheel. "Aren't you going to answer me?"

"Shut up," Ken snapped. "Brandon had nothing to do with Lynn. Nothing." His voice rose. "And I tell you this, nothing will ever keep Lynn and me apart."

"Except jail."

"She won't go to jail. I would. That's why she's confessing."

"You know this for a fact?"

"My father talked to the DA. She's going to get five years probation. The deal's already worked out."

"Just like in the story you told me."

"Just like in the story," Ken agreed.

We were now heading down West Geddes. Two more blocks and we would be at the store. I shifted in my seat. I hadn't realized it but my hands were slick with sweat. My heart was pounding. This had to work.

Because if it didn't Ken was going to kill me. Of that I didn't have the faintest doubt.

As I turned onto Otisco my hopes began to fall. My God. There were no lights at the Laundromat on the corner. The bike store was closed. It looked like Ni Mo hadn't fixed the transformer yet.

I pulled up in front of Noah's Ark.

The place was dark.

Tim wasn't there.

I was in deep shit.

I turned off the engine. My heart felt like a bird beating against a cage. Ken motioned for me to get out. I did and he slid out next to me.

The rain lashed at my face. I blinked the drops out of my eyes. Ordinarily I would have run to get out of the downpour. Now I moved as slowly as possible. My legs felt like lead.

"Let's go," Ken ordered and pressed the gun into the small of my back.

There was no need to hide it because there was nobody out on the street.

I moved toward the shop slowly. My only hope now was to stall him. Especially since I didn't even have the other thistle. I'd given the jewelry to George. It was now down at the PSB. A streak of lightning cut across the sky as I put the key in the lock and twisted it. A moment later we were inside.

The store was dark and stuffy.

Pickles was nowhere in sight. The only thing I could see was the counter and the birdcage in the middle.

I guess Tim's and Julio's plan hadn't worked out.

"Keep your hands up," Ken ordered.

We walked toward the counter.

Suddenly I saw a big black splotch on the side of the cage.

Maybe things weren't so bad after all.

"Where is it?" Ken demanded.

"How do I know you won't shoot me when I give it to you?"

"I won't. On my honor."

Now that was a laugh if ever I heard one.

"Either tell me now," Ken growled in my ear, "or I'm going to start by shooting your arm off."

I repressed a shudder. There'd be nothing left if he did that. "It's over there." And I pointed to the counter.

"Where?"

"Under the gravel paper in the cage."

"Get it."

"Don't you want to?"

"Just get it." And he prodded me with the gun.

We were now at the counter. Steeling myself for what I had to do I unlatched the cage door and reached my hand in. I lifted the edge of the gravel paper and pretended to pick something up, then I brought my hand up and caught the spider just as she was getting into the cage. She filled my hand. She felt soft. I tried not to think about what I was holding.

"You have it?" Ken asked.

"I certainly do," I replied.

Then I turned around and threw Martha in his face.

Chapter
32

Ken screamed and staggered backward.

Martha hung on, covering Ken's face with her bulk.

As he reached up to claw at his face I grabbed Ken's wrist and smashed it against the counter as hard as I could.

The gun remained in his hand.

I smashed harder.

The gun fell as Ken eased his grip.

Martha jumped off and scurried back toward the bird-cage.

I reached for the Magnum, but Ken kicked it and it went skidding across the floor.

As I went after it, Ken grabbed me and hurled me back to the counter.

I bounced off of it and dove toward him.

We both fell. First I was on top and then he was.

I scratched at his face and his eyes. I could feel his sweat dripping on me. Suddenly his hands were around my neck, his thumbs were pressing down. I gagged and brought my knee up. He moaned and collapsed. I crawled out from under him toward the gun. But then he was suddenly ahead of me. I watched his hand close around the Magnum.

He scrambled up.

My God, I thought in amazement, I'm really going to die. What a stupid way to go.

Then I felt the gun's blast.

My body shook.

My ears rang.

I could smell the cordite.

But I didn't feel any pain.

"Robin."

I looked up sure I was going to see a spirit come to take me to the next world.

Lynn was standing in the doorway. Tears were streaming down her cheeks. "I couldn't let him do it again. I just couldn't," she whispered. She ran over to her brother and knelt down. He moaned. "He's alive," she cried. "Thank God." She stroked his hair and kissed his lips, then she looked up at me.

"I don't expect you to understand but he's always been there for me, always. He was the only one who was. He used to give me baths when I was little and tell me how pretty I was. He let me sleep with him when I had bad dreams and when my mother died he held me and started stroking me and it felt good. It did. It helped me forget. Is that so wrong?" she asked defiantly. "Is it?"

But I didn't answer. I couldn't. I was still too stunned. I heard Lynn talking but it was as if her voice was coming from a long ways away.

"We had sex when I was twelve," she continued. "It just happened. I didn't think of it as bad. I thought of it as our

own little secret, something that we shared. It was only later
when I was seventeen that I realized it was wrong. I tried to
stop." Lynn's voice was now so faint I had trouble hearing
her. "I even married Gordon hoping he'd take me away. But
he didn't. And Ken was always there. I dreamt about him at
night. I saw his face whenever I slept with another man and
I slept with plenty trying to get away from him. It was as if I
was his. As if I was meant to be his." And she covered her
face with her hands and began rocking back and forth.

I couldn't think of anything to say.

Pickles came over and rubbed against my leg. I automatically reached down and petted her. Feeling her fur between
my fingers, I gave thanks that I was still alive.

And unhurt.

Finally I managed to stand up.

I was reaching for the phone to call 911 when I realized
my legs were wet.

At first I thought it was blood.

Then I realized I'd peed in my pants.

"So what's going to happen to Lynn?" Manuel asked as he
shook Zsa Zsa loose from the cuff of his pants.

It was a week later and things were just beginning to
return to normal.

George leaned up against the counter. "I'm not sure. She
could be charged with Assault With a Deadly Weapon and
Accessory After the Fact. Now whether or not the DA will
choose to do that is a different story. My guess is he'll let the
Assault go and stick with the Accessory charge. But who
knows? I can never figure out those people down there."

Tim stopped sweeping the floor. "And her brother?"

"He's got two counts of Murder in the Second Degree fac-

ing him when he gets out of the hospital. Which, as I understand it, will be awhile. He doesn't have too much of his
stomach left."

"Lucky for him his sister didn't use a Magnum," I
observed. "There wouldn't be anything left."

George turned to me. "I would think that right about now
Ken Stanley is probably wishing that she had."

"You're probably right."

"Do you think Ken's father knew?" Tim asked.

"No," I replied after I'd thought over my answer for a
moment. "I honestly don't think he did. Ken said he spent
most of his time at work and I think that was true. The man
just came home to sleep and eat. And after all," I pointed
out, "when you think about it, why should he have known? I
mean it's not as if Ken and Lynn were screwing on the dining-room table in the middle of dinner."

"True," Tim said. "But I still think he must have had an
inkling of what was going on." And he went back to sweeping.

George changed the subject. "So how long did Connelly
scream at you?"

"About an hour."

"Midgley said you could hear him down the hall."

"I'm not surprised."

"He said you kept smiling."

"Well, after you think you're going to die, listening to
Connelly isn't that bad." Zsa Zsa clawed at my leg and I
picked her up. "Tell me one thing," I asked George. "Do you
know why Joe Davis was at Lynn's house?"

"He was trying to blackmail her. Brandon had told him
what he was up to and when Brandon died, Davis put two
and two together and decided maybe he could make a little

extra money. But he didn't have any proof and Lynn told him to get out."

Tim turned to me. "You don't seem as happy as you should. Still got the heebie-jeebies?"

"No."

Surprisingly I didn't. I just couldn't stop thinking about Lynn and Ken and what their lives must have been like.

All those years together.

The passion. The hiding. The being caught in something you could never get out of. The knowing you were cut off from everyone else.

No wonder Lynn had never talked about her feelings.

She couldn't.

Not to me.

Not to anyone.

She'd been totally alone.

Picture-perfect in her white suit and blond hair.

Living in a house where nothing was ever out of place.

And yet at the end, she'd almost killed the person she sacrificed everything for to protect me.

Why?

Was it that she couldn't stand another death?

That three murders were too many?

That the cost of her love had become too high?

And then I thought about Lynn's father.

Mr. Stanley had paid me four thousand dollars to find out the truth.

Well, I had.

Only the answer wasn't what he had expected.

He'd told me he was sorry he'd asked. He'd said he'd wished he'd never seen me. He'd cried when he said that he'd rather have his family than the truth.

And then I thought of Gordon. So jealous. So possessive.

He'd kicked over a dining-room chair when he'd found out. His face had been purple with rage.

"All these years," he'd screamed. "And it was never me. Never. I tried, God how I tried to get her to love me. I gave her everything and it never mattered. The cars, the house, the clothes—she couldn't have cared less. And now I know why. All she wanted was *him*. And he was always there smiling and advising, offering to take Lynn out when I was too busy." Gordon punched the wall. "I even paid for their vacation to Saint Barts. She just needs a little time away." He savagely mimicked Ken's voice. "A little time." And he snatched a vase off the dining-room table and hurled it against the wall. It exploded in a shower of shards. Then he reached for a plate and dashed it on the ground. I left Lynn's house to the sounds of breaking glass and dishes and sobs.

I sighed and lit a cigarette as I remembered. All those years everyone had spent together had turned out to be built on a lie. Lynn's lie. I knew I shouldn't feel sorry for her. But I did. She'd never had a chance.

Zsa Zsa let go of Manuel's pants leg and ran over to me and began chewing on my sandal. I bent down and picked her up. She licked my ear and started nibbling on my watchband. I told her "no" and put her back down. She ran off to investigate the cage of rabbits sitting on the floor.

"What are you thinking about?" George asked.

I shrugged. "Just the way everything ended up turning out. It's all so tangled. So complicated."

"You could say that," George agreed. "Myself, I'll take a good clean drug bust. Spare me the family stuff. That's always the worst. You never know what you got until it's too late."

"What do you think is going to happen to Matt Lipsyle?"

"Nothing. The man's dying. What more can they do to him?"

"True." I lit a cigarette. "I wonder what Norma is going to live on now that 'Uncle Ken' is in prison?"

"I imagine welfare, food stamps. Like she would have before."

"Is the house in her name?"

"I think it is."

"Well, at least for that." I shifted my weight from one leg to the other. "You know I tried to call her the other day. I wanted to tell her I was sorry."

"And?"

"She hung up on me."

"Well, what did you expect? From her point of view things were going along okay until you showed up. Now she still isn't going to have her husband back and she's lost a good part of her income."

"I know." I thought about what Matt Lipsyle had said about justice being a rich man's thing. I had a feeling he might be right.

I was wondering if I should have just left everything alone when the front door opened and Julio sauntered in. He was carrying a rolled-up brown paper sandwich bag.

"I found a mouse for Martha," he told us.

I closed my eyes. No matter what happened I'd never adjust to her eating habits.

"She's okay, right?"

"She's fine," I reassured him.

We were washing the blood off the floor, when Tim had found her crawling under the counter. He'd put her back in her cage and called Julio. Julio had come racing over. When he picked her up he noticed she'd gotten a nick on one of her legs. He'd gotten hysterical and we'd had to take the thing to the vet. Which, considering what had just gone on, was pretty incredible.

The vet had assured Julio that on the whole tarantulas were a hardy breed—otherwise they wouldn't be able to survive on three continents—and given Julio some antibiotic ointment to dab on. Which he'd faithfully done.

As Julio went inside to check on her, I thought of how the past few weeks had been like being part of a feverish dance, a tarantella. There had been these couples whirling around and somehow I'd gotten caught up in their midst.

Lynn and Ken.

Brandon and Lynn.

Norma and Matt.

Janet and Ken.

Brandon and Janet.

All twirling round and around and round each other.

All going faster and faster and faster.

The living dancing with the dead.